Praise for Michael Bishop's
Joel-Brock the Brave
and the Valorous Smalls

"What a scary joy . . . full of frights and friends, and sports, full of pathos and lonesomeness and hard choices."
— Jane Yolen, author of *The Devil's Arithmetic*

"A unique fantasy adventure . . . the characters are highly entertaining and quirky. The writing paints a lavish world of vivid imagination."
— Lisa Kurdyla, *VOYA Magazine*

"Young readers who enjoy quests with marvels in the kingdom of the weird—mushroom warriors! mazes! time games! giant slugs!—will find much to interest, amuse, and surprise them in Michael Bishop's unusual fantasy, *Joel-Brock the Brave and the Valorous Smalls*, well and profusely illustrated in pen-and-ink by Orion Zangara."
— Marly Youmans, author of *Glimmerglass*

"Michael Bishop's *Joel-Brock and the Valorous Smalls* is a riveting read. It's the story of baseball-loving nine-year-old Joel-Brock, whose parents have been kidnapped by mysterious minions of an underground world. Into this dark and creepy place the boy must venture with two friends, a sawed-off store detective and a sassy fourteen-year-old runaway girl, to confront mysteries and monsters and—mushroom people. The three are small, but valorous—and they'll need all their courage to rescue Joel-Brock's family . . . if they can! Humor, fantasy, and adventure blend perfectly in this exciting book. Come and join Joel-Brock's thrilling quest!"
— Brad Strickland, author of *The Drum, the Doll, and the Zombie*

"Michael Bishop, one of science fiction and fantasy's most accomplished authors, hasn't lost a step. In *Joel-Brock the Brave and the Valorous Smalls*, his first book for young readers, Bishop has written a rollicking adventure story in which Joel-Brock and his diminutive companions, on a quest to find his mother, journey beneath a big box store to discover a spectacular subterranean world. Gobbymawlers and snotfeet, baseball and heaps of Southern charm—not to mention a sharp political bite—all come together to produce the most enjoyable young adult adventure I've read in some time. With beautiful illustrations by Orion Zangara, this is a treasure for the book shelf."
— Nathan Ballingrud, author of *North American Lake Monsters*

"*Joel-Brock the Brave and the Valorous Smalls* is the book I'd take under the covers with a flashlight to keep reading until I was done, regardless of my bedtime . . . [It] reminds me why I became a reader in the first place. A deeply imaginative and exciting tour of a weird world on just the other side of the ordinary."
— James Van Pelt, author of *Pandora's Gun*

Other Fairwood Press /
Kudzu Planet Productions novels
by Michael Bishop

Brittle Innings

Ancient of Days

Who Made Stevie Crye?

Count Geiger's Blues

A Funeral for the Eyes of Fire

Philip K. Dick is Dead, Alas

Joel-Brock the Brave
and the
Valorous Smalls

Michael Bishop
illustrated by Orion Zangara

The Valorous Smalls

Joel-Brock the Brave
and the
Valorous Smalls

Michael Bishop
illustrated by Orion Zangara

KUDZU PLANET
· PRODUCTIONS ·
BONNEY LAKE WA

Joel-Brock the Brave and the Valorous Smalls
A Novel for Young People, Whatever Their Age
Total approximate wordage for text of novel: 67,880

A Fairwood Press/Kudzu Planet Productions Book
June 2016

Fairwood Press
21528 104th Street Court East
Bonney Lake, WA   98391
www.fairwoodpress.com

Cover and interior illustrations by
Orion Zangara

Book design by
Patrick Swenson

Kudzu Planet Productions
an imprint of Fairwood Press

ISBN13: 978-1-933846-58-3
First trade paper edition: June 2016
First hardcover [First Edition]: June 2016
Printed in the United States of America

This story is for the big-hearted Smalls who inspired and helped with it, Annabel English Loftin and Joel Bridger Loftin: Future Oboe (and Ukulele) Player of America and Home Run Hitter of the Future, respectively. Indeed, the poem "Hope" in Chapter 22, also titled "Hope," is Annabel's original work and appears with her permission. Further, the story exists in this form because Joel wanted it to feature a shelf stocker, a private eye, and a baseball player. I thank these two siblings for their many contributions, only a few of which I've listed here.

Acknowledgments

I owe an unpayable debt to several people for reading *Joel-Brock the Brave and the Valorous Smalls* and for refusing to throw up their hands and leave me to my own devices. Annabel and Joel I cite in my dedication. Others whom I note for their proofreading skills and substantive critiques include Michael Hutchins, Klaus Krause, Jack Slay, Randy Loney, my agent Howard Morhaim and his former assistant Beth Phelan, Brad Strickland, my wife Jeri Bishop, and our daughter Stephanie Bishop Loftin, mother of Annabel and Joel. Of course, I also wholeheartedly thank Jonathan Bridger Loftin, our grandchildren's estimable dad. Further, for over a year, the illustrator of this story, Orion Zangara, worked to provide the evocative pen-and-ink drawings that ornament each of its chapters. Finally, I must give more than a mere nod to Patrick Swenson: publisher, editor, writer, book designer, and friend. Without him, this book as a physical and/or electronic artifact simply would not exist. Wholly deserved blessings on each of these kind and talented folks.

Michael Bishop
Pine Mountain, Georgia

Contents

1

Home Run Hitter of the Future

Joel-Brock Lollis secretly thought of himself as the Home Run Hitter of the Future, but on this hot summer evening he also thought of himself as the loneliest nine-year-old in the world. He had hiked nearly three miles along a blacktop two-lane from his house on Crabapple Circle toward Big Box Bonanzas, his favorite store in Cobb Creek, Georgia. Even wearing his Cubby League **BRAVES** uniform didn't turn his mind to baseball. Too much other stuff fretted him.

First, he'd seen no member of his family for over a week. Second, his stomach ached. Third, by leaving the Lollis house, he had disobeyed his mother. Fourth, hiking the road's weed-grown shoulder in the gloom of a fading sunset really scared him. Fifth, even though he'd tried to wash his uniform, it bore lots of stains and stank of boy sweat. And, sixth, he had no idea if his journey to Big Box Bonanzas would chase away *any* of these worries.

Not far from his destination, Joel-Brock stood like a wide-eyed lemur in a jungle of hungry leopards. He was at a crossing waiting for the light to change. And when the **WALK** sign lit up and he stepped into the street, headlights glared and dozens of engines snarled all around him.

"I wish I was a giant and weighed ten tons!" he shouted at the traffic.

Once across, Joel-Brock stopped on a curb beside the big store's parking lot. Its tarry surface rolled off into the twilight toward windows that blazed

like bonfires. Long ago, there had been a strip mall here, but the owner of Big Box Bonanzas had bought it and torn down all its little stores to build this humongous one. Now cars popped into and out of the lot's lined spaces like giant metal honey bees on a melting hive.

Joel-Brock skipped between the cars and into the entryway of the boxy store. He nodded at khaki-clad greeters, passed checkout lanes, and headed for Electronics, where he found Melba Berryhill, his favorite employee in the store.

"I would like a job," he told her.

Miss Melba, a chocolate-skinned woman with hair like bristly cotton, looked at him with surprise. She could not recall Joel-Brock's name, but his cocker-spaniel eyes and skinny arms made her want to hug him and tote him home. But her shift did not end until midnight, and kidnapping the boy at this moment would *not* please her boss.

"Now, why would a kid your age need a job?"

"My family's disappeared," Joel-Brock said. "And there's not a lot in our house left to eat."

"Then you should call the police or Family and Children Services."

Joel-Brock's eyes pled with Miss Melba.

"What's your name, young man?"

"Joel-Brock Lollis." He did not say Home Run Hitter of the Future because she would scoff or scold him for bragging. So far in his baseball career, he had hit only one "home run." And he'd made it around all the bases only because of a flurry of throwing errors by the boys on the other team.

"Well, Joel-Brock Lollis, you still should tell the police or DFACS."

"I can't," he said, and he yanked a note from the back pocket of his baseball pants and handed it to Miss Melba. She read it to herself. These were the words that his mama had scrawled on that grimy scrap:

Darling Joel-Brock,

If you contact the police or the Department of Family and Children Services, your teachers at school, any of your friends' parents, or almost anyone at all, the gobbymawlers who have spirited your daddy, Arabella, and me away will never let us return to you.

So please stay inside the house with the doors locked and wait. Eat all the fruit and anything else you find in sealed packages in the pantry. And every time you give thanks for your food, pray for our early release by the contemptible stooges of the worst man in Cobb Creek, and maybe they will let us come home before your next game.

Love, Mama

Miss Melba peered at the boy with a sharper look of bewilderment and distress. "I still think—"

"No," Joel-Brock said. "Not by the hair of my chinny-chin-chin."

"Joel-Brock Lollis, you've got no hair on your chinny-chin-chin."

"Okay, then—'not by my *skinny-skin-skin*.' I won't do *anything* that'll keep my family from coming home."

"But you ignored your mama's plea to stay inside with the doors locked."

"She'll know why I did that. Things are different now: I'm *hungry*."

"Then you do need a job, but a job here will turn *you* into a gobbymawler. Is that what you want?"

"When Mama says gobbymawler, she means *stinker* or *pain in the neck*, not just somebody who works here. I don't know why."

"Your mama doesn't like this place. Her name shows up a lot in our Complaints records."

"Please, Miss Melba—you'll see how hard I work."

"Okay. But when my shift ends, I'm taking you home. I'll give you a pork chop, turnip greens, and pot liquor."

"I don't drink liquor."

"With pot liquor, babycakes, you can use a spoon."

"I mean I don't *touch* it."

"No," Miss Melba said, "I don't reckon you do."

*

A clock radio in Electronics ticked over to show the digital time: **9:24** p.m. Only a few people prowled the aisles. Miss Melba said that little business got done on slow weekday nights, so she had time to spray some air freshener all around his head.

"I feel sticky, Miss Melba."

"Maybe you *oughta* feel a bit like you smell." She added, "Just kidding, mostly."

"But why do you have to do that?"

"If you want a job, babycakes, you can't smell like a sweaty-sock closet."

At that moment, Miss Melba's night-shift boss, Augustus Hudspeth, appeared. He asked who the short-stuff in the baseball uniform was and why the kid kept switching all the TVs, computers, and DVD players on and off.

"He's Joel-Brock Lollis, my nephew," Miss Melba said. "He wants a job."

"Your *nephew*? Melba, this hyperactive little fellow is *white*."

"No sir, he's biracial. That's all."

Mr. Augustus Hudspeth loomed tall. He had love handles that made his shirt look rumpled and a belly that made his tie look too short for his shirt. "Tell him we can't hire children, Melba. And nobody's supposed to bring a kid to work."

"I *didn't*, sir. My sister dumped him off. I just figured I'd give him a chance to learn something by watching me do *my* job."

"You're not working, Melba—you're babysitting."

Joel-Brock turned away from the monster FōFumm TV now showing the Atlanta Braves playing the Colorado Rockies. "Nobody babysits me," he told Mr. Hudspeth. "I'm ten—*almost* ten."

"Come on, sir," Miss Melba said. "Give us a break. He's a strack little soldier."

"'*Strack*'?" Augustus Hudspeth said.

"That's army talk. It means 'sharp as a tack.' I think."

Joel-Brock blushed at his grubby uniform.

"Okay," Mr. Hudspeth said, sniffing. "But do me a favor: Wash that watermelon-rind air-freshener stink off the boy. Somebody's likely to cut him into strips and slop the pigs with him."

"Augustus," Melba said. And then: "Mr. Hudspeth."

Yipes, Joel-Brock thought.

"And keep him out of our customers' sight. This is *just for tonight.*"

"Yes sir. Thank you, sir."

*

But "*just for tonight*" turned into every night . . . except Thursday, Miss Melba's day off. She told Augustus that her sister had left her son to join a convent, and that she, Melba, was now the boy's "temporary keeper." Actually, she had no sister.

"I'd have your sister arrested," Augustus said, but he found Joel-Brock jobs as a go-fer and an assistant shelf-stocker. He could do these jobs without much harming Miss Melba's own performance. Once finished helping Kyle Robinson restock Toys and Shel Burgess carry woks and vanilla candles to the Home section, Joel-Brock duck-walked, really low, to Electronics and clicked on the FōFumm TV to watch that evening's Braves game. Augustus, also a fan, stopped in to check out the action. But tonight the Braves and their opponents, the San Diego Padres, looked . . .

"Different," Augustus said. "And I mean *different.*"

"They're wearing shorts," Joel-Brock said.

"And skintight sleeveless jerseys," Augustus said.

"And hats with bells and floppy brims," Joel-Brock said. "And two-tone shoes with blinking blue lights."

Augustus groaned and said, "What kind of silly promotion has the Braves' front office dreamed up now?"

And both he and Joel-Brock realized that the Braves in this lineup—Sealy, Coffin, Safransky, Pfingston—were not the players they usually cheered for. They'd never even *heard* of these dudes.

"They must've called up a bunch of minor leaguers," Augustus said. "But why? It makes no sense at this point in the season."

"I have no idea," Joel-Brock said. His parents and his sister Arabella used this expression a lot. But none of the Padres had familiar names on their jerseys, either. (The name on their pint-sized shortstop's shirt was **Chou Shu-Hu**.) However, Joel-Brock did not point out these facts to Augustus because he feared that doing so would only irritate his supervisor more. "Maybe it's okay," he finally said. "We've got two runners on and just one out."

Then a Braves outfielder named Pfingston—*Pfingston?*—struck out. Augustus shook his fist. Then a slender player strode into the batter's box and took up a confident stance. The announcer identified him as J.-B. Lollis, the centerfielder batting .406 with 21 home runs, 64 runs batted in, and a .788 on-base percentage.

"*Lollis*," Augustus Hudspeth said. "What a set of statistics! You related to this guy, Joel-Brock?"

"I have no idea. I've never heard of him." And he hadn't, but the name, so much like his own—almost identical—sent an eely shiver up his back.

Miss Melba came up behind Augustus and her "nephew" to check out the game. "What stylish uniforms," she said.

"Maybe on *that* kid," Augustus said. "But some of those guys look like they're wearing silk boxers. And those shoes belong in a circus." J.-B. Lollis took a called strike. "What're you waiting for?" Augustus yelled. "*Hit* the ball!"

"He's feeling the pitcher out," Joel-Brock said.

Next, J.-B. Lollis watched a sinker drop low and away for a ball. Augustus rolled his eyes again. "Guess he's *still* feeling the pitcher out," Miss Melba said.

J.-B. Lollis walloped the next pitch into the second tier of seats in left-center. The stadium's sound system played "Eye of the Tiger," and the Braves led the Padres 3 to 0. Joel-Brock and Miss Melba high-fived. Augustus did a locomotive shuffle all around the inside of the Electronics section. "Yes-yes, yes-yes, yes-yes." he choo-chooed.

Joel-Brock's namesake circled the bases and crossed home plate into a mob of pogo-sticking teammates. The fans, too, were jitterbugging about and pumping their fists. J-B Lollis trotted free of his teammates and tipped his floppy hat.

"He's like your older brother," Miss Melba whispered to Joel-Brock. "You two favor like bream in a lake, a big one and its little twin."

*

On the next afternoon, Augustus asked Joel-Brock if he had looked up the result of last night's game in the *Atlanta Constitution*.

"No. No, I didn't."

Augustus said, "Well, I did—online—and the Braves lost 7 to 2."

"Uh-uh," Joel-Brock said. "They won on—"

"No, they *didn't*. And I couldn't find one Brave in the paper named Pfingston, Coffin, or Sassafras."

"Safransky," Joel said.

"I only found our regulars guys, guys who *always* play: Freeman, Heyward, and the rest. So I have to ask: *Who are these Braves with the funny names that we watched on TV last night?*"

"I have no idea," Joel-Brock said.

Miss Melba chimed in: "It's Braves from another reality—your big brother from a sideways universe that we got on TV yesterday by sheer freakiness."

"I don't have a big brother."

"Not here, but in that other reality—it's the only explanation."

Joel-Brock ducked out of the service area and sat down in a cave of TV boxes in front of the appliances. He was breathing like a dog that has trotted miles to find shelter from a thunder storm. Miss Melba got down on all fours, dog-walked over to the boxes, and peered inside.

"What's wrong, babycakes?"

Joel-Brock whispered, "Don't call me babycakes."

"What's wrong, Joel-Brock Lollis?"

"I don't have a big brother."

"Not in this reality you don't."

"Not in any. And in this one, I don't even have a family." He started his dogtrot-breathing again—but softly, trying hard to stifle it completely.

"Oh, honey." Miss Melba reached into the cave of boxes, but by now he'd backed farther in. "Joel-Brock?" No answer. *Joel-Brock?* No answer. **"JOEL-BROCK!"**

"what?" he said in his smallest voice.

"We'll find them. Don't fret, now: We'll find them."

Joel-Brock clasped his knees and, in a rush of bitterness, thought, *Yeah, right.*

Then Augustus Hudspeth said, "At nine-thirty I'm going to turn on that big flat-screen so we can catch up on our bubble-universe Braves. You'd like that, wouldn't you? Boy oh boy, so would I!"

2

"What Hasn't Happened Need Not Happen"

And, at 9:30 p.m, Augustus did just what he said he would. Announcers declared that last night the Braves had taken a 5-to-4 lead on a top-of-the-ninth solo homer by J.-B. Lollis: his second solo shot of the evening. Then, in the bottom of the ninth, their young closer, Poe Kalischer, had taken the mound and secured the win with only ten pitches: a strikeout and two feeble infield grounders.

Joel-Brock had long ago left his cardboard cave, but now he padded into the aisle of TV displays, where he actually did sense a funny kinship to his namesake on this other Braves team. The guy seemed a touchstone to his missing family. What if he *really* was a long-lost brother from another reality, a reality that Joel-Brock Lollis the Younger also belonged to? The players warming up on TV tonight wore the same odd uniforms they'd worn before, but they did not look quite so funny now.

An ad came on the FōFumm. It urged viewers to fly to the Sea of Tranquility on the Moon and spend two days at the Lunar Ritz-Carlton for the low price of thirty-seven *dillies*. On the Moon, they could climb craters, zip along low-gravity zip-lines, and sing to their sweethearts in the off-Earth moonglow. The shots of all these attractions looked like lovely spiffy fun to Joel-Brock.

"Today's computer-graphics people really have talent," Miss Melba said.

"That stuff did look real," Augustus agreed, and the game came back on.

J.-B. Lollis the Elder, batting cleanup, rifled a double into right field to score the Braves' first run. Lollis, an announcer said, had now hit safely in forty-seven straight games and had more votes than anyone else for this year's All-Star game, which would be held in August, midway through the season's two hundred games.

"Two hundred!" Augustus cried. "That's crazy! It's too blasted many!"

"Yeah," Miss Melba said. "A guy'd have to be a Cal Ripken Iron Man to reach the playoffs uninjured."

Joel-Brock had a thought: This TumTong TV—or *whatever*—was broadcasting their Braves game from a dozen years in the future. He, Joel-Brock, the Home Run Hitter of the Future, had grown into the slender, muscular body of the J.-B. Lollis now standing humbly on second base.

Terrific! Joel-Brock thought. I am truly the Home Run Hitter of the Future, a ball-swatting macho guy like Jason Heyward!

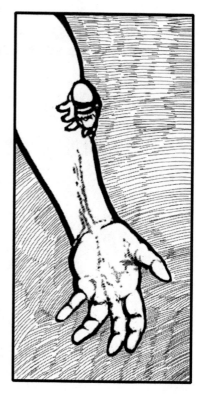

His chest swelled like a battle-ready blowfish. Then he exhaled—for he would have gladly traded his future powers as a hitter for the return of his family. He'd sell can openers for a living or teach little kids to tie their shoes. Just let his parents come back from captivity; Arabella, too, whom he loved even when she stuck a Sticky Stuff leech on his forearm and Sophia his mother could only get it off with Ooze Ouster.

But these Braves lost in the bottom of the ninth, 4 to 3, and his future self did not get another hit. But he did make several fine defensive plays in centerfield, robbing one Padres player of a double and throwing out another who had dashed from first to third thinking that J.-B. would never catch his teammate's drive. But the Braves still lost, and Miss Melba, Mr. Hudspeth, and Joel-Brock all moped around before the big TV feeling bruised and betrayed.

"That's enough for me." Augustus pointed a remote at the traitorous FōFumm.

"Wait!" Miss Melba cried. "A reporter's going to talk to Joel-Brock's brother."

"I don't have a—"

"*Shhh,*" Miss Melba shushed him. "*Shhh, shhh, shhh.*"

*

Outside the visitors' dugout, a young woman named Calla faced Joel-Brock's "brother" and spoke into her microphone: "J.-B., this defeat must have been especially tough. You had a two-run lead going into the bottom of the ninth."

J.-B. said, "Give the Padres credit. They fought back against our best closer and scratched out three hits."

"No regrets, then?"

"You can't regret a well-hit ball that doesn't drop for a hit. You can't regret not catching a long fly that surfs an updraft before you reach it."

"But you've fallen four and a half games behind Miami in your run at winning the Eastern Division. That's got to hurt."

"Plenty of season left."

"The Marlins have won eleven of their last twelve. Over the same span of games, the Bravos are barely breaking even."

Lollis rubbed his thumb on his jaw. "Is there a question in those statistics?"

"Don't you find them discouraging?"

"A month ago we won nine straight while the Marlins struggled. They had every right to get down, but they didn't."

"So you don't see this as a really tough loss?"

"It's a stumble in a long-distance race. Tough losses just don't occur in baseball—unless you think baseball has the same juice and savor as life does."

"But sports *provide* 'juice and savor' to life, don't they?"

"Sure, Calla, but tough losses don't occur on baseball fields, tennis courts, or even stock-exchange floors. Tough losses happen elsewhere."

"Like where?"

"In our daily lives, among our families and friends."

"Do you speak from personal experience?"

"Anyone with an awareness of life's various pitfalls could do the same."

"Please tell us a little more about that."

"Forgive me, Calla, but I need a shower and some rack time." J.-B. Lollis ducked into the dugout, out of camera range

Augustus clicked the set off, and both Miss Melba and Augustus looked at Joel-Brock. Their gazes fell on him like wet beach towels, as did Calla's final question about J.-B.'s personal life: Thirteen years from now, his family's kidnapping was still unsolved.

Augustus said, "You're J.-B. Lollis! J.-B. Lollis is you *all grown up!*"

"My family never came home," Joel-Brock said, as this fact sank in. "That means that . . . that they *never* will."

Miss Melba hugged him. "No, punkin. Everybody knows you *can* change a future that hasn't shaken out yet."

"*I* don't know that," Augustus said.

Miss Melba shot him a look. "It just makes sense: What hasn't happened doesn't need to. What needs to happen *can*, if folks work to make sure it does."

"Horse feathers," Augustus said. "Chicken's teeth."

Joel-Brock rubbed his eyes and considered Miss Melba's words, but all he said was, "I need a shower and some rack time."

3

Home Alone, Sort Of

On a ratty loveseat in the hall of Miss Melba's cottage on Jarboe Street, Joel-Brock lay thinking about the last time he'd seen any member of his family.

On that afternoon, coming home from Saturday's ballgame with his friend, Luc Winter, and Luc's mother, Krista, he had not thought it weird that no one in his family awaited him. His mother, Sophia, a fitness trainer, ran eight miles or more a day getting ready for the marathons that would qualify her to run in next year's Boston Marathon. His father, Bryden Lollis, worked as a computer troubleshooter, menu maker, and stand-in chef for Lollywild, a chain of sports restaurants that Bryden had started in Cobb Creek twenty years ago.

On that day, though, Bryden had driven Arabella to oboe practice. She played twice a week at a local music school, and because Arabella's oboe teacher said she had "a clever lip," she now signed all her email messages *FOPOA*, which meant *Future Oboe Player of America*.

"If I hadn't called myself *FOPOA*," Arabella said, "Joel-Brock would never have signed *his* messages *Home Run Hitter of the Future*."

Joel-Brock knew that accusation to be true and that Arabella wanted to shame him by saying so, but he didn't care. His sister was smart, especially so about words and their meanings. Once, when she was only eight and her teacher asked for an example of a noun and no one in class raised a hand,

the teacher looked at her and said, "Arabella, give me an example of a noun."
Immediately, Arabella replied, *"Abolitionist?"* And this story had become holy
Lollis family lore.

Anyway, the house stood empty when Joel-Brock got home. His
Cubby League team, the WorkOutWarrior Braves, which Sophia's business
sponsored, had won their game 14 to 2. He had reached base twice on walks
and once on an error-assisted "triple." But he did not undress or shower.
Instead, he curled up on their soft, sectional sofa, whose color—gray or
lavender—depended on which way you rubbed its upholstery. He clicked on
the TV, found a big-league game, muted the sound, and fell asleep watching
it. When he awoke, twilight had fallen and a lump of worry freighted his gut.
He called Sophia's cell-phone and got sent straight to her voicemail.

"Mama, I'm home. We won. I'm hungry. That's it. Bye."

He called Bryden's cell, which sent him to his *dad's* voicemail. He would
have tried Arabella's phone, but she still didn't have one. She was twelve.
Something else was wrong. The Lollises had three dogs: a wire-haired terrier
named Sparky, a King Charles spaniel named Leo, and a jittery old female
Chihuahua named Josie. Sophia had adopted Josie from the Cobb Creek
humane shelter. Josie had spent most of her life as a *breeder* in an illegal
puppy mill, and her ill treatment and many pregnancies there accounted for
her mistrust of human beings, especially men, and also, presumably, her near-
constant trembling. Anyway, Joel-Brock now realized that none of their dogs
had run out to meet him or curled up on the sofa next to him as he slept, and
the absence of the family dogs truly began to unnerve him.

"Sparky! Leo! Josie!"

He opened the door to the deck above the backyard, where, during the
day, the dogs played, slept, or did their business, and he called their names
again. Again, he got no response. Although deeply worried, he went to the
kitchen for something to eat. When he found nothing good, he thought

about calling his pal Luc Winter's mama. He didn't, but only because he *knew* his family would soon arrive and he'd appear a total wuss for fearing the worst. But they didn't arrive, and they *kept* failing to arrive.

Around 8:40 p.m., Joel-Brock began exploring various rooms—his own, upstairs, and Arabella's, strewn with clothes, trinkets, and books. Mama had not left a note on his pillow or propped against the fish tank. And in Arabella's sty of a room, with its bead curtain and tiny lilac-colored door into the unfinished attic, he would need a bulldozer to uncover a school bus. So Joel-Brock returned downstairs. And, under the living room's cathedral ceiling, he padded past the sectional couch toward his parents' room, which felt off-limits to him. Why? On late Saturday evenings, Bryden let him cuddle up beside him there. And Mama often called him in to feed Josie, who slept with his parents rather than in cages, as Sparky and Leo did. So, although he had no good reason to avoid this room, tonight, feeling like an intruder, he hesitated before entering.

Then he found his mother's note—not on the king-size bed or the bureau covered with family photos, but under a magnet on the bathroom mirror's outer frame. Sophia had written it in red ballpoint on a sheet of graph paper, just as she did the lists she put on the refrigerator detailing everyone's weekly appointments. The note said . . . well, just what Miss Melba had read silently in Big Box Bonanzas a couple of days ago, and what Joel had read that Saturday and learned by heart: scary stuff about gobbymawlers stealing his family away and about his need to stay inside, eating what he found in the house, praying for a happy ending, and *not* calling the police.

Restless on Melba Berryhill's ratty loveseat, Joel-Brock reflected that the BBB kidnappers still had not let his family or the dogs go. And the Cubby League Braves had played *two games without him* since he'd found Sophia's note, one during his first days alone and one soon after he'd started bunking on Jarboe Street. Maybe Sparky and Leo had run off, scared, after slipping through a hole under the fence.

He recalled that first fear-racked week. One *good* thing had happened: When he'd taken Mama's note back into his parents' room, Josie stuck her nose out of a gap between two huge pillows against the headboard. This was her hiding place when Sparky and Leo fought. The gobbymawlers had missed Josie because she'd huddled there when they burst in. Now poor Josie shook like a rough-running lawnmower engine. His reunion with her was sweet, for over the past three years, Josie had come to trust Joel-Brock. Sometimes she even slept with him. He hugged her, wishing that she'd open her gray muzzle and tell him about the kidnapping, but instead, trembling, she licked his fingers with her tiny pink snail of a tongue.

Other things that week had *not* gone well. Some fruit in the fridge had softened, but the cantaloupe wedges were as hard as cucumber rinds. He spit their mealy pulp into the trash and hurled the mushy apples and peaches over the fence into a vacant lot. As for the food in the pantry, Joel-Brock ate as many energy bars as he could stand, but tossed corn chips and stale crackers out for the birds. A tin of tuna, which he'd found under a box of black tea, resisted his struggles to cut its lid off with a can opener. And when he gave up on cereal and canned meats, he burnt the eggs he was scrambling and a horrid stench filled the kitchen.

On day two, Will S Gato, their cat, showed up at the door meowing to be let in. (Maybe he'd smelled the tuna.) Joel-Brock stroked him until the cat bit his wrist and the boy swatted him. Will S Gato flattened his ears, spat, and shot under the sofa.

"You stinker! No wonder the gobbymawlers didn't take you!"

On day four, Joel-Brock cracked the blinds on a front window and peeked out. A gobbymawler squatted on the porch staring at their door. If she wasn't a gobbymawler, she was a person wearing the pinkish-brown jumpsuit of a Big Box Bonanzas worker and a soft round cap—like a fat pancake—of the same color. Joel-Brock sidled out of sight. Even though gobbymawlers had stolen his family, he wanted to think of the arrival of this buddypard—as store managers called all their hires—as a courtesy call. He *liked* visiting the store, and maybe this buddypard had brought him a fresh pizza sample or a booklet of "valuable coupons."

Still, Sophia often said that she could shop there only if she held her nose. Joel-Brock had never seen her holding her nose, but he *had* heard her curse its lack of quality goods, the fact that stuff she liked too often vanished from its shelves, never to return, and its "disgraceful" treatment of its employees: greet-ers, baggers, stockers, checkers, gardeners, shoplifter spotters, et cetera. And, then, just this past winter, it had all gotten *serious* for her, and she began a heart-felt battle against the store. She asked friends to pitch in, and she, four other women, and two of their husbands paraded in a parking-lot picket line. Their signs screamed BIG BOX BONANZAS IS **UNFAIR** TO ALL, and LOW PRICES HERE COME AT A **HIGH** COST, and LOCAL GOODS— **NOT** TRUCKED-IN GARBAGE, and so on. Reporters covered the protest. Segments appeared on the TV news and write-ups in the papers. Several kids at school, who liked Big Box Bonanzas as much as Joel-Brock did, called his mama "eco-freak" and even some uglier names that hurt his feelings worse. A few kids sided with him, but Joel-Brock thought the whole thing a huge em-

barrassment. Why had Sophia gotten so bent out of shape?

Knock-knock, knock-knock-knock, knock-knock! Whoever had just crept onto the porch knocked, again and again, with the brass knocker. *"Boy-o, open up!"* the strange female yelled. *"I've got news for you!"*

This buddypard seemed to be a teenager, but her shouts terrified him. Did she want him to open up so that the creeps who'd snatched his family could grab him too? Go away, Joel-Brock prayed, but the buddypard kept knocking and pacing about. He peeked through the blinds again. His tormentor *was* a teenage girl—with coppery hair, emerald-green eyes, and a sharp but fetching face, even when she muttered. Finally she left and never—so far as Joel-Brock knew—came back. So at the end of that week he determined to get a job. Then he'd buy pizza and broccoli, which, although otherwise a normal kid, he really liked.

He didn't call the police or DFACS or anyone else on his mama's list, but he did wonder why no friends of his parents had phoned or come by. Hadn't they missed him at the last two games? What in the world had happened? Well, using his father's laptop one day, he discovered that Sophia had posted a FacePlace notice saying that the Lollises had gone on vacation: *"Three big and hungry watchdogs are guarding our house."* She must have posted this message—this *lie*—hoping to keep Joel-Brock safe, and she must have done so just before the BBB gobbymawlers whisked her and Bryden and Arabella out of their house.

On his second Monday alone, he put out food bowls for Josie and Will S Gato and, wearing his dirty baseball duds, left for Big Box Bonanzas. Dusk had gelled into muggy summer dark and he hiked along the road sweating. Vans, roadsters, and trucks whooshing by all seemed as tall as jacked-up Monster Mash jalopies. The driver of an 18-wheeler, seeing Joel-Brock, sounded his air horn: ***BLAAAT!*** Joel-Brock wobbled and fell over. On his hands and knees, he thought: *You. Big. Butthead. Meanie.*

He got up and resumed his march. He *liked* Big Box Bonanzas. Once, his mama had gone there for photography supplies, vitamins, scrapbooking materials, candles, and Halloween candies. In emergencies, his daddy still bought fresh meats and veggies for the Lollywild restaurants there. And Arabella still visited BBB for shampoo, paperback young-adult novels, and snap-on beads and bracelet charms.

And there, almost before Joel-Brock knew it, shone Cobb Creek's Big Box Bonanzas, a beacon in the dark.

4

Gobbymawlers vs. Sprols

On Miss Melba's loveseat, Joel-Brock jerked awake, confused.

"Hope you slept okay, Joel-Brock," Miss Melba said.

He fisted his eyes and sat up. "I walked half the night, from Crabapple Circle to Big Box Bonanzas."

"You did that a week ago. Last night you slept here on my loveseat." Miss Melba touched his forehead. "Holy Moses, punkin, you're sort of sizzlin'."

Joel-Brock wondered why he let her call him punkin when he didn't let her call him babycakes. "I didn't sleep *much*, Miss Melba."

"And why should you sleep? You probably won't until—" Here she stopped.

"I kept thinking of Mama's note. Do you still have it?"

"Sure." Miss Melba tweezered the note from an apron pocket and spread it out on her lap. "I should have gone to the police or DFACS or *some*one your folks know, but the gobbymawlers said not to, and so did your mama, and—"

"Yes ma'am?"

"Punkin, those gobbymawlers scare me. I didn't want to push them to a meanness we couldn't undo. So I didn't do a thing."

"Something that needs undoing is the Lollis kidnapping," Joel-Brock said, "*if* it can be undone. And if the gollyboogers—"

"—mawlers."

"—if the gobbymawlers jailed them. So I hope they did—put them in a place they can escape from, I mean."

Miss Melba sat utterly still, except for stroking his silky hair.

"What *are* gobbymawlers?" Joel-Brock asked. "I mean, *really*."

Miss Melba faced this expected question: "Most folks call anyone working at Big Box Bonanzas a gobbymawler, anyone wearing khakis and a saucer-shaped cap. *I* work for BBB, so I'm a gobbymawler, but *not* the grabby me-first licknickels that most people mean by that tag. Did you think I was?"

"No ma'am." And he didn't. How could he possibly?

"*Really*, Joel-Boy, the licknickels are usually the not-quite-human servants of Mr. Borsmutch, founder of Big Box Bonanzas. The nasty name for them is *sprols*, and they seem to live in or near the warehouse under our store. I *think*." She continued: "I *think* that—instead of *know* it—because Ms. Roberta Ripper-Gee says they're part person, part ghoul, and part fungus and that Pither M. Borsmutch raises them underground."

Joel-Brock lifted his eyebrows so high that his scalp tautened.

"Rumor runs that they're nasty things that *do* what Mr. Borsmutch wants, without him egging them on, but *want* what they want. One day, rumor also runs, he'll trade out his human workers for such gobbymawlers, *sprols*, and when he does, they'll take over and do everything in BBB: shelf-stocking, checking shoppers out, *everything*."

"Miss Melba, that stinks."

"Sprols do exist. I work with them. So do you. Most are okay—but some, inside or outside the store, become ghoulish things looking for rights to set wrong or wrongs to make even wronger."

"Do you see them around here . . . on Jarboe Street?"

"Not here, but in neighborhoods 'round our store, drifting like an ashy stink at our loading docks or just outside the Garden Center—*haints*, what you'd call ghosts. Do you sort of get what I'm saying?"

"No ma'am."

Miss Melba barked a laugh. "Well, it's not *just* around work, punkin. I also know they're out and about, creeping into our world."

"So we should lay low on Jarboe Street forever?"

Another hard laugh: "What a fretter you are, my worrywart orphan."

"I want my family back—but not messed up or killed. I'd also like to kick some gobbymawler butt. Or should I say 'sprol butt'?"

"You shouldn't say butt at all," Miss Melba said. "But I hear you, punkin."

"What can we do?"

"I got a notion that could maybe help—hire you a private eye."

"Miss Melba, I don't *know* any private eyes."

"I know two. One works part-time at Big Box Bonanzas."

"Doing what?'

"Shoplifter spotting."

"Gee. Could you—?"

"Oh, Lord, I smell bacon char. Yes, I could. But let's eat first, okay?"

*

That afternoon, Miss Melba drove Joel-Brock back to the store in her sporty hybrid car. It had the body of a 1950s Nash Metropolitan on the frame of a beat-up Jeep. It looked odd on the road, but Joel-Brock liked riding in it for the same reasons that a dog likes to poke its head out a car window—the sun, the wind, the street noise, the smells.

Once in Electronics, Joel-Brock fiddled with the flat-screen to pull in an afternoon Braves game featuring his grown-up self, J.-B. Lollis, and a new rival team, the Nashville Cats. When he had no luck, Miss Melba said, "Go stock shelves with Shel and Kyle until Augustus shows."

"I just bug 'em, ma'am," Joel-Brock said. "Besides, they never talk."

"You know they're sprols, don't you? *Good* sprols."

"No," he said, glum that he still had not set off in search of his family. He glared at Miss Melba thinking that *she* had somehow delayed him, but recalling that when she'd driven him to his house to pick up Josie, he had scared the Chihuahua. Figuring him for a bad guy, she'd hidden under the seat for the ride to Miss Melba's place.

Tonight, Miss Melba drew back from Joel-Brock's glare. *"What?"*

"Take me to see the detective."

"He doesn't always come in at the same times. I'm not even sure he's—"

"What's his name, Miss Melba?"

"Shoplifter-spotters don't like their names blabbed around. 'A nameless detective is an effective detective,' Vaughn always says."

"So his name is Vaughn?"

Miss Melba fanned the air, as if to dry her nail polish. "Golly-shoot, I didn't mean to blab it out like that."

"Miss Melba, you promised to help."

"I did, but—"

"Whisper his name—*all* of his name. Whispering isn't blabbing."

"Okay." Miss Melba approached. "It's a funny one. It sort of marks him out as . . . *different*." She bent down and tickled his ear with her breath: "It's Vaughnathan Valona. You got that? *Vaughnathan Valona*."

Joel-Brock imagined a big-shouldered man with olive skin wearing a charcoal-striped suit and alligator shoes. He'd once seen such a galoot in a crime show on TV, a guy nobody else called by name. Now he knew the detective's moniker and also that the Lollis family's kidnapping was almost as good as solved.

"Thanks." Joel-Brock kissed Miss Melba on the cheek.

Forty minutes late, Augustus Hudspeth lumbered into Electronics. "Why haven't you all turned on the Braves on ESPS-Tomorrow?"

Joel-Brock said, "I don't think that channel is ESPS-anything, sir."

"Yes it is: Extra-Sensorily Perceptive Sportsnews, a channel for seers and tea-leaf readers. Turn it on, boy, and tell me what mischief you two are hatching."

Joel-Brock turned on the FōFumm. "None, sir. Miss Melba just told me our store detective's name."

"Vaughnathan Valona—crafty old Vaughnathan Valona? How *is* our sneakiest gumshoe doing, anyway? I don't see him that much anymore."

Miss Melba said, "A crafty spy tries to go unseen."

"Not always," Augustus said. "Often, the obvious presence of a shoplifter spotter deters a thief—Department Store Management 101, Miss Berryhill."

Miss Melba grabbed Joel-Brock's arm and dragged him out of Electronics.

"Where are you all going?" Augustus called after them.

"To find the invisible man," Miss Melba said. "And to hire him to help our future home-run hitter get his family back."

5

Vaughnathan Valona

At a desk in Accounting, Miss Melba asked the manager, Roberta Ripper-Gee, if she'd seen Detective Valona. Ms. Ripper-Gee had a head the size of a grown male lion's and a mane of frosted tawny hair. "I saw him in the Garden Center. Or maybe in Automotive, or maybe in, uh, well—" She stuck.

"What was he wearing, Roberta?"

"That's hard to say—he's always changing. Maybe a sailor suit and an old pair of brogans. Maybe a baseball costume like your nephew's here."

"It's a uniform, *not* a costume," Joel-Brock said. After picking up Josie and some fresh clothes for him, he recollected, Miss Melba had put his uniform through her washer at least twice. It sure smelled better now.

Ms. Ripper-Gee said, "Oh! Mr. Valona was wearing tweed and riding an escalator up from the lounge to Sporting Goods."

An *escalator*? Did Big Box Bonanzas have an escalator? The building consisted of a single story on a huge slab. Shoppers either walked inside it or rode in electric carts with bulb-horns to warn others of their approach. Miss Melba thanked Ms. Ripper-Gee for this lead and tugged Joel-Brock away—from Accounting to a farther office, Product Recalls, to yet another department, Warranty Nullification, and on to another, Dunning for Dollars.

Joel-Brock sensed that *this* store was a much bigger thing than a mere link in a chain of such stores. On its outskirts and in its under-depths, he sensed, lay a complex of rooms, tunnels, galleries, dungeons, etc., that spread out beneath Georgia and possibly the entire United States. It unfurled like the roots, threads, and fruiting bodies of a continent-spanning, upside-down fairy ring of mushrooms. And if there was one "food" Joel-Brock hated, which his daddy loved, it was *mushrooms*.

In the Dunning for Dollars floor space, Miss Melba dragged him into a passage that twisted back into the main store. In this tunnel, they could see out, but customers and new hires could not see in. In fact, for most people, this corridor did not exist. Joel-Brock and Miss Melba moved through it like ghosts—until he let go of her hand and planted his heels, and she too halted. The tunnel through which they'd whisked had glassy flickering sides, and the people beyond it carried on their activities heedless of them, like fish in an aquarium. "I'm having a qualm," the boy said.

"A *qualm*?"

"Yes ma'am." His misgiving had grown from a hunch stemming from guesses about the gobbymawlers and also from a vision that had struck him, one that sprang from an odd sense of the layout of Big Box Bonanzas and its hidden branches into the world below. "I don't know, it's all awfully hinky."

"And what does *hinky* mean, pray tell?"

"I hear that word on TV cop shows. It means a kind of off-ness—you know, all sorts of fishy stuff. And I'm not just *qualmified*, I'm *scared*. This whole place is starting to heebie-jeebie me."

"Well, do you want to talk to Valona or not?"

When Joel-Brock squeaked, "yes," Miss Melba seized him again, hung a right in the flickering tunnel, and pulled him into a trunk line that took them to Sporting Goods. There they popped out like *Star Trek* adventurers materializing after a beam-down, but without terrifying anyone into heart attacks, if only because no one had seen them. Then they strolled past fishing rods, hunting gear, and baseball costumes—*uniforms*—trying to get their bearings. A hissing sound, like a basketball with a major valve leak, struck their ears: *"Psssssst, psssssst, psssssst!"*

Joel-Brock nudged Miss Melba and nodded upwards. A small adult face peered down from the top of a ten-foot-tall shelving unit. This unit held golfing items of every kind—some of doubtful usefulness, including bobble-head dolls of Tiger Woods and Phil Mickelson.

"Vaughnathan?" Miss Melba ventured.

The face overhead peered farther over the shelf edge. "Who else?" said the small mouth on this small face. "I wish you'd chosen a better time, Melba."

"A better time?"

"You've interfered with a sting. It's like you scared off the last ivorybill a single second before I could take its picture."

"Ivorybill?" Joel-Brock said.

"A rare, if not extinct, variety of woodpecker," the doll-like man said. "Don't they teach you anything in school nowadays?"

Joel-Brock winced in apology.

"I guess they're too busy prepping you for tests that maim your spirits, run off our best teachers, and soothe the consciences of pea-brained superintendents." The man had a lilting voice that could not have been sweeter if he had sung these words. Neither Joel-Brock nor Miss Melba replied. The man's high perch and cool displeasure at their arrival had stunned them to silence. Indeed, Miss Melba would have preferred a rattler's bite to the dignified anger of Vaughnathan Valona—for, as Joel-Brock deduced, this small man bore that very name.

Mr. Valona somersaulted to the shelf below him and shinnied down the big unit's other shelves to the floor. He wore a silk-lined tweed waistcoat, a tan linen-weave shirt, and tweed knickers. Although full-grown, with a head of bright flaxen hair, semicircles under his blue eyes, and a thin golden mustache, Mr. Valona stood not an inch taller than Joel-Brock, who this past year had keenly felt his own lack of height. If Miss Melba had taken them both in tow, anyone seeing the three together would have mistaken them for a foster mother and her wards on a back-to-school shopping trip.

"What," Mr. Valona said, "brings you here with such exquisitely rotten timing?"

Miss Melba hugged the detective, introduced him to Joel-Brock, and told him the boy's entire story since the disappearance of his family. She reeled off his mama's note from memory, described their goofy interactions with the FōFumm TV, and synopsized their lives since Joel-Brock's move to Jarboe Street.

"And now you come to *me*?" Mr. Valona said. He clapped a hand on Joel-Brock's shoulder. "To hire me?" He seemed tiny kin to Joel-Brock, as if you could buy a sibling in this store as easily as a plug-in nightlight. "If that's your plan, kidster, you should have hired me the first evening you came to Mr. Borsmutch's store. Your family's trail grows colder by the minute."

"Don't blame him, Vaughn. I'm the foot-dragger."

"Yes you are, Melba. But you get *some* credit for keeping him fed during your ridiculous delay." He smirked. "Now, how do you propose to pay me? Away from Big Box Bonanzas, I charge three hundred dollars a day—*plus* expenses."

"You're yanking my leg," Miss Melba said.

"Why do you think I've taken a second job with the robber baron of modern-day business bigwigs? I try to redeem its shortcomings by application and wiliness, but still I work beneath my pay grade." He sighed.

"My daddy always said the only beneath-you job is one you do poorly."

"Did your daddy ever work for Pither M. Borsmutch, Melba?"

"No. He only dug sewer lines or drove a taxi."

"I take my hat off to him." Mr. Valona pantomimed tipping a hat, and Joel-Brock decided that the man *liked* wearing disguises—for example, his old-style golfing outfit—because they kept him from having to wear the khaki jumpsuits and pancake hats that most of BBB's buddypards wore. "I'm sure your daddy brought steadiness and wiliness to both those jobs."

"I don't know about wiliness," Miss Melba said.

"I pride myself on my wiliness. I—"

"Like Wile E. Coyote?" Joel-Brock asked.

"No," Mr. Valona said. "*My* wiliness usually ends well. To date, I've avoided setting myself afire, holding a lit stick of dynamite in my mouth, or falling into a canyon pursued by an anvil."

As politeness required, Joel-Brock said, "That's good."

"Yes it is. Would you care to hear the stratagems I'd planned to deploy to catch a known shoplifter—plans that your arrival totally ruined?"

"Have we got time for that?" Joel-Brock asked.

"No, but engaging me to investigate your family's kidnapping may make up for the grim irreversibility of your procrastination." And he told them of his suspicion that a rich writer was "pilfering" golf balls from Sporting Goods. Even in summer, he wore an overcoat with deep pockets, into which he would funnel the balls and tote them out to his limousine.

"Why would a rich writer steal golf balls?" Miss Melba asked.

"*This* writer steals them because he loses half a dozen every time he plays."

"How do you know that?" Miss Melba asked.

"I've caddied for him. Moreover, *this* writer steals balls because he's a confirmed cheater who always writes lower numbers on his scorecards than he shoots. I don't fault writers as a group—only *this* particular dirt bag."

"How did you plan to catch him?" Joel-Brock asked.

Mr. Valona took his yNaut from his waistcoat pocket. "Photographic evidence."

yNaut

"That's our bestselling model!" Miss Melba seized it from him and examined it as if she'd never seen one before. "It's not only a camera, but also a phone, a text-messaging platform, a compact computer, a TV set, an electronic note pad, a GPS device, an electric razor—*with* a nose-hair trimmer—and, finally, a cocktail mixer."

"Right you are," Mr. Valona said. "A moment ago, I received word on it that *this* writer I've told you about, clad in an overcoat, was heading toward Sporting Goods. Then you all arrived." Mr. Valona grabbed the yNaut back. "But I'd planned to have *more* than photographic evidence. This thing also works as an explosive detonator."

Miss Melba frowned. "What explosives does it . . . detonate?"

Mr. Valona pocketed the device, whirled, and seized a box of a dozen Lost-in-the-Woods golf balls from a shelf. He spun back around as if the box held rubies or chocolate truffles. "Each of these boxes contains one ball full of

a colored powder I can detonate with the
yNaut. That act blows open the box,
stains the shoplifter's clothes and
skin, and thus marks that
person, indubitably, as *Lost-in-the-Woods Golf Balls*
a thief."

Joel-Brock imagined several shortcomings to this plan, but he still thought it sort of neat. His patience had fled, though, and so he asked, "Sir, how can we hire you if you want such a big fee?"

Mr. Valona put the golf-ball box back on its shelf. "Don't fret the fee, kidster. I *want* to help you. But I don't work for nothing—I'm not a *pro bono* kind of guy."

Miss Melba explained: "He's not taking you on as a charity case."

"Then how will I pay?"

"Once we find your folks," Mr. Valona said, "I'll raise the issue with them."

"Yes sir. But—"

"But what, worrywart?"

"Suppose you don't find them?"

Mr. Valona grinned like the Moon. "But I will. *We* will, together.'"

"But what if we don't?"

"Yes," said Miss Melba. "What if you don't?"

"Then I'll just put off billing the boy until he's raking it in as a Major League All-Star with the Atlanta Braves. Does that suit your cockerocity?"

"*Vaughnathan!*" Miss Melba said.

6

Adelaide-Bridget Coe

Hurrah: Mr. Valona wanted to start investigating at once. He would cease trying to catch the golf-ball-thieving writer not merely because Miss Melba and Joel-Brock had thwarted his plan, but also because he now had a more important goal.

But to Joel-Brock's dismay, before embarking on their adventure, the detective insisted that they return to Electronics. He wanted to watch the TV on which Miss Melba, Augustus, and Joel-Brock had allegedly witnessed his future self swatting home runs and doing interviews.

"But it's true," Joel-Brock said. "Don't you believe us?"

"Of course I do, kidster, but seeing is substantiating."

"Earlier, though, I couldn't quite get the FōFumm tuned in to the future."

"I've got a knack for electronics. Effective eavesdropping demands that skill. I also want to equip us for our search and its attendant perils."

They proceeded to Electronics via the aisles and cut-throughs that anyone could use—*not* via the ghostly tunnels by which Miss Melba and Joel-Brock had just rocketed to Sporting Goods. As they walked, Miss Melba asked, "Do you *really* plan to take Joel-Brock with you, Vaughn?"

"Why not? Forgive me—maybe I should say, *'yNaut'*?"

"You'll put him in danger—'attendant perils,' like you said."

Mr. Valona laughed. "Which we'll face together. I need backup, Melba. *You* don't plan on coming, do you?"

"Backup? You need an army. And I wouldn't go even if you could turn my hair battleship-gray again."

"I'd get a release from the boy's parents if I could, but . . ." He let this comment trail off. "So I got *his* permission instead. Besides, it's time."

"Past time," Joel-Brock popped off.

During this walk, a host of new buddypards in khaki uniforms and pancake berets appeared about the store. Had Big Box Bonanzas bumped into all-out hiring mode? Joel-Brock's mama often griped about how hard it was to get anybody to wait on her. Tonight, however, the store teemed with buddypards and/or gobbymawlers—of the human, not the ghostly, kind.

Joel-Brock nodded at all these workers. "What's going on?"

"A mustering of *bodily* forces," Mr. Valona said, "hinting that Pither Borsmutch has sent most of his *spectral* troops to Sporangium. These human workers will try to take up the slack."

"Sporangium?" Joel-Brock said.

"Another country."

"Another country?" Joel-Brock repeated.

Mr. Valona glanced at Miss Melba. "Is there an echo in here?" He kept striding. "Of course there's an echo—every crook and nanny of this store shelters a microphone. I should know: I installed them."

"But what about this other country, Sporangium?"

"Patience. You'll soon find yourself *exploring* that fungal paradise."

Joel-Brock could not think of an earthly place—Siberia, Somalia, Death Valley—that sounded less appealing than *Sporangium*. Maybe he should run home to Crabapple Circle—where nobody would be waiting for him but the moody Will S Gato. So he kept walking with his new-found companions toward Electronics.

There, Augustus Hudspeth had collared a small, coppery-haired girl in a denim miniskirt and a sleeveless powder-blue jersey. Mushroom-shaped metal earrings dangled from her lobes, and Mr. Hudspeth was shaking her as if to dislodge not just those earrings but also every red-gold hair on her head.

"Good golly," Miss Melba said, "Augustus has gone bonkers."

Mr. Hudspeth swung about, bringing the girl with him. Then, seeing Mr. Valona, he shouted, "*You* should have arrested this riot grrrl!"

Then, to Miss Melba: "You're late getting back. I returned to find this freaky outcast trying to steal the FōFumm on display. I couldn't believe it!"

Mr. Valona said, "The poor girl would need a wheelbarrow and a block and tackle to steal that set."

"Let go!" she cried. "I just wanted to see if it works. But it *doesn't*." She wriggled free of her captor. "*Ow!* I am *so* going to sue you."

Augustus Hudspeth said, "Even if it worked, *you* couldn't afford it."

"What did you mean, 'freaky outcast'?" Mr. Valona asked.

Miss Melba put her arm around the girl, who initially tried to resist this hug but then relaxed a little and accepted it.

Mr. Hudspeth said, "Upper management fired her about two weeks ago."

"It's been barely a week!" the girl objected.

"Her name's Adelaide-Bridget Coe," Mr. Hudspeth went on. "She sabotaged our people in Shipping for three or four months, daily."

"Call me Addi. And as far as 'sabotaging' goes, I don't dispute it.'"

"Augustus," Mr. Valona said, "if I didn't know this young woman before tonight, blame those in Management who never told me about her."

Mr. Hudspeth said, "Sorry, *Vaughn*, but I blame you," and strode away, leaving Joel-Brock to wonder where he went on his impromptu "breaks."

"You may not know me," Addi told Mr. Valona, escaping Miss Melba's hug, "but I greatly admire your work." Out from the older woman's wing, she looked smaller, but in fact stood an inch or so taller than Mr. Valona, who was almost exactly Joel-Brock's height.

Mr. Valona thanked Addi, took out his yNaut, and held it up to the flat-screen set that Mr. Hudspeth had accused Addi of trying to steal.

"Why'd you get hung up on *this* TV?" he asked her. "You could have switched on any of these. Behold: a *UBM*, a *Duende*, a *Q-Cumber*, a *Phiew*, a *Soma*, a *Kumquat*. I fail to understand your fascination with this ungainly FōFumm."

Adelaide-Bridget Coe glanced at Joel-Brock, and something curious about her eyes and mouth made him catch his breath. Meanwhile, Mr. Valona jacked his yNaut (a *Kumquat Cirkuitries* product) into the big flat-screen. The yNaut glowed crimson in his hand, x-raying his finger bones.

The TV set flickered on, showing a game between the Braves and the Nashville Cats at the Cats' stadium in Smyrna, Tennessee.

An announcer said. *"The Bravos and the Kitties are tied 5 to 5, and the toughest toms in Nashville's order are coming up again."*

"How did you do that?" Addi asked Mr. Valona.

"Which?" Joel-Brock asked. "Turn on the TV or call up the future?" Everyone looked at him as if *he* had materialized as magically as had the FōFumm's picture or the unexpected future, and he glanced about for an empty box to crawl into. Then a Nashville Cat homered to right, breaking the tie. "I should never watch," the boy said. "That *always* happens."

Addi said, "I chose this set because I heard it could do *just* as it's doing now." She nodded at the players on its screen. "Look at those uniforms. Must we all become fashion retards—like the gobbymawlers in *this* sorry place—to live in the future?"

Mr. Valona said, "From whom did you hear of the set's capabilities?"

"A friend in Shipping, and after the Lollises' kidnapping, I checked it out. Then that butthead there"—nodding in the direction that Mr. Hudspeth had gone—"showed up, and you saw the rest." No one spoke, for her words *after the Lollises' kidnapping*" hung before them all like neon-red skywriting.

Joel-Brock blurted, "What do you know about the kidnapping?"

"Who wants to know?"

"Joel-Brock," Miss Melba said, "the brother of the sweet girl those gobbymawler sprols also grabbed."

Addi looked at Joel-Brock closely. "No ma'am, I don't think so."

"You *should* think so," Joel-Brock said. "You visited our house after my family got stolen. You pounded on our door. You looked like a gobbymawler. I thought you'd come to get me too and that bunches of other gobbymawlers would leap out of the bushes to grab me."

"You were probably inside robbing the place," Addi said.

"Yeah. I stole this baseball *costume*. Then I walked to Big Box Bonanzas to turn myself in to its world-famous store detective."

"You took your time doing it," Addi said.

Joel-Brock reddened. "I have short legs and I walk slow."

"Addi, you knew the Lollises had a son," Miss Melba said. "Shipping records said so. You went to their place to tell him something, didn't you?"

"Oh." Addi peered at Joel-Brock even more closely. "Oh. Maybe it is him."

"I've got a question." Joel-Brock squinted equally hard at Addi. "What did you come to our house dressed like a gobbymawler to tell me?"

"That's my question too," Mr. Valona said.

Addi went to Joel-Brock and grasped his hands. "It's easy to say but lots harder to do something about: I know *where* those so-called gobbymawlers took your family, and I want to help you free them."

"Oh, Lord." Mr. Valona closed his eyes. "Do I need a permission slip for this one, or has she already killed her kin and set up a separate household?"

"*Vaughnathan!*" Miss Melba said.

*

As it turned out, Adelaide-Bridget Coe—whose last name could have instead been Doe, Noe, Roe, or Poe, etc.—had run away from home at age thirteen. Ever since, she'd lived apart from her biological parents, who, everyone supposed, must have treated her badly. Why else would she have run away?

In any case, Vaughnathan Valona, Joel-Brock, and Addi set off toward Sporting Goods, leaving Melba Berryhill as the lone buddypard in Electronics. As they traveled, Mr. Valona and Joel-Brock asked Addi questions, and Addi answered, or didn't, as she judged appropriate to their individual "need to know."

Of course, even before they left Electronics, they had wanted to know where the gobbymawler sprols had taken Joel-Brock's family. An answer to that question would tell them their destination. Everyone, after all, realized that they must venture underground to bring about this rescue—but *where*, exactly?

"I'll tell you once we dive down the rabbit hole," Addi had said.

Mr. Valona said, "Are you perhaps *pretending* to know, to trick us into taking you along?"

"No sir. I have a nifty personal code—I refuse to lie."

"Really?" Joel-Brock said.

"Yes. I loathe liars. So if I say a thing, either that thing is true or I deeply *believe* it's true. Don't you have similar nifty codes?"

"I'm afraid not," Mr. Valona said. "Not one such *nifty* code."

Joel-Brock said nothing.

"That's just sad," Addi told them. "If you ask me a question, I'll tell the truth, if I can, or else I won't reply at all. I have no obligation to say anything more. I call that the ABC rule of PPP, meaning *Personal Privacy Preservation*. I'll *always* tell you just what 'you need to know.'"

"But *you* decide which information we need or don't need?"

"Of course, sir, for if it relates to me, who else would know better?"

"What if it doesn't relate to you?" Mr. Valona asked.

"I still wouldn't answer if you really didn't need to know."

Mr. Valona said, "You understand what a person's refusing to answer can lead to, don't you, Miss Coe?"

"More courtesy and kindness, I would hope."

"Often," Mr. Valona said, "torture."

"What?" said Addi, scandalized.

"Mobsters, terrorists, and even governments use it to squelch the virtues you've just cited," Mr. Valona told her.

"And *you* call people ugly names," Joel-Brock pointed out.

"Only if they deserve it," Addi shot back. "And I'll bet you do too."

When Mr. Valona laughed aloud, Joel-Brock asked him, "Are we really going to take her with us?"

Mr. Valona told Addi that if she indeed wanted to go, she *must* answer his next question with total honesty.

Addi narrowed her smoky green eyes. "What is it?"

"Augustus says you sabotaged the people in Shipping. He claims that's what led Management to can you. What did you do, *exactly*?"

"Ah." As they entered Sporting Goods, Addi relaxed. "Nothing much: I

sent Big Box Bonanzas shipments to the wrong places. An order of lingerie
for a fashion show in Atlanta arrived at a convent in Kentucky. Some ice-
fishing gear flew to an orphanage in Costa Rica. A disabled widow near the
Mojave Desert got a set of water skis. You know, that sort of thing."

Joel-Brock mulled this confession, but Mr. Valona gave Addi and
him backpacks and let them fill them with canteens, casting rods and line,
flashlights, beef-jerky packets, Frisbees, Lost-in-the-Woods golf balls, etc.
During this spree, Mr. Valona shot photos with his yNaut. These he emailed
to the checkers upfront, charging every item to his own buddypard Dock-Me
Card. Joel-Brock and Addi, warily stink-eyeing each other, stooped farther
and farther over under their backpacks' increasing weight.

Mr. Valona asked Addi: "Did you enjoy sending merchandise to these
slyly off addresses?"

"Of course I did—it was fun."

Joel-Brock said, "It was *lies*, despite a *personal code* that doesn't let you lie."

"But I did it for bigger reasons than just mis-sending stuff."

"Yeah? Like what?"

"Before, I was talking about *in my personal relationships*. But in Shipping, I was saying something about unfair hiring practices, our putrid pay, or how Big Box Bonanzas makes every town they show up in look like every other place they've ever built a store. Besides that—"

"How does sending people's stuff to the wrong places say all that? My mama held protests outside BBB with signs that said *exactly* what she meant. She never gave *anyone* a wrong address. She never just *lied*."

Recalling how he'd hated his mama's outspokenness—or his *embarrassment* at her complaints about a store he liked—Joel-Brock felt a hot shame, a battle between his fondness for Big Box Bonanzas and his anger that sprols from the store would kidnap his family because Sophia wanted Management to behave better.

"Okay, okay." Addi shook her head. "I did it because I *wanted* to get fired. I hated working here, but I needed the money. I still do."

"So do you want to go with us just for *something to do*?" Mr. Valona challenged her. "Or do you expect us to *pay* you for your services?"

"I want to *help*, to make up for the bad crap I did earlier."

"The bad crap you took pride in—until Joel-Brock called you on it?"

Addi gazed at the floor.

"Are you acting *now*? Trying to flimflam us again?"

Joel-Brock felt a twinge of guilt. "Let her come, sir. She's confused. So am I."

Maddeningly, Addi kept her lips clamped tight.

"You sure that's what you want, Master Lollis?"

Joel-Brock nodded.

"Okay, then, kidsters. Follow me to the Garden Center."

And so they headed toward it—but before they got there, Addi detoured into an alcove selling hairdryers and bought a big, battery-powered hairdryer that Joel-Brock regarded as a truly stupid purchase—why not put an anvil in her backpack? Afterward, though, *he* detoured into Toys to add to his pack a double handful of cute wind-up pigs, three to each hand. Mr. Valona immediately asked him what he was doing

"We'll need some distracters, sir—for us, when we're bored, or for the bad guys if we get into any tight spots."

"Distracters?" Mr. Valona said.

"Yes sir—distracters."

At length, they did reach the Garden Center, a department stocked with plants, fertilizers, wheelbarrows, hoses, and so on. There, Joel-Brock realized that Mr. Valona had meant all along for Addi to go with them. Why else give her a backpack and let her load it before she satisfied his curiosity about her motives? Only if he had already made up his mind about Addi would he have done that. But Mr. Valona had also wanted *Joel-Brock* to want her to go with them, so he'd set up their walking interview to let him voice his doubts about her, but also to *forgive her* for breaking her own code of behavior, and *then* to ask her to go with them. Mr. Valona was one smart man.

7

A Hidden Moving Staircase

The Garden Center had a high roof and no outer walls except for curtains of green mesh that buddypards rolled up or down with pretty silver ropes. Joel-Brock, glancing about, took a grateful breath. The Center smelled of pine, mint, and honeysuckle, of gardenias after a good gobbymawler misting.

Addi turned in a wide circle, extending her arms to embrace the sweetness. "This almost makes up for all the gobbymawling Big Box Bonanzas does when they move into town. I mean, they *clear out* the native plants, all the animals and bugs that rely on them, and then they pour acres of concrete."

"Not always," Joel-Brock said.

"Oh, yeah?" Addi said. "Where didn't they?"

"Here in Cobb Creek. The concrete was already here. Mr. Borsmutch bought an old strip mall, tore its stores down, and built this box on top of them—the very first Big Box Bonanzas in North America."

"Yeah. That I *do* know. Every ten minutes, some grinning buddypard tells you, *This is the First Store in the Most Successful Discount-House Franchise in the Whole Stinking World.*" Addi swung into an animated cheerleading bit: "*Who's Bonanzic? / We're Bonanzic! / Sis-boom-bah! / What's Bonanzic? / We're Bonanzic! / Sis-boom-shush!*" She bent, put a finger to her lips, spread her arms, leapt up, and cried, "*Pither Borsmutch, / Knock on Wood! / He Went and Did It / 'Cause He Could!*" Her arms and legs formed a limber X. "*Yaaaay, Piiitheeeer!*"

Visibly, Mr. Valona winced. "Please, a little *less* enthusiasm."

Addi curtsied and obeyed. Relieved, Mr. Valona led his charges back toward the main building and a row of Carolina cypresses in tubs. These hid a shelving unit full of rubber trashcans and their shield-like lids. On the way, they passed a metal trough packed with black humus, leaf mold, sprigs of moss, and shredded scrap paper. Several kinds of mushrooms grew in this trough, but not in orderly rows. Mr. Valona pointed out a morel, a destroying angel, a honey mushroom, a turkey tail, a chanterelle, and a king bolete. The chanterelle smelled like ripening apricots. The destroying angel rose inside a plastic box with a chunk of granite atop it. Across the box shone a duct-tape strip on which someone had printed in permanent marker: **DO NOT TOUCH—POISONOUS**.

"They're all gross," Addi said. "Except the turkey tail—it's sort of cute."

"They're interesting looking," Joel-Brock demured, diplomatically.

"If you're interested in gross garbage," Addi said. "But if I ever have a daughter, I *might* name her Chanterelle."

"Very pretty," Mr. Valona said.

Joel-Brock said, "Very hoity-toity." A favorite putdown of Arabella's.

"Let's go down," Mr. Valona said.

Finally, Joel-Brock thought. He and Addi fell into step behind Mr. Valona. He led them through several Carolina cypresses before the only substantive wall in the Garden Center and, pushing their branches aside, squeezed between two saplings. The children followed, and all three stood before a dazzling watery glow, like you see on the sides and floors of a well-lit swimming pool at night.

Stretching down, farther down, and farther down yet, was a moving staircase with coppery steps and rails like huge rolled strips of licorice. It plunged into the abyss below them. The steps kept plunging, the staircase's reddish sheen often touched with pulses of deep-ocean blue. Alarmingly, Joel-Brock could not see the bottom of the vanishing steps, which glided down-down-down but emerged again from the Garden Center's floor, so that he decided, well, if *steps* could recycle, maybe *bodies* could too—an uplifting sort of notion if also a kind of crazy one.

Beside him, Mr. Valona said, "Who wants to go first?"

"I do!" Addi briefly teetered before grabbing a rail.

To avoid looking like a wuss, Joel-Brock stepped onto the stairs, and Mr. Valona eased on behind them. "Use the rail and balance on your heels," he advised.

And, as if in a dream, they rode into a ginormous space that Big Box Bonanzas used for storage: a warehouse for its gigazillion products, a horn of plenty for all the loyal customers of Pither M. Borsmutch.

Thirty yards away, there rose an up-bound escalator with see-through sides and flickering blue-and-coppery pulses very like their own. That staircase, with its crowd of riders, moved abreast of theirs, ever ascending. The figures on it were buddypards in pink khaki, either old hires or newcomers assigned to carry items up from the warehouse. But Joel-Brock saw them as imposters—beings with tiny differences from what a *real* person would view as genuinely human. Hadn't Miss Melba told him that sprols had both fungal and ghostly traits, just as these rising figures did?

First: Their uniforms looked like outgrowths of their bodies rather than distinct pieces of clothing.

Second: Their pancake hats had *gills* underneath—*gills* teeming with tiny spores. The spores sifted out in powdery varicolored spills. One gobbymawler had a halo of red spores behind its head; another, a long plume of lavender motes.

Third: These quasi-humans popped in and out of view like teleporting ghosts, a talent that Joel-Brock checked out as they ascended. A sprol with a white face abruptly vanished, but another, sixty feet below in a plum-colored cap, faded away in a lingering half-minute.

Fourth: Gobbymawler sprols, Miss Melba had said, were all mutes. They could no more talk than a daisy. But she swore they could e-mail, text, tweet, and project their "voices" into animals and human beings.

Fifth: —

But four examples of gobbymawler oddities were enough for now. Joel-Brock had too many sad worries already, especially with his unremitting grief droning like a vacuum cleaner in a distant room.

At the foot of the staircase, a wide enameled floor rose toward them. To the sides of both escalators curved rings of well-padded chairs, places for older buddypards to prop their feet, sip lemonades, and chat before returning surface-side to work. Addi, heedless of her lopsided backpack's weight, tap-danced down the moving steps.

Mr. Valona called, "Careful, Miss Coe. Careful!"

"Got to go," Addi called back. "Really, *really* got to go!"

"Me too," Joel-Brock said. "This is the *longest* escalator ever." Given the length of the trip, he half-expected a group of buddypards to greet them with snacks. Instead, Addi found a restroom under the escalator and waited outside it, hopping from foot to foot, for its current occupant to emerge. Joel-Brock jumped in line behind her, and an old song, "It Must Be Raindrops," played loudly over a nearby sound system. The person in the restroom finally came out, but the door clicked shut before Addi could catch it and hop inside. When her one attempt to pry open the door failed, she struck it with her fist—whereupon a small mouth-like hole in the door spoke:

"To enter, you must answer a simple history question or slide a dollar bill into the receptacle to your right."

Addi gawped at the door. "You'd charge me to pee?"

"Only if you fail to answer my question," the door said—reasonably enough, in Joel-Brock's opinion.

"Okay, okay. Ask your stupid question."

"Mind your tone and vocabulary, miss."

Through tightened lips, Addi seethed.

"Ready? Good. Here goes: In what year did Pither Borsmutch open the first Big Box Bonanzas store in Hawaii?"

"Hawaii? How should I know? How many college *professors* would know? It's a ridiculous question."

"Wrong," the door said. *"Next."*

"Wait. Who at *any* university could answer that question?"

"Business students *at hundreds of fine schools could answer it. So I ask again, young miss: **What year?**"*

"1066! 1492! 1999!"

"I asked for an answer, not three guesses. Next."

Joel-Brock eased Addi aside. "Please, Mister Door, give me what you promised Addi—'a simple history question.'"

"Okay. Ready? In what year and city did Mr. Borsmutch open our country's first Big Box Bonanzas store?"

"That's *two* questions," Joel-Brock said.

"What a farce," Addi grumbled.

"Take your pick," the door said. *"Answer whichever you like."*

Over Joel-Brock's shoulder, Addi shouted, "Cobb Creek, Georgia!"

"A disqualified person has answered the second half of your question," the door told Joel-Brock.

"That's all right, Mister Door. I would have said the same thing."

"Honestly?"

"Cross my heart." Joel-Brock crossed his heart. "You asked me a simpler question than you asked Addi, Mister Door."

Mister Door triggered a mechanism to free its latch, and when the door swung open, Joel-Brock caught it and nodded Addi in. Blinking her thanks, Addi slipped past Joel-Brock into the restroom and closed its door. Joel-Brock sighed. But he could stand the pressure. And, if he couldn't, somewhere in the lounge he'd find an out-of-the-way redwood planter and water the sapling in it.

8

The Valorous Smalls

When Joel-Brock and Addi rejoined Mr. Valona between the lounge's two escalators, he nodded toward a nearby food bazaar. Its ceiling, however, capped them at such a height that Joel-Brock viewed it as limitless night sky. Staring upward at it, he put a crick in his neck. Immediately, he began shrugging his shoulders to dislodge it.

"Are you okay, kidster?" Mr. Valona asked.

"Maybe he needs to take a whiz," Addi said.

Joel-Brock turned a disbelieving glare on Addi. "Actually, I *don't.*"

Mr. Valona persisted: "Then what's the trouble?"

"I feel small down here, *really small.*" He nodded at the rising staircase. "Let me go back up to help Miss Melba in Electronics."

Addi jumped all over him. "*Miss Melba?* She can take care of herself. Don't you want to find your family?"

Joel-Brock hung his head.

"You're giving up before we've even started?" Addi asked.

Mr. Valona knelt in front of Joel-Brock, his head now lower than the boy's. "I'm a grown-up—supposedly. Does looking down on me make you feel just a trifle *less small* in this huge place?"

"No sir. A grown-up ought to be bigger than a kid. Otherwise . . ."

"He's trying to say size matters," Addi interpreted.

"He's already said that, Miss Coe, but in the low mood he's in, he didn't need to say anything—nor did you." Mr. Valona remained in his squat. "Master Lollis, you're wearing a uniform with *Braves* across its front and the name of your mama's business, *WorkOutWarriors*, across its back."

"Yes sir."

"If your baseball coach ever gives you and the guys pep talks, aren't they verbal kicks in the pants meant to encourage you?"

"Yes sir."

"Okay. Here's *my* pep talk." Mr. Valona glanced at Addi. "Don't worry—you don't need to compose a *cheer* to go along with it."

Addi patted Mr. Valona's head. "Bless you, my son." Mr. Valona glared at her, and she snatched back her hand.

"Okay, Master Lollis, we're a team. Most teams have names. Well, *I* have a name for us, and although you may not like it at first, I don't really care."

Addi said, "For Pete's sake, Mr. Valona, what is it?"

"The Valorous Smalls."

Addi and Joel-Brock said nothing.

"Write it on your hearts. And when we run upon a stumbling block, call upon it and *believe* it. If you do, we—the Valorous Smalls—will leap that obstacle and press on to our goal." Mr. Valona nodded at the food bazaar: a tangle of booths, carts, and vending machines lit by rays of pastel light crisscrossing from projectors in the ceiling. "Now get yourselves something to eat—on me."

*

Vaughnathan Valona led Addi and Joel-Brock into the gloomy food bazaar. Eventually, they reached a gypsy wagon set up on potting urns, not wheels. Its fare included gyros, subs, franks on egg rolls, and pizza by the slice.

To Joel-Brock, the attendant looked like what he figured a gobbymawler sprol would look like. If so, it was the first sprol he'd seen close-up, possibly, despite all Miss Melba had told him about these creatures since his family's kidnapping. The figure in the wagon had a spotted beige pudginess and a flat personality that weirded him and Addi out. They could not tell if he/she was dude or chick, teen or geezer. And this lumpy-faced person's clothes—a cook's hat, a coat, and a cape—seemed of a piece with his/her face, neck, wrists, and hands. This person did not talk, but handed them small electronic slates on which to tap out their orders.

Mr. Valona said, "Chow down big-time for our travels, okay?"

After ordering a gyro, Addi teased Joel-Brock for choosing ordinary root beer and two slices of lukewarm pizza. Mr. Valona's kosher frank with sauerkraut and a bottle of warm dark beer she dismissed as "Yucky!"

Mr. Valona paid with his buddypard Dock-Me Card, and they found a metal patio table on the shadowy edge of the dining area. The table had a hole through its center for a canvas umbrella. They sat there in the brooding twilight and ate. Masted with umbrellas, other tables floated nearby or staggered out into the dusk. Joel-Brock, gnawing his pizza, spied two figures several tables away, like two gray posts in the muddy light. He nudged Mr. Valona's knee.

At length, the taller of the two figures resolved into . . . *Augustus Hudspeth*, Miss Melba's boss! Maybe this was where he retreated every evening for his breaks—this vast foyer to the subterranean warehouse of Mr. Borsmutch's first Big Box Bonanzas. What did Augustus do down here? Answering that question might require X-ray vision. Well, Mr. Valona drew from his pocket a device that Joel-Brock thought of as an *ocular*, half of a pair of binoculars. Mr. Valona put it to his eye and focused on Augustus and his companion, without trying to disguise his spying. Maybe he just hoped to make the two of them uncomfortable. And he succeeded.

Mr. Hudspeth leaned forward and stared back. Mr. Valona, seeing that Augustus had seen *him*, lowered the ocular, stood, bowed in apology. Augustus arose and dashed toward the Smalls, ending with a slide and a palm slap atop their table. This slap scared the bejabbers out of all three Smalls.

"What nerve—showing up here with this turncoat!" he said to Mr. Valona while glowering at Addi. "Given Joel-Brock's claim that we had his family abducted, I figured you and the boy might, but *this one*"—a new palm slap, in front of Addi—"that takes the red-velvet cake, Vaughnathan!"

Addi shrank into herself.

Now, Augustus's mysterious friend approached them. This *personage* had the bearing of a king or a cardinal. But, except for his tall, slender build, his wide bowl-like hat, and his clear maleness, he looked a lot like the person in the food wagon. Also, he carried in his arms a large black bird. The bird lent the only vivid colors to its bearer's person—it had *yellow* wattles, an *orange* beak and legs, and really *white* wing patches.

"That's a hill mynah," Mr. Valona said. "Such birds can talk."

The personage reached Augustus's shoulder, the bird in his arms repeatedly cocking its head, as if assessing them. Its owner—a sprol overlord?—stood before them at once human and not quite. His flesh—spotted white, pale brown, even a muted orange—was alien-looking, but the crowns, brims, buttons, and drapes of his clerical garb lent him, nonetheless, a handsome dignity.

"Your Eminence," Mr. Hudspeth intoned, "I present to you Vaughnathan Valona, Adelaide-Bridget Coe, and Joel-Brock Lollis. Mortals, I present to

you Archbishop Basil Sydney Meece, primate of the Holy Sub-terranean Assembly of Greater Sporangium."

Mortals? Joel-Brock thought. Who, nowadays, calls people *mortals?* And wasn't a *primate* some sort of monkey? This guy was more like a walking mushroom. And the bird on his sleeve—what was *that* all about? In a brash whistling voice, the mynah said, *"Pleased to meetcha, yep. I know I speak for both of us when I say, 'Pleased to meet-cha, yep-yep.'"*

Looking at Augustus, Mr. Valona whispered, "How should I address the bird?"

"I call him Mortimer," the my-nah more or less whistled.

This reply confused Joel-Brock. Why would the bird say *him* instead of *myself?* And it dawned on him that Archbishop Meece had spoken *through* the mynah. Its smart-alecky whistle undercut his dignity, but maybe a mynah suited the *primate* better than a ventriloquist's figure would have done. The Archbishop pulled an inchworm out of his hat and fed it to the bird.

"Your Eminence," Mr. Valona said, "maybe you should have chosen a cardinal instead of a hill mynah."

"*Very funny,*" Mortimer said. Or the archbishop said through the bird.

"Not as funny as naming your mouthpiece Mortimer, Your Eminence."

Augustus sighed disgustedly, but the presence of Archbishop Meece, the sprol clergyman, kept him from further rudeness. Joel-Brock found Augustus's grating attitude harder to understand here than upstairs in Electronics. There, he often detected a creamy nice-guyness in the black coffee of his surliness—like when he got caught up in a Braves game. Maybe, down here, he was actually conducting a high-level interview with this big shot in the East Sporangium church.

Mr. Valona said, "Your Eminence, what brings you to our buddypard lounge?"

"*Free inquiry beats free beer, but they never give Mortimer a sip of the suds, so I just don't know.*"

"Stop it, Mortimer," Augustus said. "You know our talks are confidential."

Archbishop Meece and Mortimer shook their heads, and then Mortimer whistled, "*We have no secrets, except the age and size of the subsurface mycelium from which our peoples spring.*"

"What's *MY-see-lee-um*?' Joel-Brock asked.

"*The tiny white filaments,*" Mortimer crooned, "*making up the vegetable portion of a fungus like a mushroom.*"

"And your people come from *that*?" Addi quickly added, "I mean Archbishop Meece's people—not yours, Mortimer."

"*Yep-yep,*" Mortimer said. "*They burst forth from the mycelium and separate into two-legged creatures of almost-human face and form.*" The mynah looked accusingly at Augustus. "*But what ugly name do you later bestow upon them here, sir?*"

"None, Mortimer—none at all."

"*Come,*" Mortimer cawed. "*Spit it out, Augustuss Hudssspeth!*"

"Gobbymawlers," Augustus said grudgingly. "But only jealous detractors use that term. No one in Upper Management condones it."

Archibishop Meece leaned into Augustus, and the bird said, "*You lie again, eh?*"

As white as vanilla yogurt, Augustus said, "That's harsh—very harsh."

"What do the peoples of Sporangium call themselves?" Addi asked.

With a menacing flap of his wings, Mortimer said, "*A persspicacious quesstion, Miss Coe. We call ourselves sssporules.*"

"Meaning . . ?" Addi pressed.

"*A small spore, a living bit of the mycelium-sprung population of Sporangium's own blessssst commoners.*"

The Archbishop put an arm about Addi and lifted Mortimer closer to her ear, even though everyone could hear Mortimer just fine. "*Our current issue with Mr. Borsmutch of Big Box Bonanzas,*" he said, "*stems from what we can only term the psychological press-ganging of our younger sporules into menial jobs in his stores. This gives them an above*ground *but hardly an above*board *sort of employment. Such work offers irresistible temptations—the stars, the glamour of commerce—but no real opportunity. We consider this practice unfriendly, exploitive, and very, very . . . bad.*"

"That's a narrow take on the reality," Augustus said.

"Especially," Mr. Valona said, "when Mr. Borsmutch also provides these young sporules—whom no one in BBB management *ever* addresses as a *buddypard*—a chance to *disappear* anyone hostile to his business practices."

"Like my mama," Joel-Brock said. "Gobbymawler sprols took my family because Mama hacked off the Boss." He stink-eyed Augustus, who now knew that he wasn't Miss Melba's nephew. "If *I* had been at home, they'd've taken me too."

Aware of their growing anger, Augustus took the cleric and his bird back to their table, where he regaled them with a speech about the diversity of Sporangium's peoples and the Archbishop's failure to grasp Mr. Borsmutch's motives in letting young sporules pass through the GillGate into his warehouse and store.

If Joel-Brock weren't lying, Augustus said, he could only assume that the sporules who'd stolen his family were maverick fungi acting on motives at odds with the Boss's. He asked the Archbishop to stay seated while he conferred a last time with the distraught Smalls, who had just caused him and his bird a powerful distress.

"Thanks loads," he then told the Smalls. "With buddypards like you, or with *ex*- or *mock*-workers like you, who needs bomb throwers?"

"You've already fired Addi," Mr. Valona said. "You can fire Joel-Brock and me when we rescue his family from Sporangium."

Mr. Hudspeth paced. "You may *not* use our warehouse to enter Sporangium! So return your butts back to from whence they came—"

"*Whence?*" Addi said. "***Whence?***"

"—that is, to the Garden Center and back into Cobb Creek, or I'll ask Security to toss you out on your puny posteriors!" Augustus shot Addi a bitter smirk.

Mr. Valona said, "If you fire us and turn us out, we'll go to the police and—"

"Wait," Joel-Brock said. "Wait, sir."

"—and tell them that, on Pither Borsmutch's orders, sprols kidnapped this young man's family and put them in a jail in a country next to this warehouse. We'll identify the sprols as terrorists under Mr. Borsmutch's authority."

"Suppose I just kill the three of you?" Augustus drew a Glomtock pistol from a holster under his shirt and pointed it at each Small in turn.

"Disperse and deploy," Mr. Valona said. Joel-Brock and Addi leapt to either side of Augustus, and Mr. Valona leapt in front of the bore of Augustus's pistol. "Frisbees to the fore. Sail Saucers out." The children grabbed Sail Saucers from their backpacks and held them by their edges, level with the floor, ready to fling.

"Don't be dunderheads. This baby"—Augustus shook the pistol—"will drop you all so fast you won't know what did it."

Mr. Valona said, "A nanosecond after your first shot, our Sail Saucers will behead you, Augustus."

"That's bunk, Vaughnathan. It's impossible. It's—"

"These Saucers have stainless-steel edges as sharp as new razor blades. Their rims are weighted to make our throws as deadly as cobra spit."

"What a lie. Big Box Bonanzas has never stocked—"

"Yes, it has. Put down that *thing*, Augustus. Or risk losing your head."

Augustus lowered his ugly Glomstock. "Can't you midgets figure out when a guy's just kidding?" The Smalls gaped at him with evident skepticism. "I just can't let you all proceed," he told the trio. "If I did, my shrimpy big boss would—would—well, he'd wax wroth!"

"Who's Roth?" Joel-Brock said.

"And why would the Great Borsmutch wax Roth and charge it to your Dock-Me Card?" Addi added.

Mr. Valona urged Augustus to *call* Mr. Borsmutch on his yNaut and ask him if he would keep the Smalls from entering East Sporangium on their Mission of Mercy. "Don't begrudge this boy a chance to reunite with his mother and urge her to drop her hostility to everything Big and Bonanzic."

Archbishop Meece approached Augustus and put his arm around him. With one finger he drew something on his brow, maybe a mushroom cap. Mr. Valona gave Augustus the yNaut. Archbishop Meece helped him enter the number for Mr. Borsmutch, and soon—to everyone's surprise but Augustus's—Mr. Borsmutch and Mr. Hudspeth were talking. The Big Boss agreed to the Smalls' request and ordered Augustus to go with them through the warehouse to the GillGate, but only to let them enter Sporangium if they answered three questions at the GillGate without any help.

"Holy manatee," Addi said. "The game's already fixed."

Joel-Brock inventoried his own stores of knowledge: He knew about dogs, plastic building blocks, video games, the *SpookY SpanieL Dog Detective* series, porpoises, and baseball . . . sort of. He *hoped* that Mr. Valona had a vaster store of facts than the size of his head would lead a pessimist to suppose. And Joel-Brock was no pessimist. Hadn't he traveled three miles to BBB looking for a job, and hadn't he found a job, along with two new buddypard friends?

Yes—yes he had.

9

At the GillGate

To reach the warehouse, Augustus led the Smalls down a corridor wide enough to hold a cargo aircraft . . . toward a pair of monstrous retractable doors a hundred yards from the moving staircases. Joel-Brock thought this corridor might extend out beneath the western parking lot of Big Box Bonanzas, but how could anyone be sure without a map? Their wanderings through BBB and the food bazaar below it had turned his sense of direction all-whichever-ways.

On either side of the corridor, inset metal doors of various sizes appeared. Most bore a stenciled message—**AUTHORIZED PERSONS ONLY**—that struck Joel-Brock as useless because only someone with the right sort of key or crowbar or blowtorch had any hope of opening them. So Joel-Brock asked Augustus what lay behind these doors, and Augustus said, "None of your business."

Addi hurried to walk backward in front of Augustus. "*'None of your business'* is an unacceptable reply," she told him. "You could have said, 'That's classified knowledge I lack authority to share,' or 'You must first have a *need to know*,' or 'Actually, owing to my duties elsewhere, I *have no idea.*' You could have said—"

"Thank you," Augustus interrupted, "I get your gist."

Still walking backward, Addi said, "It irks my chain when a big shot behaves like a butthead to an innocent kid," and Mr. Valona chuckled resonantly.

When they passed numbered shelving-unit stations, Augustus bent back a finger for each station. "*One:* cleaning supplies. *Two:* uniforms, tennis shoes, umbrellas. *Three:* shopping carts, some battery-powered. *Four:* overnight suites for buddypards visiting from other stores. And *Five:*"—bending back his thumb—"'classified knowledge I lack authority to share.'"

Grimacing, Addi dropped back again and walked to Augustus's far left, beside Mr. Valona, and the four strode forward abreast, like a rank of soldiers. "I've got it," she told them. "I'm Dorothy. You guys are the Scarecrow, the Tin Man, and the Cowardly Lion. We should *skip* to make it to the GillGate faster."

"Who's supposed to be who?" Joel-Brock was okay with skipping, but no one had started yet.

Addi said, "Augustus is the Tin Man—our own froze-up robot."

Augustus halted. "I could've shot you, but I didn't. So *take that back!*"

"I was *joking.*" Addi appealed to her fellow Smalls, but Augustus would not buy her excuse. "Okay, okay, I take it back."

Hard-eyed, Augustus resumed walking, but no one skipped. As they neared the big retractable doors, Joel-Brock imagined that those doors were the gates to an island fortress inside which grass-aproned natives hid from periodic raids by the giant ape King Kong. He kept this notion to himself, and as soon as they reached the doors, the doors began to retract into the walls so that a tall crack formed—a slender gap for their band to squeeze through. Indeed, Joel-Brock soon expected to hear tom-toms and bloodcurdling kookaburra calls and spider-monkey screeches.

*

With Augustus leading, the Valorous Smalls entered the warehouse. Its interior hit them with puffs of oily air and visions of stacked crates, catwalks, and big bonanzic products hung by cords from steel ceiling tracks: riding mowers, fiberglass showers, golf carts, bicycles, small hybrid cars, and colorful parasails. Elsewhere, additional stacked crates appeared to vanish into infinity.

"Beatific Brahman bull!" Addi said.

Joel-Brock furrowed his brow. "What?"

"I think she's riffing on holy cow," Mr. Valona told him.

Addi said the warehouse had just caused her to flash back to another film, *Raiders of the Lost Ark*, to a scene revealing that the long-sought Ark of the Covenant now dwells in a Smithsonian Institution storage facility just as a redwood curl might dwell in a cedar-chip pile—deeply, secretly, undiscoverably.

Joel-Brock said, "How do we know the gobbymawler sprols didn't put my family in one of *these* crates?"

Augustus whirled on him. "Because they didn't!"

"But take a look, Mr. Hudspeth," Joel-Brock said. "*Why* wouldn't they?"

"Because this is BBB property—*it's not allowed.*"

"Kidnapping isn't either," Joel-Brock noted.

"Take my word for it, okay? And if you want to get to the GillGate before we all turn into pumpkins, follow my lead." He turned into a broad aisle and marched right up to a forklift with a caged cab and a back *as well as* a front seat. He gave each of the Smalls an orange hard hat and the Smalls put them on.

Mr. Valona rapped his. "If it's hunting season, no one will mistake us for

Bambi and shoot us dead."

"Shut up, Vaughn," Augustus said. *Rudely*, Joel-Brock thought.

With the children on the forklift's rear bench seat and Mr. Valona up front beside Augustus, Augustus drove them back to the central aisle, making room for other forklifts trundling toward them. And, cruising at less than ten miles an hour, they still reached the GillGate—Augustus announcing, "Toys & Games," "Kitchen & Dining," "Patio, Lawn, and Garden," or "Women's Clothing"—in just over seven minutes.

The main aisle to the GillGate had some turns in it, denying them a straight-on view, so Joel-Brock could not see the gate clearly until after their forklift made several course corrections. Surprisingly, the GillGate was small—ten feet tall and a little over three feet wide. It consisted of polished bamboo for the entry, but of white-spotted orange thatch for the awning.

"Look," Mr. Valona said. "That thatch resembles the cap of a destroying-angel mushroom, *Amanita biosporigera*. I used to hit upon that species in youthful summer treks through Maine."

"How do we get through?" Joel-Brock asked Augustus.

"We may not," Addi said. "I had only one question to answer in the lounge, but here we've got three. If they're all about mushrooms, I'm doomed."

"Don't worry," Augustus said. "There are no mushroom questions."

"How do you know?" Addi asked.

"I just do, okay?"

He asked everyone to undo their seatbelts and approach the GillGate. The Smalls did so. At the GillGate, a niche beside it contained a screen, a keypad, a credit-card slot, and a drawer for dispensing—well, what?

The drawer seemed to be a kind of Automatic Teller Machine. On the mock-ATM screen shone the face of a spooky fortune-telling gypsy just like the one inside an antique boardwalk machine in a favorite movie of Joel-Brock's, *Big*.

"Wow," Joel-Brock said. "There's our Asker."

"Good old Boogerbeard," Mr. Valona said.

Helplessly, Joel-Brock and Addi began to laugh.

Augustus snapped, "Forgive me, but I'm going to rejoin Archbishop Meece and his stupid bird now." He backed the forklift up and headed off toward the lounge. With many conflicting emotions, the Smalls watched him go.

*

"Do either of you have a credit or debit card?" Mr. Valona glanced at the piratical gypsy peering at them from the mock-ATM beside the GillGate.

Joel-Brock and Addi chorused, "No sir.".

"As I figured." Mr. Valona fetched his Dock-Me Card from his wallet and slipped it into a slot next to the gypsy's bearded face. The whirring slot thrust it back out, took a better grip, and schlurped it back in. Boogerbeard winked at him before he looked down at the machine's keypad. Then the face vanished, and this message appeared:

EACH OF YOU MUST STEP FORWARD FOR A CIRCUMNAV-IGATIONAL BODY SCAN.

"Really?" Mr. Valona said.

IN YOUR CASE, FIRST PLACE YOUR yNAUT NEXT TO THE KEYBOARD WITH ITS SCREEN FACING MINE.

"Why?"

WE MUST DISARM YOU OF ARTIFICIAL AIDS.

DON'T YOU THEREBY DEHUMANIZE US? Mr. Valona typed, but he placed his yNaut on the mock-ATM and turned before its scanner to prove he had no other iCheats on his person.

Arms out, Addi and Joel-Brock also turned circles before Boogerbeard.

"We're doomed," Addi said.

"Oh, no," Mr. Valona said. "We're the Valorous Smalls. What one of us doesn't know, another will. Buck up, Addi, buck up."

Boogerbeard reappeared. He spoke, his words out of synch with his lips, which did not move at all. As if for backup, this text shone below his devil's face:

YOU MUST ANSWER THREE QUESTIONS. ONE WRONG ANSWER ENDS YOUR SESSION. GOT IT?

GOT IT, Mr. Valona typed.

NO NEED TO TYPE YOUR REPLIES, Boogerbeard said aloud

as well as in text. I HEAR YOU THROUGH BUILT-IN AUDIO RECEPTORS.

"As we can through ours," Mr. Valona replied, *without* typing.

"I *like* the texting," Joel-Brock said. "That guy has a really heavy accent."

I DO **NOT** HAVE AN ACCENT, Boogerbeard texted.

"No accent there," Addi said, "unless we count the bold type on **NOT**."

"We won't," Joel-Brock said, not wishing to make Boogerbeard self-conscious, unless doing so would bring the Lollises safely home.

YOU ALL MAY CONSULT, BUT ONLY ONE MAY ANSWER, the pirate-gypsy decreed. WHICH OF YOU WILL SPEAK FOR ALL?

"Joel-Brock," Mr. Valona said.

"Of course," Addi agreed. "It has to be Joel-Brock."

Joel-Brock preferred for Mr. Valona to speak, but his fellow Smalls had outvoted him, and he was all right with that. After all, they would never have come to Sporangium but for his problem. . . .

OKAY, the gypsy texted. FIRST QUESTION: WHICH PRO BASEBALL PLAYER INVENTED THE BUNT?

Addi said, "What in the world is a *bunt*?"

Mr. Valona said, "Let the boy think."

By their widened eyes, Joel-Brock knew that utter cluelessness had fallen upon his friends. Everything seemed to hinge on his nine-year-old memory. He stepped up to the plate—no, to the screen—and spoke with all the grit he could muster: "Dicky Pearce, sir. Dicky Pearce invented the bunt."

CORRECT, Boogerbeard texted. BUT WHAT ELSE CAN YOU SAY ABOUT THIS LITTLE KNOWN SPORTS FIGURE?

Mr. Valona eased Joel-Brock aside. "Is that our second official question?"

NO, the pirate-gypsy texted. I'M JUST CURIOUS.

"Well, then, as a writer I admire used to say, *Ask the next question.*"

OKAY. SECOND QUESTION: WHO WAS EDDIE GAEDEL?

AND WHAT EVENT GAVE HIM HIS BRIEF PUBLIC FAME IN THIS COUNTRY?

"Isn't that two questions?" Mr. Valona asked.

"They do this all the time," Addi said. "They *want* us to fail."

ONE WOULD NOT KNOW THE IDENTITY OF EDDIE GAEDEL WITHOUT AN AWARENESS OF THE EVENT RESPONSIBLE FOR HIS FAME. SO I WOULD CALL IT ONE QUESTION WITH A . . . **BUILT-IN CLUE**.

Trembling with excitement, Joel-Brock said, "I know that one, too."

Mr. Valona seized him and set him again in front of Boogerbeard's rouged face. "Okay, Master Lollis: Drop it on him like a bomb."

"Even though a grown man," Joel-Brock said, "Eddie Gaedel weighed sixty-five pounds. He was three feet seven inches tall, the smallest player ever to bat in the Major Leagues. In the second game of a double-header in 1951, sixty years ago today, he wore the number *one-eighth* on his St. Louis Browns uniform. He pinch-hit for a regular-sized player who hated having Mr. Gaedel do that for him, and he walked on four pitches. The Detroit Tigers' pitcher had no control because he couldn't stop laughing."

Speechless, Mr. Valona and Adelaide-Bridget Coe beheld Joel-Brock Lollis as if he'd just recited the entire Declaration of Independence.

CORRECT, Boogerbeard texted.

"How in holy heck did you know that?" Addi asked.

Blushing, Joel-Brock lowered his chin.

"Another baseball question," Mr. Valona marveled. "I couldn't be more useless if I were a pink wriggler in a slam-dunk contest."

"Or if I were a Tahitian assembling an igloo," Addi said, and Mr. Valona and she joyfully high-fived.

When the Smalls finally got serious again, the gypsy asked, ARE YOU READY FOR QUESTION THREE?

"If it isn't about baseball, as ready as I'll ever be," Joel-Brock said.

QUESTION THREE: WHO INVENTED THE OBOE?

"Holy wow," Mr. Valona said, deeply discouraged.

Arabella has an oboe, Joel-Brock told himself. But what do I know about it? Just that, hearing her play at seven in the morning, it makes my gums ache. Who *invented* it? Why would anyone have bothered? Addi stepped up and told Boogerbeard that she knew the answer. However, she really needed to gather her thoughts.

YOU HAVE *THIRTY* SECONDS, Boogerbeard said. STARTING NOW: TWENTY-NINE, TWENTY-EIGHT . . . And he continued the countdown.

"Wait!" Addi said. "I remember . . . from a music class I loved . . . two people invented the oboe! They were . . . French! Their names were . . . wait a second, wait . . . their names were Hotteterre and Philidor!"

WHAT WERE THEIR *FIRST* NAMES? Boogerbeard shot back.

"That's not fair!" But Addi screwed up her face in concentration and thought. "I know this, I know this . . . Michel and Jean, that's it!"

WRONG. YOU SWITCHED THEIR FIRST NAMES.

"What? *What?* On *Jeopardy* I could have said only their last names and I would have been right! You're trying to cheat us to keep us out of Sporangium." She added, "I gave you more facts than you asked for! Besides, since I said *Jean* Hotteterre's last name first, I purposely said *Michel* Philodor's first name last!"

NO. AT FIRST, CHILD, YOU JUST DID NOT ANSWER FULLY.

Joel-Brock bopped Boogerbeard's visage with his palm, and Mr. Valona seized him and pulled him back.

The gypsy wiggled his swatted nose. THAT BRAT STRUCK ME . . . TOTALLY WITHOUT PROVOCATION!

Mr. Valona said, "Your disqualification of Addi's answer is provocation!

Joel-Brock misses his family, man! He wants to get them back!"

BE THAT AS IT MAY, THE RULES REQUIRE—

"A pox on your rules!" Augustus Hudspeth cried from his forklift, which he had just driven within hailing distance. "Let them in, you virtual tyrant!" he shouted. "The Smalls have done more with your ludicrous questions than anyone would have thought possible! So *let them pass! Now!*" And Booger-beard melted away.

The GillGate split along its stem and peeled back on either side. Through this portal, the bones of another world took shape, and Joel-Brock stared into the inky black contours of Sporangium. He recalled a car trip as a tiny kid to Sweetwater, Tennessee, and a nearby site called the Lost Sea. His family had hiked into caverns where this "sea" occupied some six acres of that attraction. In a glass-bottom boat, they'd floated above fairy-land grottos washed by spotlights. They saw half-blind trout that developers had released into the water when those rainbow-sided fish had still had their eyesight. Their guide flung liver pellets, and those half-blind fish lunged at them, greedy for a taste of the exiled sun that still surged within them. . . .

Mr. Valona waved at the crack in the GillGate. "Get out your flashlights," he said. "And squeeze on through!"

10

Into Sporangium

Going through, Addi pointed her flashlight up and lit the gills beneath the white-specked cap of the destroying-angel mushroom—a *built* thing, not a real mushroom—making up this door into Sporangium. Its spore-holding gills looked like accordion pleats, and the spores once trapped in them, loosened by the splitting of the GillGate's stem, sifted down on Addi like baking flour.

"Oh, yuck!" She brushed this strange dandruff away. "*Yuck-O!*"

"Easy," Mr. Valona said. "It's a special effect, and whoever built the Gill-Gate—Mr. Borsmutch, I'd guess—wanted it to creep us out."

"He did a terrific job."

As Addi pushed through, more fake spore dust drifted down on her and her fellow Smalls from the gills beneath the cap of the Sporangium-side portal. Once beyond the re-sealing door, all three brushed this dust, now more ivory than snow, from their bodies and backpacks.

Inside Sporangium, Joel-Brock struggled to adjust. The air smelled fresher than the air in the warehouse, but with a faint scent of rocks, pebbles, and ores—smells like those in the wondrous Lost Sea. He recalled, too, the smells of the trout moving toward eyelessness in those waters. If not for the electric lights down there, people would have seen only nerve-triggered flashes inside their own heads.

Here on its eastern edge, Sporangium did not seem to have electricity, but the glowing lichens or fungi on the cavern walls kept absolute darkness from stealing their eyesight. *And*—thank goodness—they had flashlights!

"See the GillGate from this side." Joel-Brock shone his flashlight upon it. "It's different from the destroying-angel frame on the warehouse side."

Mr. Valona agreed. "I'm not a trained mycologist, but I've done some mushroom picking, and being near the ground, with a sharp nose and even better eyes, always helped me. Anyway, the designers of the GillGate's Sporangial side based it not on a poisonous mushroom but on the edible *Agaricus bisporus.*" He then talked a long time about many kinds of mushrooms, including the Portobello, the white, and others with *really* difficult Japanese names. Addi and Joel-Brock gaped as if he were an alien. "Sorry—maybe I *am* a sort of *amateur* mycologist."

"If you ask me, there's no such thing as a *non*poisonous mushroom," Joel-Brock said. "I *hate* mushrooms."

"*Hate*'s a strong word, Master Lollis. Good people *hate* deceit and injustice, but they usually just *dislike* mushrooms."

"Well, I must be a Very Good Person because I *really* dislike mushrooms."

Addi put her arm around Joel-Brock. "You're not exactly getting the distinction Mr. Valona's drawing between *hate* and *dislike*." She cocked her head and asked why the GillGate's makers had put a destroying angel on the far side and an edible mushroom on this one.

Joel-Brock set his flashlight on the ground, lens-first. "Maybe they didn't want buddypards entering Sporangium, but they didn't mind sprols visiting the warehouse."

"But did they want a *mob* of them visiting it?" Mr. Valona asked. "There's not even a guard by *this* portal, much less a Boogerbeard counterpart."

Joel-Brock looked westward into the high recesses of Sporangium and out over its long and wide central valley. Bright hillside fungi enabled the Smalls to see farther here, as many lit candles inside a cathedral can make it feel at once vast and cozy.

Addi sang, *"The rocks are alive / With the light of lichens. . . ."*

The other two Smalls grinned, delighted by Addi's words and voice.

"Grin all you like," she said, "but I see nothing inviting to head toward—unless we gather some fungi and smear our faces with their bioluminescence."

When Joel-Brock and Mr. Valona stopped grinning, all three felt their weariness. Tired to the point of punchiness, they needed to trudge uphill to the rocks' "firefly sheen" and make camp there.

And then Joel-Brock remembered something. "Okay, Addi, we're in Sporangium. Tell me where my parents are. You said you knew."

"They're in a mushroom dungeon, just like Mr. Valona said earlier."

"Yeah, but where?"

"Under the ball field where you play your Cubby League games."

"Then why didn't we *drive* over there from Big Box Bonanzas and find it that way?" He shook his head. "Instead of coming all the way down here?"

"We *had* to come down here to find it," Addi said. "It's really hard to get to from the upside, or it would be for me. Anyway, we can't get there tonight." She extracted an orange nylon windbreaker from her pack and shrugged it on. "Right now," she said, "we should rest."

Maybe that made sense, but Joel-Brock didn't like it, so they discussed which side of the valley to make for. Then they set off to the south, if they weren't goofily turned around. So by flashlight beam and lichen shine, they picked their way over rocks and up a gentle grade.

*

They made camp high on a southern rock ledge, where the valley rolled away to the north of their perch and westward to places uncharted. Joel-Brock laid his backpack aside and sat on the windbreaker he'd brought from

Sporting Goods. It seemed that the Smalls were spectators in a stadium with all its lights off, but for crimson EXIT signs, cigarette-lighter flames, and the faint tiny lamps of glowworms.

Addi's windbreaker hung from her like a cloak with extra-long sleeves. She sat down beside Joel-Brock and clasped her knees. Mr. Valona walked to the edge of their campsite terrace, lit a tiny pipe with his lighter, and blew smoke over the tumbled rocks. Neither Addi nor Joel-Brock had suspected him of such a foolish disregard for his own health. Although not exactly shocked, Joel-Brock felt anxious about Mr. Valona. Addi just grinned at the poor man like a sinister Siamese.

"That'll stunt your growth," she said.

"Too late," Mr. Valona replied. "Far, far too late."

"You should give *me* a puff," Addi said cajolingly.

"No I shouldn't."

"Then you're just another do-as-I-say-not-as-I-do hypocrite."

"To deny you a vice of mine? That's an odd standard for a charge of hypocrisy." He sucked hard on his pipe. "We've had a long evening, and I am *not* the noble soul I strive to shape from the human materials at my disposal." He spread his arms in resigned self-display. "But I try. I try."

Addi laid an arm over Joel-Brock's shoulders. "*You* got us through the GillGate," she said. "You answered two of three questions Boogerbeard asked us." Her hand did a funny knuckle-roll on his head.

"A batting average of about .666," he said dully.

"While *I* batted zero," said Mr. Valona, who then blew a smoke ring.

Addi asked Joel-Brock, "How did you know the name of that guy who started the bunt? I'm positive not every ballplayer learns such stuff."

"I—" Joel-Brock began. "I—" he tried again. Finally, he sighed to reset his mood. "Today is my birthday." Before he could say anything else, his shoulders hiccupped, and he sobbed, a veritable homeless orphan, until he

could make himself stop.

"Your birthday?" Addi snugged him closer. "What's that got do with answering Boogerbeard's baseball questions?"

"*Your birthday?*" Mr. Valona emptied his tiny pipe, walked over to the kids, and squatted before them. "You should've told us," he said fiercely. "*You … should … have … told … us.*"

Joel-Brock opened and closed his mouth like a hooked bass. "Until Boogerbeard's second question, I didn't *remember* it was my birthday."

"Explain that," Addi said.

"Last year on my birthday," Joel-Brock began, "Daddy told me the story of Eddie Gaedel for a *present*—not so I'd worry about never growing taller than he was, but so I'd know that something neat once took place on my birthday: Eddie Gaedel pinch-hitting for the St. Louis Browns on August 19, 1951, almost sixty years ago.

"Today, it was *exactly* sixty years ago. So I was born, Daddy told me, on the half-century anniversary of Eddie Gaedel's pinch-hit walk for Frank Saucier, a normal-sized outfielder. Every American League big shot thought this walk by a midget—they called him a midget, but Daddy said he had dwarf in him too—was a disgrace. And all these big shots decided that no three-foot-seven-inch-tall midget would ever play in the American League again.

"But Eddie Gaedel walked on my birthday—what would later *be* my birthday—and Daddy showed me in a big baseball book where he has a career on-base percentage of one thousand. Who else has that? Anyway, because I answered his question about the inventor of the bunt, I think Booger-beard asked his next question as, well, *a birthday gift*. But until he asked it, I didn't even get that it *was* my birthday."

"How'd you know the inventor of the bunt," Addi asked, "whatever a bunt is?"

"You bunt," Joel-Brock said, "when you face the pitcher and hold your bat out in front with one hand on its handle and the other halfway up its thicker end—not so your fingers will get smacked, though—and you drop or push the ball into fair territory with the fat part. Then, Daddy says, you run like hell and hope no opposing player pounces on the ball and throws you out at first.

"My first hit in a Cubby League game, I got bunting . . . like Daddy had told me to do. Guys in our dugout cheered like I'd hit a homer. Later, Daddy said I'd been a 'regular Dickey Pearce up there, just shorter.' Pearce was five-three, and that first bunt proved a little guy could think as well as play. I knew that, but, well . . ." Like a batter refusing to run out a dribbler back to the mound, Joel-Brock stopped.

"Good story." Mr. Valona reached into his waistcoat pocket and pulled out three items that, at least at first, resembled coins. "Here. Let's have a birthday party, even if it's a sort of rinky-dink one."

Addi recognized her coin as a chocolate truffle sold in Big Box Bonanzas under the brand name D'Lisssh. "Oh, I *love* these!" She looked at Mr. Valona expectantly. He said to go ahead and unwrap it, but also to read the fortune stamped inside the wrapper, and Addi did as he said.

Mr. Valona turned back to Joel-Brock. "So how old are you, slugger?"

"T-t-ten."

"You don't look a day over twenty-three." Joel-Brock gaped at Mr. Valona, and Mr. Valona added, "Sorry. I just had a picture of you at that age."

"At least you didn't say, 'You don't look a day over six.'" Addi shook her head. Then she ate her D'Lisssh, swallowing its pieces politely.

Mr. Valona ate his chocolate too. Then he sang a Beatles birthday song that starts, "*They say it's your birthday.*" Addi joined in, harmonizing with him.

Joel-Brock chewed his D'Lisssh until the other two Smalls finished. "Thank you." He rolled away from Addi onto his side, pulled his knees to his chin, and slept, making a noise like a mosquito's nearly inaudible whine.

"What does your fortune say?" Addi asked Mr. Valona, who seemed far away . . . in another life, maybe. "Your fortune, sir," Addi tried again. "What does it say?"

"Oh." He opened the tiny ball into which he'd wadded his tinfoil wrapper, spread it out on his palm, and passed it to Addi. This is what Addi read there: "*You probably wish / That this note from D'Lisssh / Would make you feel easy / Instead of just queasy. / Drat. / Sorry 'bout that.*"

"'*Drat,*'" Addi read aloud. "'*Sorry 'bout that.*' Well, that's rotten. Gremlins in the wrapper-making factory, I guess. Want to hear mine?"

"Sure—yNaut?"

Addi popped the foil wrapper taut and read from it. "It says, '*Forget all your days lost / At regrettable cost. / Now you truly exist / In an age angel-kissed. / Pow! / Go show them how, gal.*'"

"Very nice," Mr. Valona said quietly.

"Joel-Brock didn't read us his." Addi nodded at the boy's curled-up form. "Is it okay if we check it out for him?" Mr. Valona nodded. Addi opened Joel-Brock's fist and removed his D'Lisssh wrapper. She read its message aloud: "*'Go home if you have one. / You're out of your league, son. / The sooner you know it / The less badly you'll blow it. / 'Bye. / It's a dread thing to die.'*" She gave Mr. Valona a disapproving grimace. "Whoa. That's really going to freak the kid out."

Mr. Valona seized the wrapper and set it afire. Its tip blazed up blue, silver, and red in his fingers. Then he shook out the flame. A faint metallic char lingered. "There's no need to freak anybody out," he said. "That's a threat with no heart or bowels, and we Smalls don't heed such. Understand?"

"Yes sir."

"Lie back. Close your eyes. Sleep."

*

The next morning (if anyone could know the coming of morning in Sporangium), Joel-Brock awoke having to pee—*his* sign that morning had come. He stood and leaned back, hands on hips, to unkink his spine. Then he walked upslope to the cavern wall. There he made water for what seemed an hour, but was probably only fifty-nine minutes. Over his shoulder, a rustle of windbreaker told him that Addi had awakened. "Is it raining?" Then she glanced about and found neither the boy nor the detective where last she'd seen them. She waited for her eyes to readjust. "Joel-Brock, is that you?"

Joel-Brock finished and faced her. "Good morning." He returned to the ledge on which they'd slept and seized the hand sanitizer in his backpack.

"Ah, you all are up." Mr. Valona climbed toward them through a rift in the upland slope. "Morning duties tended to and accomplished."

"Whoop-de-do," Addi said. "Guys have all the luck."

Mr. Valona said, "Live to fifty *as a guy* and see if you still believe that."

"You're not fifty."

"Nearlybout." He foraged in his backpack, shrugged it on, and looked out over the valley, where the younger Smalls could see nothing but darkness and specks of flickering light, a snow-globe domain with its power cut. "Joel-Brock, are you bright tailed, bushy eyed, and rarin' to go?"

Joel-Brock felt a curtain drop behind his eyes. A surge of dizziness buffeted him, but he tried to reach Mr. Valona—to show his gratitude to the man for acknowledging his birthday with a D'Lisssh and a happy-birthday duet with Addi. However, in trying, he tripped and fell into a rift that did not quite align with the ravine that Mr. Valona had just climbed up through. Mr. Valona made to grab him, Addi screamed, and the boy plunged toward a surface that would likely burst his skull, or shatter his back, and he would die at ten, a victim of one of this world's gazillion nasty pitfalls.

11

Quagslip

"J oel-Brock," a man's voice called. *"Joel-Brock!"*

"C'mon, Joel, stop kidding around! Moan or something!" Addi feared that he could no longer kid around or moan, either one.

And he couldn't. He just couldn't.

*

After going back into the crevice he had just emerged from, Mr. Valona could not find a smear of blood or a scrap of clothing, much less a broken body. Meanwhile, Addi stood high on their ledge casting a flashlight beam into the rift. Mr. Valona admired her effort, but wished she'd stop braying like the issue of a songbird and a burro. He had scrabbled down the rift in an all-out panic. The last time he had felt this scared, the greyhound he'd bet on at the track in Pueblo, Colorado, had started running on three legs with his $10,000 wager on its scrawny shoulders.

"Addi, for Pete's sake, knock off the laser show!"

"But where is he? This is a *nightmare*, you P.I. with no diploma, you detective in a coma, you—"

"Miss Coe, you're not helping."

And you are? But before Addi could shine her flashlight into his face, a feathery missile flew at *hers* and, by raking its talons through her hair, sent her to her knees. Like Poe's raven, it ended up perched atop a head—hers.

"Need some help? Need some help?" the bird whistled. *"Yep-yep."*

"Mortimer, is that you?" Addi tried to pull Mortimer down, for her scalp felt like a pin cushion. "Hey, you mite-infested feather duster, give me a break."

"Give her a break, but spare the fool who's fallen." The bird's squawk lowered in pitch, and its message signaled a new speaker: *"Anyone who calls his brother fool will be baked in a pie, with or without three-and-twenty other blackbirds, Mortimer."*

"I am not *a blackbird, Your Eminence, and I, I, I asked you to* spare the . . . the boy, didn't I?" the mynah said, dancing.

"Get **OFF** my head!" Addi swung her flashlight, but missed.

And then through Mortimer, at a great distance, Archbishop Meece, said, *"Return to me, Mortimer. Return to me. Return to me."*

Addi, whose pupils had grown as big as black marbles, actually saw Mortimer returning to the cleric at top speed, but distance and the dimness of East Sporangium still hid the Archbishop. How far off was he? How had he seen them on their sleeping ledge? Why had he sent Mortimer to harass them?

Addi peered into the arroyo that Mr. Valona had just reentered to search for Joel-Brock and shone her flashlight on his back. He, in turn, swung around to stare up at her in dismay. "I don't see him. It's like trying to find a BB in a pile of pea gravel."

"But where could he have gone?" Addi asked.

"I don't know, and I need more light."

Annoyed because she had to struggle to hear him, Addi yelled, "What?"

"I need more light!"

*

BLAAAM!

Somebody somewhere threw a switch, a big one. And either dawn or full daylight flooded East Sporangium like eye-stinging water. Mr. Valona, in the arroyo, and Addi, up on the ledge, shielded their eyes against the glare—light that blotted out the sheen of the cavern's glowing lichens and fungi.

Kneeling, Addi shut off her flashlight. "I didn't know light could hurt so much."

"Stay like that," Mr. Valona called up. "Let your pupils readjust."

Addi looked up through spread fingers as she did when viewing a scary scene in a horror film. She didn't want to see the ugly thing about to occur, but, still, she cheated—not just by peeking through her fingers but also by rising, lowering her arms, and gaping at the sky. Its black expanse almost stopped her breath. *"Awesome!"* And it struck her that, for once, anyway, she'd used that word correctly.

By now, Mr. Valona's and her pupils had sunk to pin-hole size, and both realized that a magnesium-bright "sun" had flashed on. It moved on tracks running from the east, where the cavern's outer wall joined with the BBB warehouse, to the far west, deeper into Sporangium. This phony sun slid westward like Apollo's chariot, but with the bulk of a compact car and the brightness of a polished shield.

Mr. Valona now had more light. The boy had not landed in *this* crevice—unless he'd also fallen into a hole that had swallowed him entire. That seemed unlikely, so he scrambled up the ravine's eastern slope and walked its ridge back to Addi on the lip of their campsite. She pointed to a place on the valley's eastern floor where a pony and its rider had halted on a rock-strewn upward grade facing the Smalls.

"It's Archbishop Meece and Mortimer the Mynah," Addi said. "Do you see?"

"The rider and his mount, yes, but not the bird." Mr. Valona peered as hard as he could, and Addi pointed to a gully running alongside the crevice that he'd already twice explored. At the bottom, it had a white powder more like salt or snow than sand, but with a peculiar liquid quality that Addi could not account for.

"Maybe Joel-Brock wound up in that pitfall," she said.

Mr. Valona tried to focus on the parallel-running rift. Its sands showed no signs of having received a human form—no dents, no nail scratches, nothing at all—but a second glance revealed a sneaker wedged in a cleft near its bottom. Thank God for Sporangium's fake sun, thought Mr. Valona. It now hitched westward like a roller-coaster ratcheting uphill. But he looked down again at the sneaker, which had surely belonged to the boy. And when Addi prepared to leap to a rock in the crevice, Mr. Valona reached out to stop her. "Think! You don't see Joel-Brock, only his shoe. That pitiless stuff has closed over him and evened itself out, just like water."

"More like quicksand," Addi said. "Anyway, he'll smother."

"If it's quicksand, but it's something else, a thing *Sporangial*, a thing friendlier than quicksand." Mr. Valona *had no idea*—as the boy would've said—where this notion had come from, but it kept him from panicking.

Addi had her own revelation. "It's quagslip. And it won't kill him."

"Quagslip?"

"Something like that. He's okay—if he didn't get freaked out sliding into it, and if the darkness hasn't driven him crazy."

Mr. Valona pondered options. Oddly, neither he nor Addi had any panic, but both felt the urgency of Joel-Brock's plight. "Maybe the stuff has the ability to flow," he said, "but not to fill your mouth or nostrils, lethally. It's not liquid mercury—quicksilver—but a substance with lots of space between its grains."

"You think?"

"Yeah, pretty much. Get my backpack, would you?" He would have gone

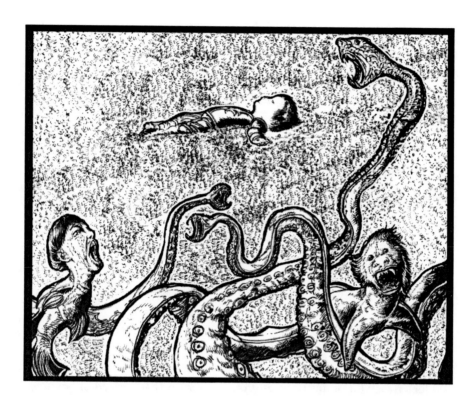

for it, but feared that Addi might use his absence to leap into the quagslip. He felt her distress and her hope as strongly as she did and did not want to lose her to either one. But she did as he asked, and as she returned, the animal carrying Archbishop Meece pointed its nose their way and came toward them at a healthy clip.

"Here." Addi gave Mr. Valona his backpack.

He set it on the ledge and pulled out a shrink-wrapped box of golf balls. He then found the parts of his collapsible casting rod, along with a batch of nylon fishing line. He assembled the rod and fed out enough line to rig the ball box with an under-slung basket of line that would hold the box horizontally.

"Hurry," Addi said. "We can't waste time."

But Mr. Valona had to be certain that when he lowered the golf-ball

box to the quagslip, its weight did not drag out so much line that he lost
the tension necessary to reel Joel-Brock in when he grabbed it as if it were a
towline. Then he'd have to beach the kid like a two-legged, land-going marlin.
Addi dismissed his plan's chances of success, but he kept working. He had no
other ready option. Wading into the quagslip would pose too much risk, and,
besides, he had one more addition to his "bait" to make, an instrument of his
own devising that he'd used in dark waters to catch mudcats. He stuck a blue
dome-light on the box's bottom, a lure that blinked, beeped, and shook. Then
he reeled out just enough line to set the box down softly beside the sneaker
in the rocks.

"Finally," Addi said.

"I hope not," Mr. Valona said. "I hope we're just beginning."

*

Joel-Brock hit on his back, as if on a waterbed that, instead of bouncing
him off, caught him like a bathrobe thrown onto a mattress. He felt the
white grains draw his body into them, not swallowing him like quicksand but
sifting past him and *easing* him down. He didn't fight this liquid capture, but
yielded to it, finding it pleasant.

Weirdly, Joel-Brock could still breathe as the quagslip pooled in his eye
sockets, crept in at his lip corners, and eked into his nostrils. It flowed and
dissolved, promising changes that scared him but did not bring about any
odd alterations. And so he floated, a slain knight stretched out on his shield,
in a dream that held him horizontal in its grasp, like a carpenter asleep on a
door atop two sawhorses. Joel-Brock *was* that door, also a being that could
open it and pass through into a world where he would become something
other. This change, at once liberating and scary, kept him from opening the
door . . . for the otherness he passed into might be a rain of spores or the

permanent death of his Joel-Brock Lollis self.

He could see nothing in this blackness where sight fled and his body sank into a sweet ignorance of its parts. He, or his body, had become a gate—just as the GillGate let a traveler pass from one odd country into a stranger one.

But he could not *see* the gate to open it. He was a half-blind trout in the inky waters of the Lost Sea. Beneath him, denizens of the quagslip tugged at him, to pull him farther down so that the old Joel-Brock—*old at ten!*—could sink through the space its grains had made and unite with the bright critters. So he tried to roll over in the quagslip, to let its grains help him sink deeper. But he could not overcome his satisfaction with his current state to even try, and so the darkness stamped him **MADE IN SPORANGIUM**, and he seemed *finished* in every sense.

And then . . . *BLAAAM!*

All at once, the blackness of the quagslip got an injection of light . . . or several injections, for the grains around him began to gleam. Air rushed in along with light, and the accident that had befallen him no longer seemed attractive or cozy. He could hear, but not well. He could see, sort of, and he could breathe even with his mouth and nostrils full of the slip-sliding grains. He yearned in every atom to resume the quest that had brought him and his friends down into Sporangium. He wondered if this gully and its quag-slip could work as an On-Demand Object Maker, like those devices that "printed" on demand such things as small plastic gorillas, metal can openers, or Jason Heyward bobble-head dolls. So could he escape from this rift if he first escaped as a New Improved Joel-Brock the Brave? Or would he drown in the grainy muck?

And then a faint beeping sounded and some blue sparkles lit up the goop around him. He sort of swam beneath the beeps and the slippery blue sparkles. A baby porpoise could not have done better. Still, he sank as he swam, feeling pinches on his buttocks and back. These pinches meant that other sprols growing here—but not him, himself—hoped to add him to their mass and . . . *what?* Turn him into a sprol too? Fearing that, he refused to get off his back or to sink lower.

Then he felt a weight on his chest—a box of Lost-in-the-Woods golf balls from Big Box Bonanzas. Surely Mr. Valona didn't want him to sink beneath the weight of this heavy little box? Before he could think more, the ball box rose several inches. As it rose, a gizmo on its base made it beep, blink, and wriggle. Joel-Brock feared it was deserting him, and, adrenalin-driven, his hands rose through the quagslip and clasped the ends of the box . . . just as Mr. Valona had hoped they would.

Even when his fingers got tangled with the fishing-line basket supporting the box, he did not let go. Instantly, he arose from the gulley through its dry goop into such a rush of light and landscape that he closed his eyes. Doing so burned an image on his retinas: Vaughnathan Valona, Adelaide-Bridget Coe, and even Archbishop Meece hoisting him to safety. As buoying grains dropped from him like mica flecks, he had no doubt that he had arisen and that all three Smalls would succeed in their mission.

*

The fake sun had moved a third of the way along its tracks toward West Sporangium. Joel-Brock lay on a rock staring into the faces of Mr. Valona, Addi, Archbishop Meece, and Mortimer, who hopped about on the Archbishop's shoulder.

Another shaggy face—a muzzle with a mane of hair so black it seemed powdered with coal dust—also peered at him. After snorting quagslip from his nose, the boy spat out more grains and squinted at his many rescuers. The horse face—eyes on either side of its snout—he *really* didn't know. But he wanted to.

Addi leaned over him. "Joel-Brock, are you all right?"

"Yes, except for my ankle and a headache. I hit the gully wall falling." He sat up, but the pony stepped back.

That pony's mine, he thought: It's Christmas Day, and that pony's mine.

Somebody said to take it easy, he had plenty of time. When he said, "No, I don't," that person only shrugged. Then Joel-Brock stood, his head low. He backed up two steps. The pain in his right ankle said his ankle did not want to hold him. He willed it to and studied the land stretching out like a moonscape. Mr. Valona and the Archbishop helped him keep standing.

A thousand gullies ran toward the central valley, dirt-dull on some of their walls but glinting with veins of ore, lichen shine, or fungal glow-gills in the shadows thrown by their steep sides. Farther on, big structures arose in East Sporangium, near the walls, rifts, and rock piles in the central valley. They resembled old stone monasteries in Turkey that Joel-Brock had seen on TV travel shows. They implied human, or quasi-human, builders and also the menace of their unseen residents.

"You may have to go back," Mr. Valona told him. "If you can't walk, Addi and I don't have the strength to carry you, kidster."

"I'll hop," Joel-Brock said. To Addi he said, "How far to my family's prison?"

She scrunched her shoulders: "Too far to hop."

Mortimer leapt up onto the Archbishop's tall tan hat and clung there. "*The scamp need not hop at all,*" Mortimer whistled, his master speaking through him. "*Let him step into stirrup and set forth on Pit Pacer.*" The Archbishop indicated the shaggy black pony that he'd ridden to their campsite.

Pit Pacer, the pony, eyed Joel-Brock skeptically.

And Mr. Valona began second-guessing the Archbishop's plan: Could the old cleric walk to *his* destination? Was Pit Pacer tame enough to tote a squirmy boy? If the trip took over a day, where would they find food or water?

As kindly as the Archbishop meant his offer, his whole plan seemed pitted with holes.

"Nonsense," Pit Pacer said. *"The Archbishop has ways you know not of."*

Everyone looked at the old pony, understanding that Archbishop Meece had just switched mouthpieces. Good—Mortimer sounded like a leaky balloon, while Pit Pacer had a nice baritone. But the fact that the pony spoke through his nostrils did undercut that lovely baritone a tad.

"Pit Pacer will carry you where you need to go," the pony said, or appeared to say, the Archbishop providing hand gestures. *"He knows where to find food and water. He isn't used to the weight of adult humans, but for years he pulled coal carts through a mine. He should have no trouble toting the boy or resisting the impulse to unseat him. In fact, I rode Pit Pacer to your warehouse to show him we value him yet."*

"Why would you loan us your pony?" Addi asked.

"Well, we both have our issues with Pither M. Borsmutch," Pit Pacer said for the Archbishop. *"If I help you, maybe your mission will benefit my interests."*

Addi changed tacks: "Why don't you heal Joel-Brock's ankle?"

"Heal him? I don't do healings. Or should I say, 'We don't do healings'?"

"Why not?" Addi pursued. "Aren't you a holy man?"

"Insofar as I'm a man. Moreover, the Holy Subterranean Church of Sporangium forgoes physical healings because they have only a fleeting influence on us sporules. Our various fruiting bodies—the forms you see before you as inhuman gobbymawlers—are just temporary containers for our minds and souls."

"I don't get that," Addi said.

"Their bodies don't last long enough for a physical healing to mean much," Joel-Brock said. "What matters are their ties to the underground root system that gives rise to their physical forms."

Addi looked at him as if he'd snapped a hummingbird to life between two of his fingers. "Whoa, J-Boy!"

And Joel-Brock realized that a rare thing had happened to him during his dunk in the quagslip, and neither Addi nor Mr. Valona would ever fully get it, even if he found the words to explain the transformation to which his time in the gully had treated him. He had absorbed this knowledge through his cells, as he may have zapped some of his own to the disembodied beings drifting in the quagslip. Maybe, despite his ankle injury, he'd had what Sophia liked to call "a happy accident." But Addi and Mr. Valona did not seem to share this optimistic opinion.

"I'm okay," Joel-Brock tried to assure everyone. "Look, I'm really okay."

"*Of course you are,*" Pit Pacer said. Or the Archbishop said through the pony, adding, "*Mortimer, fly down there and get this young man's tennis shoe.*"

Mortimer considered this and then swept into the gully after Joel-Brock's shoe. He took it by a lace and lifted it free of its trap by will and wing power. The shoe swung about beneath him like a canoe under a helicopter, but Mortimer easily returned it to the campsite. Then the lace pulled free of its last eyelet, and the sneaker landed with a plop in front of the Archbishop.

"*Well done,*" he said through Pit Pacer.

Addi picked up both shoe and lace and handed them to Joel-Brock.

"*Auwk, I'm a stalwart again,*" Mortimer whistled. "*I've got his voice back and mine too of course. And we've business elsewhere to attend to, yep-yep.*"

Pit Pacer shook his mane, relieved that he was no longer a mouthpiece.

Back on the Archbishop's shoulder, Mortimer told the Smalls, "*Make use of your light. Eat something. Repack your bags. Find a trail for Pit Pacer to follow.*"

We will fly, so make use of your light."

The "sun" had not yet moved halfway across the "sky." It wouldn't enter the vault defining *West* Sporangium for hours, but they did as asked, eating an energy bar apiece and drinking water. They repacked their backpacks. They studied the terrain and found a trail out of the foothills for Pit Pacer to lead them westward. Then the Archbishop nodded at Mr. Valona, and Mortimer told him to take out his yNaut.

"My yNaut?" said Mr. Valona. "It won't work down here, will it?"

"Not yet, but jusst you wait, Misster Sstore Detective."

This sspeech led Mr. Valona to believe that the mynah had inssinuated ssome of itss own perssonality into the Archbisshop's words. But he found the yNaut in his vest pocket and gave it to the Archbishop, who took the device and felt about his robes for something. At last he found a wafer of circuitry the size of a thumbnail. He flipped open the yNaut and snapped out its circuit board. He waved for Mr. Valona to take the yNaut's old circuit board. Mr. Valona did, and put it in a knickers pocket. Then the Archbishop slid the mystery wafer into the dead yNaut to make it live again and returned the device to Mr. Valona.

Mortimer whistled, *"As a ressult of transsformationss to its visscera, thiss device will now work ssuccessfully down here."*

"Really?" asked Mr. Valona.

The Archbishop somehow stopped Mortimer's lisping: *"Oh, yes. Did you suppose we had no electronic systems like yours aboveground? Well, we do."*

"I'm glad, especially if my yNaut will work."

"It will. It does now. Unfortunately, we must fly. But first I must put out the sun."

"Put out the sun?" Addi said.

"Yes," the Archbishop said, through Mortimer. *"Make it dark again."*

"But why?" Mr. Valona cried. "The 'day' isn't half over yet, is it?"

"Because we must fly, and because mushrooms and mynahs love the darkness . . . for their deeds are unbelievable." The Archbishop spread his arms, and his fleshy robes swayed from his arms like wings. The Smalls gazed on in awe. Then, again through the mynah on his shoulder, Archbishop Meece said, *"Let there be night . . . again."*

BLAAAM!

The sun blew out, and Joel-Brock lifted a hand to his face. He could see neither his hand nor the gill-glow seeping from under the Archbishop's hat or the bright lichens and fungi gripping the rocks all about them. And Mr. Valona and Addi could not see a whit better than he.

But all could hear. And all heard a deep inhalation of breath, the collapse of the Archbishop's body, and a rush of wind. The cleric and the mynah moved too rapidly for sight to overtake hearing, so Joel-Brock had to imagine the Archbishop's transformation into a white crow not much bigger than Mortimer. Speed ribbons flowed from the white crow's wingtips and tail, and Mortimer sped after in the ribbons' fluttery wake. And how both crow and mynah enjoyed astonishing them!

"What sort of prelate would leave us here in the dark?" Mr. Valona wondered.

"A mushroom," Addi said. "A flying sporule."

But Joel-Brock had no idea if she was talking rot or responding to a question that he'd just asked himself.

12

A View from the Blueberries

Their eyesight came back . . . in stages that let them see lichen shine again and a lingering glow in the black sun still trundling west.

Joel-Brock rode Pit Pacer. Mr. Valona and Addi walked on each side of the pony, the whites of whose eyes resembled slices of big boiled eggs. The Smalls trudged down from the foothills on a trail crisscrossing gullies and carrying them past mileposts, weird rock sculptures, and many jumbled stones. Far off stood castles or cliff dwellings—or so they seemed in the twilight—but Pit Pacer showed no desire to go to these places, and the Smalls took comfort in his attention to the trail—now tight, now wide—as it cut through the valley leading toward what the girl assured them was the hidden prison holding Joel-Brock's family.

"But how do you know?" the boy asked from Pit Pacer's back.

"Beats me. I just, uh, remember the place—also that gobbymawler sprols probably took captives there. It's all like a dream of a hint of a memory."

"Do you take drugs?" Joel-Brock asked.

"Joel-Boy, I resent that question."

"Hey, you asked to smoke Mr. Valona's pipe."

"That's not a drug, is it? Anyway, I was acting at being a riot grrrl."

Mr. Valona studied Addi intently. "Pipe tobacco contains nicotine, Addi, an alkaloid that's addictive. Chemical companies put it in insecticides."

"So it *is* a drug," Joel-Brock said.

Addi asked Mr. Valona: "If you know all that about it, why do you smoke?"

"Now and again, I puff on my pipe. Anyway, I'm not an insect and it won't kill me." Mr. Valona's grinning teeth shone in the twilight.

"Not fast it won't," Joel-Brock said. "But it'll kill you slow."

"Thanks for the reminder. Maybe Miss Coe will take it to heart."

Pit Pacer's recurrent *clop-clop* echoed hollowly. Joel-Brock's ankle throbbed. He leaned to touch it. Addi said to leave it alone or he'd fall and wind up with a knotty head as well as a knotty ankle. He sat up again. Water trickled through a nearby runnel. Other drips and gurgles etched the echoey silences. Pit Pacer clopped on purposefully. But was he going where they needed him to go?

"Addi," Joel-Brock said, "how do you know what you know? How do you know there's a secret prison under my Cubby League field?"

"A short nap in quagslip," Mr. Valona said, "and our boy's the Grand Inquisitor."

But Addi wanted to answer. She held her hands clasped behind her, like those of a pacing philosopher, and kept pace with Pit Pacer, mining her memory.

"Well?" Joel-Brock said.

Addi seized the pony's bridle and looked up at Joel-Brock with a crazy gaze that alternately caught and released him. She wobbled his kneecap, scarily.

"Lots of things suggest themselves. After I started in Shipping, a boy in Health and Beauty—a teenage *boy*, I thought—may have taken me to the food bazaar. I think he did. I liked him. He was most likely an evolved fungal being, fully vested and always in pink-khaki BBB uniforms."

"A gobbymawler sprol?" Joel-Brock asked.

"Maybe. Probably. We ate at a Yucatan food booth, fried squid in pita bread. I got sick and fainted. Some of Manny's buds—Emmanuel Obello

was his name—Manny and those guys carried me into Sporangium to try to treat my food poisoning."

Mr. Valona said, "Whatever you ate probably contained mushrooms."

"Did you answer any questions at the GillGate?" Joel-Brock asked.

"I don't know, but why would Manny and his buds have to, if they were returning to help a kid he'd accidentally got sick. The Yucatec got me sick, not Manny. Anyway, later they found some gingery stuff down here, ground from the mycelium of a toadstool, and I took it in some water."

Joel-Brock peered at Addi. "Did you shrink to toadstool size? Or grow so big you hit your head on the cave roof?"

"No. I woke up in the trailer I rent with two other BBB girls, but they weren't there when I woke. Nobody was."

"Did your trip to Sporangium *really* happen?" Joel-Brock persisted.

"I may have dreamt it. I can't say for sure what happened and what took place in my dream. But the mushroom poisoning happened, and the ginger I took helped me, so I have a real memory—from early days at BBB—of coming here before. I don't know the place as well as Pit Pacer does, but I *do* know it."

"What else?" Joel-Brock said.

"Someone may have wanted me to lose my memory of visiting. So they may have done something to me to blur it all together."

"Who? What did they do?"

"I don't know," said Addi. "Hypnotized me. Gave me a potion. Or, after I got sick in the bazaar, I may have visited Sporangium as a spirit. I may've simply escaped to it as a healing place while my body got better in Cobb Creek."

"*Simply*?" Mr. Valona said.

"Okay, maybe it isn't simple. But it still boils down to three possibilities. First, Manny Obello and his buds—sporules, all—brought me here to make me well. Second, I dreamt my visit in a fever. Or, third, I came here as a spirit, guided by Manny's knowledge of the place and his promise I'd get better here. Then I forgot it all until a panel truck stopped in front of the Lollises' house and some sprols got out, and I saw them approach the house."

"How many?" Mr. Valona asked.

"Three from up front, four or five from the back, all dressed in BBB beige, with pancake hats and tan tennis shoes."

"Males or females, Addi?"

"I couldn't see their faces."

"Why not?"

"I was across Union Church Road from Joel-Brock's subdivision . . . too far away to tell male from female."

"Couldn't they've been true people and not evil sprols passing for human?"

"I guess—until I saw them doing some grossly inhuman stuff."

"Hold on," Joel-Brock said. "What were you doing across Union Church Road? Staking out my house?"

Addi glared. "No. I'd gone out Union Church to Eatonton Farm, across the road from your house, to pick blueberries. I told the attendant I had no money, but if I could have a pound of what I brought back to her at the end of the day, their Farm could have the rest—five or six pounds, maybe—to sell at a higher price than they ask of folks who pick their own. She took pity and said okay."

"What did they do," Mr. Valona asked, "to prove they were real sprols?"

"They surrounded the house. Once they'd fanned out, I couldn't see them well. I pushed some blueberry branches back to see three gobbymawlers on the front porch, and I assumed they were making a delivery."

"Addi, what did they *do*?" Mr. Valona said.

"My view of the porch was blocked. I thought Joel-Boy's mama had answered the door. Seeing the buddypards' truck out front, she must've shut and locked that door and got Joel-Brock's dad and sister to lock the others. Then the gobbymawlers from the porch came back into the yard and huddled there. Then they spread their arms like Archbishop Meece and started to spin. The light in the yard blurred. They didn't transform into dust devils—no grit swirled around them—but into *gust* devils, which thinned and blew into the attic vents spinning on the roof. They all swept into the house through those vents . . . except the driver. He took the truck up the drive on the house's far side where I couldn't see it until it backed into sight again, onto Crabapple Circle, its nose pointing at me and the blueberries. Then it roared back toward town on Union Church Road."

Mr. Valona said, "How do

you know they took the Lollis family to Big Box Bonanzas and on through its warehouse into Sporangium?"

"I told Manny Obello what I'd seen and asked what it all meant. He couldn't talk without a go-bespeak, so he used a yNaut with a vocoder. And just as he had on our food bazaar date, which may or may not've happened, he jacked into the vocoder and talked to me. This time he ratted out the gobbymawlers that had done the deed on Mr. Borsmutch's order. He told me details about the kid-snatch—stuff that matched what I'd seen from the blueberry bushes—and others about where the family wound up. He said the sporules had blown a big part of their mission by failing to grab Joel-Boy with the other Lollises. That slipup, he said, had really hacked off old Pither."

"And how did Manny Obello happen to know these details?" Mr. Valona asked.

"He drove the panel truck."

"I'll kill him," Joel-Brock blurted.

"Good luck with that one," Addi said. "He vanished after telling me his story. I've never seen *him* again either."

*

Pit Pacer snorted. This pause on their trek to West Sporangium at first agreed with him, but the longer it lasted the more he stamped and blew hay-scented air from his nostrils.

Easy, Joel-Brock whispered: *Take it easy, fella.*

Mr. Valona shook Pit Pacer's reins, and the Valorous Smalls set off again, each aware of how *exposed* they were in this many-tiered cavern. It shimmered with low-level light, echoed with plinks and gurgles, and smelled of loam, quagslip, slate, mildew, hay, and growing or decaying fungi. Also, the trail wrinkled, rose, veered, and smoothed out so often that traveling it was like a camel journey over the tracks of a tumbledown roller coaster. In fact, the Smalls advanced like this for two hours, according to the yNaut, and covered less than five miles, as the hill mynah flies.

"Could we maybe take another rest?" asked Addi Coe.

"Hmmph," Joel-Brock said. "Tired already?"

"Says a guy riding like a rajah in a howdah," Addi rejoined.

Joel-Brock and Mr. Valona began to guffaw. *"Rajah,"* the boy said. *"How-dah,"* replied Mr. Valona. They repeated these funny words back and forth.

At length, Addi put her hands over her head and cried, *"Aauurrrgggh!"*

Then she stalked away, climbing one steep slope in ten seconds. When she crested it, she came upon a lichen-lit mesa the size of a basketball court. She stared across it with pleasure, as if she knew it from another life or a half-remembered spirit visit as a preteen. She figured that she'd left Joel-Brock and Mr. Valona hundred of yards behind and below her. Still, the weirdness of these sensations did not distress her. She'd achieved a strange, but also strangely calming, homecoming.

Also, she had more light here.

Looming over this mesa was a big rock building much like a monastery, a church, or a school. Anyway, it had lanterns in its window arches, each in blown glass like a giant specimen of the edible mushroom *Amanita chepangiana.* This mushroom Addi had never before seen or heard of, but now its Latin name flashed on her inner eyeballs as if written in Nepalese calligraphy. She read the words, connected the words to the lanterns, and the lanterns to the mushrooms they resembled. Then the lanterns caught fire and blazed away over the mesa. Addi marveled. Who requires a sun—real or phony—when the church of *Amanita chepangiana* has become a house of fiery stars? Then her pupils shrank against this light, and the wonder of her vision faded, almost reassuringly.

"Addi!" Mr. Valona shouted. "Come back! All is forgiven!"

She looked over her shoulder and down. "No it isn't! *Come up here!*" To

herself, she thought, As if you deserve what you'll see.

Pit Pacer climbed the rising trail, and Mr. Valona, holding his reins, appeared on the switchback's last slope. Joel-Brock clasped the saddle horn and held his knees hard against Pit Pacer's flanks. Lantern light flickered in the pony's eyes as he stepped onto the edge of the mesa. He had been here before, but because he now had some age on him, the climb had tested his strength, stamina, and temper.

"My, my," Mr. Valona said. "Somebody set a twelve-story pewter cake on fire." He tugged Pit Pacer and Joel-Brock along behind him toward Addi, a glow of awe and pleasure on his face.

Abruptly, Pit Pacer reared, nearly unseating Joel-Brock. Mr. Valona dropped the pony's reins, grabbed Joel-Brock under the arms, and set him down without jarring his ankle. Pit Pacer trotted off toward a dainty brick bridge connecting the mesa to one floor of the lantern-lit building. A robed figure met Pit Pacer on the bridge, seized the fallen reins, and raised a beckoning hand to the Smalls.

Come, the gesture said: *Follow me.*

13

The Spawnifice

Seeing this monk-like figure beckon, the Smalls exchanged glances.

"Let's go," Addi said. "I want to see the inside of that building." She gestured at its window arches containing mushroom-shaped lanterns and its lofty corner-set towers. Who wouldn't want to enter such a magnificent place?

"Hold on," Mr. Valona said. "The people of Sporangium are different. We could fall victim to foul play or death."

"You talk like you think anyone wearing a turban has a bomb inside it."

"Spoken like the girlfriend of a two-legged mushroom," Mr. Valona said.

"Manny isn't my sweetheart, but if he was, I wouldn't deny him because a hateful person called him a sprol."

"And you shouldn't, Addi. But these fruiting bodies—the Sporangians—may not act as moral agents in the same way we do . . . or, at least, as we *should*."

"What are you talking about?"

"Addi, they grow from a thready mass of vegetation, a network of runners and nerves that they may never completely separate from. They—"

"Stop. If we don't go soon"—Addi gestured at the dainty stone bridge—"we'll have no one to guide us through that building."

Joel-Brock asked, "Have you both forgotten my family?"

"We'll find them," Addi said. "But do you plan to *hop* the rest of the way there? Just relax for a bit."

"Look." Joel-Brock hopped on his left leg thirty feet across the mesa beside the sporule palace. Then he stopped, turned, and stood on his good leg, arms spread, as if to say, *I'm faster on one foot than either of you on two.* Then he hopped back toward them until he tripped and fell headlong.

Addi ran to Joel-Brock and helped him up. Mr. Valona said that because they could not reach his family's prison without transportation for Joel-Brock, they might as well follow the monk into the fastness. Joel-Brock grunted a glum okay, and Mr. Valona swung his backpack around to his chest to let the boy ride him piggyback. And the three Smalls, on two pairs of legs, hurried after the departing monk.

*

The bridge did not lead straight from the mesa into the palatial structure, but funneled any traveler down into a stone court at the base of the many-tiered building.

As they descended, Joel-Brock found Mr. Valona's footfalls more jolting than Pit Pacer's, for he had to fight the pull of gravity. Addi, however, skipped. At the foot of the bridge-ramp, the monk awaited with Pit Pacer. A stone lane led from the court to a series of stalls and a large paddock beyond, where they saw eight or nine more ponies. Like Pit Pacer, two had black or dark-brown coats. White and caramel spots marked all the others. The smells of hay and horse droppings drifted to them.

"*Welcome!*" This word from Pit Pacer sounded more nasal than had the pony's voice when speaking for the Archbishop. "*I am Miles Lee Umphrees, the canon of this place, the Spawnifice. We could have called it the Hotbed or My Lyceum, but Spawnifice has a higher tone, don't you think?*"

"What do you do here?" Mr. Valona asked.

"*Prepare bedding trays, spawn sporules, and grow them to term as members of the upright non-photosynthesizing vegetable class.*"

"I thought maybe you bred ponies," Addi said.

Canon Umphrees smiled, but his smile did not make his misshapen, spotted face more handsome. Still, he politely replied, "*Our ponies we keep as mounts for visitors and riding enthusiasts such as—"*

"Archbishop Meece," Addi guessed.

"That's right, but also as producers of manure and turners of compost. We work them hard but otherwise treat them well. Compare us to mesa miners who force them to haul coal-laden carts without ever letting them go aboveground again, except for burial or shipment to glue-making factories."

"My God," Mr. Valona said.

Canon Umphrees seemed not to hear. *"Let me show you around. To relieve you of that boy's weight, Pit Pacer will let him ride."*

Mr. Valona said, "Why not feed Pit Pacer and get Joel-Brock another pony? I'll pay to take one of your steeds to Mr. Borsmutch's place in West Sporangium."

"I'll arrange it now." The pony swung about and clopped off toward his stable mates, his tackle lopsidedly swaying.

Canon Umphrees shrugged as if to look smaller in his robes. But he could not see himself as others did, with the result that Joel-Brock gave off a low-level disgust that he did not even notice. Then the Canon turned and chased down Pit Pacer to undo his tackle and put it on another pony.

Joel-Brock told Mr. Valona, "I don't want to tour this Spawn-'n'-Fuss, sir."

"*Spawnifice*, Master Lollis. But the Canon's giving us another pony. We can't just leave after accepting it."

"No," Addi said. "That would qualify as eating-and-running."

 Miles Lee Umphrees slouched back leading a pony

with white and caramel spots, like big, glowing amoebas. When they arrived, the pony opened its mouth and said, *"Call him Shaftoe, a gentle mount that has worked down here almost as long as Pit Pacer. The boy may ride him safely. Once at your destination, leave him with any worker at another spawn source or compost paddock."*

Addi said, "Ah, a Subterranean Hire-a-Horse, with drop-offs everywhere."

The Canon, through Shaftoe, said, *"Except that we charge no rent, a policy that Mr. Borsmutch has personally authorized."*

"Very kind of him," Mr. Valona said. "It suits our cockerocity."

"But he can withdraw this concession at any time," the pony said throatily, *"and, if he knows who you are, he'll place his fee on your Dock-Me Card. So have a care about what you say and how you treat our gentle Shaftoe."*

Joel-Brock, still piggyback, shuddered. He could not get used to a pony speaking for a sprol and referring to itself in the third person. But he got off Mr. Valona's back and hopped over to the pony.

Neighing softly, Shaftoe let Joel-Brock, with Mr. Valona's help, climb into his saddle. *"Sit me easy,"* the pony himself said.

Canon Umphrees took Shaftoe's reins and led the Smalls through an arch into a Spawnifice corridor with composting rooms on either side. Helical bulbs burnt in their ceilings, illuminating piles of wheat-straw-bedded manure in long two-sided boxes that he referred to as ricks. The Smalls felt the heat radiating from the piles and drew back from the acrid stench of the ammonia fumes.

"Whew," Joel-Brock said. "That stink hit me like a flamethrower blast." As a kid, he'd once rummaged among his mama's cleansers under the kitchen sink as she washed dinner dishes. Annoyed, she undid the cap on a plastic bottle and asked him if he'd like to smell something "really different." He agreed, and Sophia lifted the bottle to his nostrils. One whiff staggered him.

He grabbed his face and dashed to the bathroom to put his head under cold water from the bathtub faucet. His mama apologized. She hadn't expected him to react so violently to the pungent fumes.

Today, however, Joel-Brock marveled at the number of fungal drudges in the Spawnifice. White-spotted, dun-hued persons with stubby bodies and blobby faces, they toiled near or inside the ricks. They wielded pitchforks to turn the compost, leaving the piles' centers loose as they worked dung, peanut hulls, and shredded bark into the mix. In some rooms, they watered the steaming piles or added more filler to cut the grease in the compost, for this material would serve as food for the "spawn" that, on another floor, the sprols would rake into the ricks later.

After preparing the compost, the sprols killed worms or other pests still in it and rid it of the ammonia formed as it fermented. Then they forked the stuff into trays—like big wooden coffins—and loaded the trays onto wagons that pit ponies pulled up the ramp to a higher level. There the sprols stacked the trays several feet high in de-ammonifying chambers with steam nozzles and box fans that Mr. Valona knew for industrial versions of a fan sold in BBB's Home section for $15.00. Not until this process had cleansed the beds of ammonia and dropped their temperature from 145° F to 75° F, said the Canon via Shaftoe, could the planting phase of mushroom growing begin.

Because Shaftoe was wheezing now, Joel-Brock felt sorry for the pony. He was both a beast of burden and a four-legged speaking device, and as they climbed, Shaftoe resumed the Canon's explanations:

The compost is useless until we seed it with mycelia from mushroom spores grown like vegetables in the piles. Bricks of sterilized pony dung serve as hosts for our spawn. The spawn also contains rye, water, chalk, and wheat, and other matter as food for its roots. Once the mycelium spreads through the grain, it qualifies as spawn. We've never used any of the commercial products popular aboveground.

"I know that fish spawn," Addi said, "But how do *mushrooms* spawn?"

"*They don't,*" Shaftoe said. "*Our workers act as spawn distributors, adding it to compost mounds by breaking up the bricks, seeding pieces of it throughout, and raking it into the cleansed wheat straw, pony dung, and peanut hulls.*"

"Mushrooms don't spawn themselves," Mr. Valona told Addi. "They grow in a medium that others have injected spawn into."

Joel-Brock stopped paying full heed to Shaftoe because many more sprols were climbing the ramp or coming down it. These were humanoid beings with tan flesh and omnipresent brownish freckles. They glanced at the Smalls as if angry. Many elbowed Addi as they passed, but ignored Mr. Valona because he walked beside Canon Umphrees, who led Shaftoe. Also, Mr. Valona hugged the right wall, where the gobbymawlers-to-be had to use great agility to gouge anyone. Joel-Brock mostly escaped these pokes because he rode Shaftoe. Still, the Spawnifice grew more hostile the higher they climbed, and because the Canon did not notice or care, the Smalls felt relief when on the third or fourth level he diverted them into a spawning room.

Although younger than Pit Pacer, Shaftoe must have worked longer and harder than the older pony. He wobbled past the trays in this room. Head down, he chuffed like an old furnace. Tenderly, Joel-Brock rubbed the pony's sweaty neck.

Finally, the Canon spoke through Shaftoe: "*This is where we add mycelial cells to the grains in the mix so that the different networks can spread and connect—like roots meeting and forming tangles as hard to undo as the Gordian Knot.*"

"What's the Gordian Knot?" Joel-Brock asked.

"*Something Mr. Borsmutch told me to say,*" said Shaftoe.

"Then he not only knows we're here," Mr. Valona said, "but he's also tracking our every step on our way to his underground villa?"

"*I suppose so.*"

Shaftoe crumpled to his knees, his posterior high to relieve the pressure on his lungs. With Addi's help, Joel-Brock got down and stood beside Shaftoe on his left leg, until that leg went prickly numb and *he* collapsed beside the pony.

Mr. Valona asked, "How far from the Spawnifice to the Lollises' prison?"

Voiceless, the Canon knelt between Joel-Brock's legs, ripped his left trouser leg from instep to calf, and felt his wound. Joel-Brock winced, but did not try to twist free. The Canon let go of his leg and tapped his chest. Half-standing, he then gestured for Joel-Brock to stay down, but nodded at a coffin-like compost tray and limped to it, pulled out a clump of wheat straw and thready mycelium, patted it into his palm, returned to Joel-Brock, and stuck it to his ankle. The poultice then crawled around the ankle to the boy's wound and clung there without a bandage.

"Wow," Addi said. "You know what that means, don't you?"

Bewildered, Joel-Brock merely grunted.

Addi lectured: "That gunk on your leg will suck your brain into it, a sprol will eat it, and you'll wake up tomorrow as a—*Slave of the Spawnifice!*"

"Not funny," Joel-Brock said.

Painfully, Shaftoe got his front legs under him and stood as the Canon made *stay-still* signs at Joel-Brock to imply that if he obeyed, his injury would heal. Joel-Brock felt heat, a focused fever, a chill, and then a sweet firmness and lack of pain. When the Canon nodded, he peeled the poultice off, amazed by how gently its tangled threads let go, and placed it aside. It shrank and burst like a puffball, shooting white spores into the air. Joel-Brock stood, tentatively, and offered everyone a thumbs-up.

Canon Umphrees grinned in a ghastly way, a grin apparently signaling his joy in the healing, *not* in a sick secret plan to deliver them all to Pither Borsmutch. Joel-Brock could not help grinning too.

"I can walk," he said. "I won't need Shaftoe any more."

The other two Smalls stared at him as if they had just witnessed a living centaur separate into its human and horsy parts.

"Then I'll get a sprol to take Shaftoe back to the stables," Canon Umphrees said in the pony's throaty voice.

14

Two Unexpected Calls

Out on the ramp, the Canon caught a sprol and talked with him in mute lip speech. Other sprols hurrying by and some clattery carts added to the hubbub, all reminding Joel-Brock of the chaos of a kicked fire-ant mound.

"Is Umphrees up to something?" Addi asked Mr. Valona.

Mr. Valona shrugged. "I don't know."

"Well, who's our enemy here?"

A song called "Watching the Detectives" began playing in Mr. Valona's waistcoat pocket. He took out his yNaut. "Vaughnathan Valona—private eye, store detective, quest facilitator, and all-around good guy. State your business."

The caller spoke too softly for the other Smalls to hear.

"Okay." Puzzled, Mr. Valona handed the yNaut to Joel-Brock. "It's for you."

Joel-Brock, who hated to talk on phones, whispered: *"Who is it?"*

"The ever unpredictable Augustus Hudspeth. I didn't know you guys were such Big Bonanzic buddies."

Joel-Brock frowned and spoke into the yNaut: "Yeah?"

"'*Yes sir,*'" Mr. Valona said. "Mind your manners, Master Lollis."

"Yes sir?" Joel-Brock said into the yNaut, thinking it weird that Mr. Valona was being polite to a man who had waved a gun at them.

"Tell me exactly where you all are, Joel-Brock," Augustus Hudspeth said.

"In the Spawnifice." A pause. "Sir."

"I said, 'Exactly.' Where? What level? What suite of rooms?"

Joel-Brock specified their location.

"That's better than the stable court, but still not good. As soon as you can, get to the upper floors, at least to the mycohumanification chambers. Got me?"

"Yes sir, but why?"

"If Canon Umphrees is still with you, tell him that you and your friends want to see the mushmorphosis rooms. Say you want to skip everything else and go straight up-ramp to sprol production."

"Mr. Hudspeth, I can't remember all that."

"Just get Vaughn and that red-haired Addi brat moving, okay?"

"Yes sir."

"Keep your yNaut switched on. This is important."

Joel-Brock returned the yNaut to Mr. Valona—to whom, surely, Mr. Hudspeth should have given his message—and quickly told his friends.

Meanwhile, the sprol who'd been "talking" with the Canon started down-ramp with Shaftoe, and the Smalls popped out of that spawning suite as if pushed from behind. Mr. Valona put head locks on Addi and Joel-Brock and marched them upward, close to the right-hand wall, apparently fearful that Augustus and Canon Umphrees had plotted how best to do them in. Maybe they should be traveling down, not up. Should they trust Augustus or fear that all he had said via the yNaut was setting them up for a cruel Pither M. Borsmutch booby trap?

Despite lacking a mouthpiece, Canon Umphrees scrambled after the Smalls. The sprols on the ramp moved in graceless clumps at speeds faster than the old Canon could go. Although he tried his best, he was lucky to keep the Smalls in view. But Joel-Brock, Addi, and Mr. Valona were taller than many of the Spawnifice sprols and thus provided him with heads to focus on as he lurched after them. Joel-Brock also limped along, not because his ankle continued to hurt, but because he had still not pulled on the sneaker that Mortimer had fetched for him.

He hated the headlock in which Mr. Valona had put him and Addi, to keep them both safe. They were yoked to him like a team of small oxen. Mr. Valona tugged them along and let them tug him too. They all had to believe that Augustus would not lie to them about a terrible danger from the Spawnifice's sprols—if, that is, they failed to reach a mysterious suite of rooms on one of its highest levels. Whose side was Augustus on? Did *Augustus* even know? And why had Augustus asked to speak to him, a ten-year-old, about so urgent a matter?

Climbing, they passed stone-floored suites devoted to the last stages of mushroom growing. Sprols marching up-ramp beside or ahead of them broke from the general surge to enter these rooms, but sprols bent on spawning or composting heel-walked down in grim silence. Even in a head lock, Joel-Brock glanced into various suites and spied sprols spraying the trays and laying top-dressings of mashed clay and sifted loam on the wheat-straw piles. All the sprols watering these piles seemed able and efficient. Did they really *know* what they were about? Or had they been modified in the spawning stage to labor mindlessly up here?

Who knew?

Maybe Canon Umphrees knew. He wheezed microspores from his nostrils and signaled the Smalls that he was still trailing them, that they must halt and let him guide them again. But they ignored his urgent gestures.

Mr. Valona tugged Joel-Brock and Addi past a suite where the trays showed white pins on their casings. These *pins*—as he knew from gathering fungi in wet Appalachian forests—would turn into *buttons*, which would soon turn into genuine mushrooms, edible or inedible, depending on their type. The sprols here looked to see if the stringy mycelial masses had started lacing their casings. They examined the white pins growing from the encased rhizomorphs and charted their growth by stages. Pinning was a crucial stage. It foretold the yield and quality of the coming harvest.

The Smalls climbed and climbed. Sprol traffic had thinned, as if the workers had taken their posts or returned to their dorms. Abruptly, Mr. Valona released Joel-Brock and Addi. Joel-Brock glanced back. On a less crowded ramp, Canon Umphrees hitched along like the Mummy in an old black-and-white flick—one arm reaching forward, the other stuck to his side as if too heavy to lift. Addi yanked Mr. Valona's wrist as if it were a pump handle.

"Let the poor galoot catch up," she pled. "He's treated us okay, hasn't he?"

"Augustus said to *get to the top*. He urged us to *climb*."

"Maybe he should have told us to 'get to the bottom' of things."

"Cleverly put, Addi, but we can't take a chance on going down."

"Do you think the Canon plans to absorb us into him so that *we* turn into sprols?"

"No," Joel-Brock said. "We're not that far from the mycohumanification suites. We've got to do what Augustus said."

"The what-kind-of suites?" Addi asked.

Joel-Brock ignored her. "If he's planned something bad, we'll know soon, but if we go down, we won't. And lots of hacked-off funguses will surround us."

"*Fungi*," Addi said.

"Either plural is acceptable," Mr. Valona said. "Besides, Joel-Brock votes with me and I with him. That's a majority, Addi."

"A majority of *males*, and look at what all you men have done for the world."

The Canon had now drawn many rooms closer, so Mr. Valona seized the Smalls' arms again to hurry their march up-ramp.

At the first cropping room, Joel-Brock delivered a surprising lecture:

"Mushroom growers call the times of the cropping stage *flush*, *break*, or *bloom*. They last about forty-two days, but sometimes as many as a hundred and fifty. It's a lot chillier in there," Joel-Brock nodded into the room, "because cooler temps aid growth, but also engender more insects and bacteria."

They passed another cropping room.

"The sporules control its humidity level. If it's too high, the mushroom caps get slick and clammy. There's got to be *some* moisture in the air, but if there's too much, the casings seal shut."

"What's gotten into you?" Addi said. "You sound like a professor."

Joel-Brock clamped his lips shut, *tight*. His talkativeness confused him. What had loaded his all-baseball brain with facts about a food—a *lousy* food—that he would never even eat? Ah, yes: his baptism in a quagslip-filled gully, his sense that it caused strange changes, and his feeling that it acted as a food for funguses created outside the building—all *that* hinted at the stages in mushroom growth marked by the Spawnifice's different levels. *Quagslip* accounted for his sudden expertise about all things mushroomy. But *how* had it boosted his knowledge of these matters?

Joel-Brock walked. The ramp had few sprols on it. How weird, then, that so many had swarmed it earlier. Behind them, the Canon resembled a cartoon prospector crossing a desert in quest of water—on legs that seemed shorter with each new step.

"Here's a mycohumanification room," Joel-Brock said.

When they entered it, "Watching the Detectives" began playing, and Mr. Valona brought his yNaut out. "Hello!" he said.

Addi and Joel-Brock looked around. This suite had not only mushroom lamps in its windows, but also fluorescents on the ceiling. Although he'd never before set foot in a mycohumanification chamber, he recognized every ripening cabinet, body modifier, figure trimmer, ensouling machine, and cohort extruder by its design elements, because the chambers looked less like the insides of an

old-style factory than they did the galleries of a modern art museum.

On the walls between the stations of the mycohumanification process hung large 3D photos of fungal humans. Most reminded Joel-Brock of aliens in classic sci-fi films, but how else should they look? They were creatures quirked into near replicas of human beings by lovely machines, DNA magic, a pinch of poetic license. The suites used more than one process to create these beings, which ranged from *fully fungal* to *sort-of human*, from *sporule* to *near-buddypard*. Besides the poster-like photos, the suites held statues sitting on slate bases or on short granite columns. Joel-Brock couldn't tell if they were plasticized mushroom people who had emerged stillborn from the process, or handmade works of art. Maybe only a philosopher could have made a telling distinction between the two. Joel-Brock shuddered.

"Joel-Brock," Mr. Valona was saying. *"Joel-Brock!"*

"Sir?" He looked as if he'd been yanked from a paralyzing dream.

"It's Augustus. He wants to talk to you again."

Joel-Brock accepted the yNaut. "Hello."

"You're in the mycohumanification suite, right? Vaughn just told me. Good. Now you've got a small chance of escaping the trap you-know-who has set for you."

"I *don't* know who," Joel-Brock said.

"Think, J.-B. Think!"

Well, of course. He looked at the fabricated sprols on display about the room, the *cohort extruder* that made their living counterparts, and the *ripening cabinet* in which they, well, *ripened* into sort-of-intelligent beings.

"When the attack begins, go up," Augustus said. *"Several more levels sit above*

your present one. When you reach the roof, you'll—" Augustus broke off.

"We'll what?"

Addi reached for the phone, but Joel-Brock pivoted away from her.

"You'll know what to do," Augustus said. *"Earlier this afternoon, I got a Braves game from tomorrow on the FöFumm—a game against the Birmingham Barons."*

"What happened?"

"J.-B. Lollis the Elder went hitless in four at-bats and made a throwing error in the top of the ninth that cost his team the ball game."

"Gee, Mr. Hudspeth, thanks for telling me that."

"After the game I jacked a Kumquat laptop into the FöFumm, hacked the Braves site accessible via the TV a decade-plus from now, and found an email address for your future self. I sent him some pointers about his swing and news that you and two others had entered Sporangium to fetch your family home."

"J.-B.'s swing is almost perfect, sir."

"When he emailed me back, he asked if he could contact you guys down there. I gave him Vaughn's yNaut number, but said not to call until you leave the Spawnifice."

"Can my future self really do that? Call me?"

"You'll find out. Right now, though, someone here wants to say hello."

A pair of bumps indicated that his caller's cell had just switched hands.

"Is it on?" a familiar voice said. *"Hello, babycakes, you there?"*

"Miss Melba! I'm here!" yNaut static crackled like a campfire, but the signal was audible, mostly. Joel-Brock and Miss Melba talked. She first asked what his parents did when Josie got down in the mouth and stopped eating.

"Feed her tiny pinches of peach till she's eaten all of one, okay?"

"Yeah, yeah," Miss Melba said, *"I'll do that."*

Augustus took back his cell. *"The sprols will attack soon. Remember what I said about getting to the roof. Godspeed, kid!"*

The mycohumanification suite hummed with the sounds of mushmorphosis. Some of the statues moved on their stands, or appeared to, and Canon Umphrees flopped rather than burst through the suite's main door.

15

The Ramp Mistakenly Taken

Mr. Valona waved Addi and Joel-Brock toward that door, and Joel-Brock thrust a thumb into the air, to stress that they must go *up*. Addi also ran toward the up-ramp. But Canon Umphrees spread his arms and made fish mouths to imply that he wanted to talk, maybe even to apologize for suckering them into the Spawnifice. Then he pointed at a TV screen showing an animated cartoon of the Canon.

When the sound came on, his pudgy stick figure said, *"I didn't plan this attack. I knew nothing about it until I received a text message about the uprising from Archbishop Meece."* The stick figure lifted a tiny stick-sided rectangle, but the real Canon held up a more or less real yNaut.

"Let us by," Joel-Brock told the living, not the cartoon, Canon.

"But—" the Canon mouthed, and his animated figure "actually" said.

"Let us by!" Mr. Valona yelled. "Do you want our efforts to rescue Joel-Brock's family to end in failure?"

The Canon moved aside. He wanted to do the right thing even if—from a sprol's perspective—it seemed to insult his own kind. The Smalls edged into the corridor and then joined hands on the ramp to sprint upward on it. But Joel-Brock had a qualmifying pang and turned back to the Canon.

"Thank you, sir," he said. "And bless you too." Back in the corridor, he heard the distant tramping and chuffing of sprols as the sprols marched upslope.

"Let's amscray," Addi said.

The ramp steepened, alarmingly, and they passed rooms whose purposes suddenly seemed more military than agricultural. They did not stop to see, but pushed on against the cries of their reluctant bodies. Mr. Valona was gasping, Addi panting, and Joel-Brock suffering a sharp stitch under his right ribs. Still panting, Addi suggested that they "take a breather."

Mr. Valona gasped, "I've never had such pain on a hike."

Addi patted his back. "It's *not* a hike, it's a *climb*. You can't call the conditions ordinary." She was right—Sporangium had the depth of an ocean trench, lots of bleak uneven terrain, and mazy buildings like the Spawnifice. They heard the sprols again—the tramping feet, the echoes of this tramping, the chuffing of their breathing, and their own pounding hearts.

"Let's go," Joel-Brock said, and the Smalls arose and climbed until they reached a fork where the ramp split like a **Y** into two ascending prongs. Neither path gave a clue as to where it might end, nor did the ramp have any signage. Joel-Brock remembered long-retired catcher Yogi Berra's advice, *"When you come to a fork in the road, take it,"* and *wished* they could do just that.

Addi said, "Maybe two of us should go one way and the other another."

"Oh no," Mr. Valona said: "All for one and one for all."

"Then which way do we go?" asked Joel-Brock.

"I'll toss a coin." Mr. Valona dug out a quarter and laid it on his thumbnail.

"Call it, Addi," Joel-Brock said. "Heads right, tails left."

"But if I call it wrong, our failure will fall on me," Addi said.

"No," Mr. Valona said. "The burden becomes the coin's. Please call it, Addi."

So he flipped the coin, and Addi called it, *"Heads!"*

The tramping grew louder, more menacing. The sprols' breathing was a mounting *hum*, the droning of a thousand hive-bound bees.

Silver-bright, the quarter atop Mr. Valona's hand showed tails. "And so," Joel-Brock said, "it's up the left fork we go." They angled up the leftward ramp into a long hallway that, after sixty yards of switchbacking, dead-ended at a wall, which they had not foreseen. And when they tried to locate push points in it to a hidden territory beyond and found nothing, they despaired. "The coin's fault," Joel-Brock told Addi. "You called heads, but the coin took us tail-ways."

"Back down to the neck of the **Y**!" Mr. Valona yelled. *"Hurry!"* They hurried and, dashing downhill, reached it quickly and halted below the **Y** juncture to see sprols trudging toward them like ghastly soldiers, their faces blank or hostile and their bodies agleam with fury. Each sprol carried a stave or a sling. When they saw the Smalls, those in the front rank—which crossed the whole corridor—whirled their slings or rattled their staves. One stave,

a sharpened plank, landed with a smack at Addi's feet and bounced up the right prong of the **Y** they must climb to reach the roof . . . *if* Augustus had given them good advice about how to escape the fungal hordes.

"Those sprols are *serious*," Mr. Valona said. "Make a bunny-hop circle and yank the golf-ball boxes from your backpacks."

Joel-Brock had never *heard* of a bunny-hop circle. But he and Addi formed a sort of circle with Mr. Valona, and they all yanked golf-ball boxes from one another's backpacks. Because Mr. Valona had pre-removed their shrink wrapping, they got into these boxes quickly and freed several balls.

"Pick a target and bombard the suckers!" Mr. Valona said. "*Now!*"

Joel-Brock, occasionally a pitcher, hurled a golf ball into the first rank— at the sprol who'd thrown the stave. It hit this creature in the brow, stuck like a huge third eye, and knocked him into the rank behind him.

The injured sprol's comrades caught and held him up, as a shield rather than a kindness. Still he fell, tripping his comrades, even as Addi and Mr. Valona got off tosses of their own. Addi's ball bored into the belly of a doughy *Amanita* mushroom soldier, but Mr. Valona's short-hopped harmlessly through their ranks. The skittering ball upended a sprol farther down. This sprol toppled five or six others. By this time, Joel-Brock had blistered yet another with a fastball and clipped one more with a sidearm curve. Several mushroom warriors dropped their staves to assist the fallen. The sprols coming up behind them tramped in place, stomping either the wounded or their weapons.

Joel-Brock flung another ball. "Let's hightail it!"

"My cinnamon mints exactly, kidster."

"Wait." Joel-Brock got Addi to rummage in his backpack for six metal windup toys, which she set on the ramp facing the foe. These toys resembled pigs: cartoon pigs, razorbacks, Spotted Poland China swine, etc. Joel-Brock turned the keys in their backs until their springs almost popped and let them go—as "distracters," he told his friends—and the pigs came on as if their legs and feet, clicking and clacking, were the drumbeats inspiring their march.

"The sprols will just kick them aside," Mr. Valona warned.

"No sir," Addi said. "It's pig versus mushroom, swine versus truffle. I admit it's not mongoose versus cobra, but sometimes even a goofy idea will work."

The windup swine advanced on the sprols, and the sprols, once the windups were near enough to be seen as swine, no longer cared that these fake pigs were teensy-weensy jokes. They fled in panic, even though one well-aimed stave swing would have sent all the windups flying.

"Well, I never," Addi said, truly surprised.

"Genius," Mr. Valona said. "It's an enacted parable about the efforts of us Smalls to overcome the obstacles that Sporangium sets before us in our quest to—"

Joel-Brock broke in: "Once the pigs *stop* moving, sir, the sprols will *start*."

The Valorous Smalls darted up the right-hand fork, thankful that their distracters had distracted and hopeful that Augustus had not lied.

*

At length, they spied some spindly stairs rising to a metal platform and a door. If nothing else, the stairs would prevent the sprols from bursting through that high door in crushing numbers. They'd have to climb up single-file and step through carefully—to keep a Small on the far side from golf-ball-bopping them.

Below the stairs, the Smalls again rested. They resolved never to climb the steps in the Statue of Liberty, the Eiffel Tower, or the Giralda belfry in Seville. Huffing like asthmatics, they climbed the staircase, Joel-Brock coming last, and halted beneath the door they thought would open onto the Spawnifice's roof.

"I hate it when guys in movies run up steps to a rooftop or a clock tower," Joel-Brock said. "It's dumb."

"Yeah," Addi said, "why do screenwriters think escaping means going up?"

"Bear cubs climb trees to elude predators," Mr. Valona said.

"Maybe so," Addi said, "but what works for a bear won't work for a crook fleeing the cops. Of course, the bad guy has a long way to fall and the director gets to run closing credits over the bloody *schplatt* he makes."

"Thanks," Joel-Brock said, "for reminding us."

Mr. Valona shushed them. "Listen. What do you hear?"

Addi said, "Tramping feet and a million mouth-breathing sprols."

"Open the door," Joel-Brock said.

Mr. Valona pulled hard on its bolted handle. Nothing happened, except that he grabbed his own arm and bent over in pain.

"*To access this roof,*" the door said, "*you must answer three questions of a highly specific nature about your tour of the Spawnifice.*"

"NO!" Mr. Valona cried. "No, no, no, and NO!"

"I'll second that," Addi said.

"*We require payment in the form of smart answers. That's what distinguishes doors in Sporangium from anywhere else in the world.*"

"I would have thought," Addi said, "that merely existing as *a door in Spo-*

rangium would single you out from doors anywhere else."

"*Ah,*" said the door, "*excellent point. Besides, I've already asked these questions a hundred times. You may pass.*"

"But ask the next group that shows up," Mr. Valona said. "You don't want to get out of practice."

"*Another good point. I'll do as you suggest.*"

Click! The door opened—inward—and the Smalls eased through it one at a time, with Joel-Brock pulling it to behind them: *Click!*

16

The Getaway

Once the windup toys wound down, the sprols stepped on them like Godzilla or the Beast from 20,000 fathoms squashing the folks fleeing them underfoot—but not quite, because the windups had menaced the sprols rather than vice versa. Ironically, no sprol had seen these movies, so this bad comparison had never occurred to them and they could mangle the windup pigs as they pleased.

Then they resumed chasing the Smalls and got to the base of the spindly staircase just as Joel-Brock pushed its door shut on them. Now the sprols had two choices: go back down or continue their pursuit. They chose the chase, which required them to dash up the steps a sprol at a time, like kids in line to visit Santa Claus. They jostled for places and fell into a file that zigzagged down-ramp for a hundred yards before spreading out again into straggly clumps. At the stairway door, two older sprols, cabinet polishers rather than manure rakers, tried to pull the door open.

"To access the roof," the door said, *"you must answer three questions of a highly specific nature about your duties in the Spawnifice."*

One sprol, Amanmu Tablas, had a level of intelligence rare among his kind but a level wasted among polishers of ripening cabinets. He realized that even if he knew the questions' answers, he must answer them telepathically. He wondered if the door could receive his answers via brain waves. But Amanmu Tablas still broadcast the door both his dismay and a highly specific threat: *"If you fail to open for us, O esteemed and otherwise admirable door, our Maker, Pither Borsmutch, will have you snatched from your hinges and flung into a quagslip gully."* The esteemed and otherwise admirable door gobbled its pride and clicked open to Amanmu Tablas, who stepped out onto the wide slate roof. Dozens of his fellow sprols prepared to follow.

But instead of the rooftop vista that Amanmu Tablas had expected, his eyes met the back of a shovel blade that Joel-Brock swung with all the force his ten-year-old body could muster. Amanmu Tablas crumpled into the sprol behind him, who knocked over the next one *ad* (not quite) *infinitum*, until most of the sprolish army had fallen like—reader, forgive me—a file of dominoes. Joel-Brock stared down into the interior of the Spawnifice at the toppled sporules and, nearer to hand, at Amanmu Tablas. Tablas's body kept the door from fully closing. Also, the wound inflicted upon him, a member of the species called *Amanita mutabilis*, had caused a stain to spread over his face and down his broad neck and chest like melted raspberry sherbet. Joel-Brock beheld this magenta stain with will-weakening horror.

With his shovel he pushed Tablas's body back onto the stairway platform, trying to imagine himself working a pair of robot hands hundreds of yards from this upsetting reality. But he could not imagine it because he felt pity for the mushroom man and all the sprols sprawled behind him. Moreover, he *really* needed to get the door shut to give the Smalls a chance to flee this nightmare. Many sprols below the staircase had begun to stand. He used the shovel—not to disfigure the body blocking the door, but to move it—and nudged it just far enough aside to push the door to. *Click!*

Then he thought on what he had done. He had killed the sprol with the raspberry stains on his chest. He had no idea that the slain sprol bore the name Amanmu Tablas, but he knew that a real name of some kind attached to the mushroom being. A shovel blow had ended his life; hence, what he had just done had little in common with J.-B. Lollis's hitting a curve from

a pitcher over a fence and defeating the other team. This sprol would never arise again, whereas the pitcher and his teammates *would* play again. The stakes in Sporangium were higher than those—

"Joel-Brock!" Addi yelled.

He laid down the shovel and turned to Addi. As if someone had left it behind for him, he had found the shovel propped against a nearby wall and had stepped to the door with it planning to do just what he'd done—protect Mr. Valona and Addi as they strove to escape. But, having just slain this innocent sprol, he wondered if their *means* of escape would hasten their own deaths too. Innocent? Well, that was—

"Joel-Brock, come *on!*"

In the lichen-lit darkness, he ran toward Addi and Mr. Valona. Some fifty feet away, they sat in the front seats of a flying trike. Mr. Valona turned its motor over until it caught. The motor chugged as if certain of its ability to launch them into the night. The flyke had a strut-fixed parasail above it—a rectangular canopy of shiny blue, orange, and gold. Its lightweight body resembled that of a large, but thin and hairless, tarantula. The parasail's stripes shone like neon signs. Joel-Brock fixed on them as guides to sidestep the vehicle's propeller and to vault into its back seat. Like Addi and Mr. Valona, he had already turned his pack around, so that just before he hopped aboard, Mr. Valona had set the spidery craft rolling.

"We can't see any better than a mole," Joel-Brock yelled. "How much runway do we need to get, uh, uh—?"

"—airborne?" cried Addi.

"Right!" Joel-Brock figured the towers on the corners, black-on-black silhouettes, lay a hundred yards away, but the flyke was closing on them—*fast.*

"Easy," Mr. Valona cried. "I'm a paraglider pilot licensed by both the USPPA and the USUA. I do this all the time, just for fun."

"Underground?" Joel-Brock shouted. "At night? With passengers?"

"No. But I've worked through the pilot syllabi of both those groups and flown in some really heavy weather."

"*Underground?*" Joel-Brock said again. Behind them, the door to the roof burst open. A swarm of sprols—all with names—stumped after the laboring vehicle. Not one, he knew, considered itself a faceless pawn or a bale of cannon fodder.

Addi shouted, "There's a wall ahead! Lift us *now!*"

"Leave it to me," Mr. Valona called.

One of the sprols—the winged Mercury of sprols—gained on the wobbling and yawing paraglider. This sprol, Philo A. Cigara, wanted everyone in his native country to know his name, especially Pither Borsmutch, the founder not only of Big Box Bonanzas but also of this Spawnifice, Cigara's incubator. Perhaps Cigara, a child of the fly agaric toadstool, reacting to his body's weird alkaloids, believed he could fly unassisted. In any case, Joel-Brock glanced back and saw Cigara coming.

"Give her some gas!" he yelled at Mr. Valona.

Mr. Valona did, and the flyke lurched forward at a speedier clip. The silhouettes of the corner towers grew in height, and Mr. Valona began to doubt their chances of clearing the wall between them. Also, the darkness around them, broken only dimly by bioluminescent fungi and the glow of their parasail, had begun to unnerve him. What if they lacked enough speed to clear the wall?

God help me, Mr. Valona thought: God help us all.

BLAAAM!

Off to the west, Sporangium's fake sun burst into eye-stinging splendor, and their flyke bounced eastward over the roof, so that the glow of this sun did not smite them with full force. But this fact also held true for Philo A. Cigara, who knew that another shot of adrenalin would let him seize the boy's trundle seat and keep their craft from escaping. And so he grabbed for its aluminum piping.

Mr. Valona saw that the wall ahead had a twelve-foot gap in its center. He must get their wheels off the roof and angle for that opening to clear it. Then they'd have time for an updraft (if any blew down here) to slip beneath the parasail and lift them enough to avoid plunging to the rocks. Mr. Valona gave the paraglider more gas. It bumped and began to rise. But Cigara, who had leapt before this acceleration, seized Joel-Brock's seat. Because he weighed little more than a bag of leaf ash, the flyke fluttered through the gap in the wall. The Smalls gasped when it sank, their guts rising like fists inside them, the craft pitching and yawing in the building's shadow. Cigara seized the boy's face from behind and gouged his eyes with wormy fingers.

"Stop!" Joel-Brock cried. "Stop, you *jerkweed!*"

Addi turned and reached for the sprol's arm, but her lunge, along with Cigara's effort to blind Joel-Brock, made the flyke's swerving even worse. Mr. Valona shook his head, cautioning Addi not to rock the glider further and telling Joel-Brock to elbow their attacker into the abyss. Cigara's incessant eye-gouging led Joel-Brock to grab one of the sporule's spongy hands and to cram it into his mouth.

Then he bit it, hard, and tried to do seize Cigara's other hand. He failed because the sprol yanked his hands away and fell from the flyke like a sack of leaf ash. No scream escaped him, for Cigara could not scream as humans and invested gobbymawlers could, and he plunged into a gully where no one ever found him.

Of course, no one ever looked for him, either. . . .

Joel-Brock's mouth filled with a vile taste he reckoned was poisonous. He knew better than to gulp such saliva. So he spit it over his shoulder into the abyss that had just received the sprol. He spat and spat until he had no more spit and just the aftertaste of the sprol's poison to remind him that life is not all fine unless you enjoy suffering as much as you do health, love, and creation itself.

Whoa. Woe. Joel-Brock had killed two sprols within a span of ten minutes. Many dismissed sprols as vermin, but he believed that idea hurtful, not solely to its victims but also to himself. He had done what he had to, but he would never despise his victims. Of course, he had just turned ten, and who could say what life would hand him in the span of breaths still allotted to him?

Meanwhile, the Smalls' flyke bobbed upward in the cavern under a glary sun that blew a lacquer-like sheen on everything beneath it—even as it daubed stark shadows into places better left unlit. For fear of hitting the stony roof, they could not rise too high, nor land without fear of colliding with a spire or dropping into a gully of quagslip. Joel-Brock began to cry, again. But please, reader, do not condemn him. Most likely, he is already a saner creature than you or I.

*

Despite Mr. Valona's cautions, Addi reached back and grasped Joel-Brock's shoulder. Wiping his eyes with one chilly hand, he refused to look at her. Their ultralight—or not-quite-ultralight, given that it had a pilot and two passengers and no longer qualified for that status—tilted as it rose. Buzzing like a telephone-pole transformer, it cast a spidery shadow on the landscape below.

Addi could not process all that had just occurred—from the behavior of Canon Umphrees, to their tour of the mushroom-growing suites, to Mr. Hudspeth's cell-phone calls, to the hostility of the sprols and the rooftop presence of a flyke that Vaughnathan Valona knew how to pilot. And how about the powering-up of that phony sun at the very moment when Mr. Valona needed light to clear the wall? Did the lords of this realm wish the

Smalls to fail or to succeed, to end up prisoners like Joel-Brock's family or to remain free and rescue the Lollises?

Clearly, Pither Borsmutch had a sadistic yen to foil their mission. He was sort of like God, occasionally involved, occasionally so aloof that he must have died. Anyway, if he stood behind all that had happened, or if he stepped away and merely watched, Addi knew the pattern as one that had played out in her own life, until she'd cried in her heart, *"Enough!"* and run away.

Now she shouted, "Circle the Spawnifice, sir! Take us west!" Mr. Valona seemed to have zoned out. "West!" she hollered. "Go west!"

Mr. Valona banked their flyke to the left—to come back around the Spawnifice and set their course to West Sporangium. Doing so would entail passing through a portal connecting the two halves of this dark domain. The fake sun moved toward that portal and hung near it, illuminating a tall vertical gap that would demand luck as well as skill to thread in this craft.

Now, though, they flew west beside the front edge of the Spawnifice's roof, and every sprol that had tried to thwart the Smalls stood at its northern wall watching them stutter past. To Addi, the sprols resembled cartoons, with squat bodies and squinty eyes under their pancake hats. They shook their fists, rattled staves, and leaned toward the flyke as if to board it like freebooting sky-pirates. They did not, of course, but did hurl their staves. The staves bounced off the parasail. One grazed the flyke before falling into the court where Pit Pacer and the other ponies sheltered. Because the sprols had shot off so many stones earlier, only a few used slingshots. One stone flew past the Smalls—a stone big enough, had it hit them, to do real damage. Almost miraculously, the flyke passed beyond these inept warriors and buzzed westward above quagslip gullies and the stone hovels of sporules from places other than the Spawnifice. Addi told Mr. Valona several times that he'd let their craft rise too high, and he heeded her. Still, she feared that he'd lost some of his sharpness during this last encounter. The flyke had few features beyond its sail, motor, stick, seats, and wheels. It had no instruments—no speedometer, altimeter, or fuel gauge, and no ailerons on its wings' rear edges.

So when Addi asked Mr. Valona how much fuel it had left, he truthfully said, "I have no idea."

Purple half-moons underlay Joel-Brock's eyes, but a breeze stirred by the parasail had dried his tears. Addi touched a half-circle, lifted her finger to her lips, and tasted it. How sweet that Joel-Brock Lollis could snatch from the nerve-fraying misadventure of their getaway a small tatter of sleep.

*

"How will you know when we need to land, sir?"

Mr. Valona looked at Addi sidelong. "When the motor starts sputtering."

"Worse than it's doing now?"

"That's no sputter. That's a smooth continuous buzz."

"It is?"

"Relax. I won't fly that high. You've already told me the folly of doing so."

"Shouldn't I keep an eye out for a flat place for you to land?"

"Sure," Mr. Valona said. "But let's try to get through that pass"—nodding at the gap ahead—"into West Sporangium. Let's use the flyke while we have it."

Addi asked Mr. Valona what it had been doing on the roof, gassed up, and how he had happened to know how to fly it.

"It must belong to Canon Umphrees or Archbishop Meece," he replied.

"Meece can fly *without* a machine," Addi pointed out.

"Yeah. And maybe Umphrees can too." Mr. Valona studied the unfriendly terrain. "As for my knowing how to fly these things, well, that was indeed lucky."

"What if someone wanted us high up in the air so that—?" Addi stopped.

"Go on."

"We'd have that much farther to fall—if and when we fell."

"Good lord, Miss Coe, are you a conspiracy nut?"

"Hello," she said. "Didn't a conspiracy against Joel-Brock's family bring us down here, sir?"

Mr. Valona said, "Ah." Addi relished his agreement. Structures amid the rocks to the north hinted at buildings like the Spawnifice, but so well camouflaged by the geologic features around them that she could not be sure they actually existed. Once, a sporule family gazed up from a quagslip gully in the cavern floor. Its members belonged to the same species as the Spawnifice sprols, but may have been grown in natural cave settings, specimens of *Homo basidius,* a term meaning "human fungal spore bearer." In any case, Addi shuddered to detect these mycohumans peering up, shading their eyes as the Smalls cruised by less than a hundred feet overhead.

The tunnel into West Sporangium grew wider and taller.

"I'm scared," Addi said.

"Of what?" asked Mr. Valona. "Of crashing? Of the sprols and the overlords of Big Box Bonanzas? Of our perilous journey? Of the specter of failure?"

"That pretty much covers it."

"I would hope so."

"But I have thought of something more specific to fear."

"Okay," Mr. Valona said, "tell me."

"What if Sporangium's overlords pull the plug on the sun while we're airborne?"

"Why would they do that? Didn't they zap it on to help us escape?"

"If you say so, but what if the Westies don't have a fake sun on their side?"

"Why wouldn't they?"

"Sprols love the darkness for their seeds are evil—their *spores*, I mean."

"Well," said Mr. Valona, "we'll soon find out." He banked the flyke into the foyer of the pass, where the tracks for the fake sun did not extend. Then they buzzed into the gullet of this gap, into an area still dimly lit by the eastern sun. Addi prayed, wishing for Mr. Valona a change of heart that would reverse their direction, or a pair of night-vision goggles to improve his sight, and shut her eyes and prepared to pass from quasi-darkness into unending—

BLAAAM!

A lever somewhere had just put out the sun.

17

A Blessing

Vaughnathan Valona *believed* that even in this pass between East and West Sporangium, he'd have light enough to fly safely. He *knew* he had the piloting skills. He *trusted* they had enough fuel to arrow through the pass before their tank ran dry. If not, he'd land with such care that all the Smalls would walk away unharmed.

One advantage of flying underground was that heavy crosswinds did not exist. In their absence, the flyke's low speeds did not pose the perils that they did aboveground, where a crosswind could blow up and swat you out of the sky. Down here, though, old-style seat-of-the-pants flying worked 98% of the time. Blessedly, this passage between East and West *did* have light—from bioluminescent fungi and in the roving searchlight beams at each tunnel's end. One big, low-set searchlight behind them picked out crucial topographic details in the west. Another swept the pass from its western portal, showing carved cliff dwellings on both walls. Until this evening, he'd never realized that such a subterranean civilization existed, and, pondering this, Mr. Valona smiled into the flyke's mild prop wash.

"Hey, where are we?"

Mr. Valona glanced back. Joel-Brock had not slept *that* long, but owing to the snuffing of the fake sun, he awoke confused and fearful.

Shouting over the flyke's prop noise, Addi explained all that happened.

"Neat," Joel-Brock shouted back.

Mr. Valona chuckled, hopeful they'd see their mission through. He lifted them to avoid a rock spire, squinted when the western searchlight struck him face on, and fretted over the light available in the next cavern. But his spirits remained high even as they flew out of the pass into West Sporangium and a series of dry metallic hiccups fluted from the lawnmower engine.

"What was that?" Addi demanded.

Joel-Brock said, "Hiccups—we should scare the hiccuper."

"How do we do that, Joel-Boy? The hiccuper is a *machine*."

Joel-Brock sat back grinning. So Addi hit Mr. Valona on the shoulder, glaring at him all the while. When he said, "Ouch," she hit him again.

"Get usss down," she hissed.

"Easy, Miss Coe. If my bursitis flares, there's no telling where I'll drop us." He surveyed this second cavern, which, even without a sun, was lit with a mother-of-pearl dusk, as if giant slugs had crisscrossed it, tracking cat's cradles of mollusk slime all over. The sight put him in mind of some bushes he had seen one dawn, laced with spider webs, when that pocket landscape sparkled like a realm of faerie. Despite his disbelief, it had all been real. This landscape was also real, terrible beneath them—except for the rock piles and jagged cliffs on either side, it lay so flat and broad down its middle that it resembled a fallow field in Nebraska.

Joel-Brock leaned forward between Mr. Valona and Addi. "Wow."

The flyke was now hacking horribly, so Mr. Valona worked its brake toggles and throttle to keep it from pitching out of control. Joel-Brock fell back into his seat. Addi's hand had applied a tourniquet to Mr. Valona's arm. "Easy," he said to the flyke. "Easy," he said to his passengers. "Easy," he said to himself. Declining to panic even when the propeller stopped, he used the fixed parasail to glide them to a three-point landing. They buffeted along, but finally stopped, upright and alert, on what seemed a granitic ice floe. Mr. Valona expected white bears to lumber over to see if they were harp seals. Stunned by the quiet, the Smalls also held still and silent. They had survived what Addi believed to be the first half of their perilous journey.

*

Joel-Brock walked around the flyke like someone admiring a sculpture. Its sail loomed over it like a canopy over a bed. But until they had more gas, it was useless. They would have to walk to his family's dungeon. He could do that because he had shoes again and because baseball had kept him in shape. But flight, its dangers aside, seemed the best way to end their travels *quickly*. Both Mr. Valona and Augustus Hudspeth had stressed speed in their mission. Ironically, then, they sat on jagged rocks near the flyke foraging through their backpacks or nibbling at energy bars.

"Hey," Joel-Brock yelled.

"Hey yourself," said Addi sourly.

Hmm, thought Joel-Brock. Maybe the answer lay in their clever yNaut. He asked Mr. Valona if he still had his cell.

"Why? Do you need it?"

"Maybe you could call Mr. Hudspeth."

"Augustus? Do you really think that would help?"

"You could tell him where we are and ask for more gas."

"Ha-ha," Addi scoffed.

To ease his annoyance with her, Joel-Brock recalled several times when

Addi had tried to rescue or reassure him.

Mr. Valona raised his yNaut like a tiny torch, its message panel alight. "Here," he said. "Just remember that Augustus has shown no keenness to talk to me."

Joel-Brock's cell-phone phobia arose in him, but maybe Mr. Hudspeth, whether friend or enemy, did sort of like him, even if that affection came only from their shared interest in the Atlanta Braves. So Joel-Brock walked from the flyke to Mr. Valona to take the yNaut. As he did, the yNaut's message panel flashed again. Mr. Valona spoke into the cell to whoever had called and then held it out to the boy.

"For you," he said, "but it isn't Augustus."

Joel-Brock accepted the yNaut, and things immediately got curiouser.

*

"Hello," Joel-Brock said.

"Hey, is this me as a kid?" a slightly familiar voice asked.

Although the question sounded like a joke that a Cubby League Brave might try to pull, the voice clearly belonged to his future self, J.-B. Lollis. Joel-Brock *had* expected this call, but his armpits started turning musky anyway.

"Yes sir," he said. "I'm ten today."

"Yeah, I figured. I'm twenty-three today. Make that yesterday. A couple of my buddies took me out for wine and sushi."

Joel-Brock blurted, "Gah."

"I know how you feel." J.-B. Lollis laughed. *"But I also hit them up for a fresh broccoli salad."*

"Yes sir. That sounds a little more like me than—"

"Sushi?"

"Yeah." Joel-Brock had seen Bryden and Sophia eat sushi without any-one holding a bullwhip over them, but adults belonged to another sort of humanity, like Neanderthals or, well, mushroom people.

"Nowadays I eat it for the texture and the flavor," J.-B. Lollis said as if his kid self deserved a reason, *"and for the pleasure of appearing sophisticated."*

"Yes sir."

"Joby, please drop that 'sir' crap with me."

Because only Bryden called him Joby, Joel-Brock replied honestly. "I can't. It's just what I'm supposed to call adults—'sir' and 'ma'am' and so on."

"You're right. That doesn't go away, either."

The other two Smalls gawped at Joel-Brock, who, flustered, returned to the flyke and sat down near it out of earshot.

"I guess you haven't found them yet—our parents, I mean," J.-B. Lollis said.

"No sir, we're still on our way."

"Find them. Free them. Don't do anything foolish, if you can help it, but don't let these people disappear from your life." J.-B. Lollis swallowed, audibly.

"I will, sir."

"Not having them here—" His elder self stopped again.

"What?"

"It spoils the sushi. It turns a homer in the bottom of the ninth into a stupid pop-up to the pitcher."

Joel-Brock's head ached. What must it feel like, to J.-B. Lollis, to speak to *him?* Was the guy as desperate for something to say as he was? If so, Joel-Brock spoke aloud a thought that he'd had at the start of this daunting mission: "Anything that happens to me down here will happen to you, sir."

"Joby, I wouldn't be too sure about that."

"If I die, you'll die. And so will all the future you've lived into."

"That's some hefty thinking you're doing there, Joby, but I really don't think you should over-think it."

Joel-Brock paused before asking, "Are you mocking me?"

"*No, I meant it, Joby—you're doing some* truly *heavy-duty cogitating. And who'd know better than you how much I hate to be mocked?*"

"Thanks." He felt free to say more: "If we rescue our family, you won't be the same you who hits homers in the Bigs thirteen years from now. You'll be a J.-B. Lollis who escaped this mess in a way that just makes things messier."

"*Possibly.*"

"You could wind up a lawn-service dude—if you get out of Sporangium at all."

"*If* we *get out of Sporangium, you mean.*"

"Yes sir. If *we* do. Are you *really* okay with that, given all you've got now?"

"*Joby, I'm* really *okay with that. But you're forgetting one important fact.*"

"Yes sir?"

"*What you and your pals do may not end up strictly good or strictly bad. But let's assume it's good. The rescue happens, and you—we—wind up in a better place than the good one I'm supposedly in now. And even if by some yardsticks it's not* quite *as good as mine is now, by other measures it could be* better. *Understand?*"

"I don't know. That's sort of hard."

"*Life can still be good, terrific in fact, even if I—we—don't end up a big-league Brave. Do you see?*"

"I think so, Mister Joby."

"*Okay then. Get to it.*" And J.-B. Lollis ended the call.

And Joel-Brock sat behind the flyke, *cogitating.* His thirteen-year-older self had given him and the other Smalls leave to rescue the Lollises, if possible, and to alter his own future life of riches and fame in startling ways, all on the off-chance that the rewards would prove greater than the penalties.

It made sense to Joel-Brock because he wanted to regain what the gobbymawler sprols had stolen from him, but it posed a problem for poor J.-B. He could lose as much as he gained. His telling the Smalls to go ahead with their quest was like giving them his blessing, and Joel-Brock realized that he *needed* his older self's blessing. But to bestow it, J.-B. had needed Joel-Brock to take a mortal risk, and so, across time, they had reached a truly heavy accord.

Mr. Valona appeared beside the flyke. He tousled Joel-Brock's hair. "Everything okay?"

"Yes sir, but we need to get going." He peered up. "Mister Joby says so. And he gives us his permission."

Mr. Valona started to say one thing, but instead said, "Ah. Okay. I'm very glad he did that."

18

Gorgástrogons

Addi ambled over to the flyke. West Sporangium differed from East Sporangium, as the democratic state of South Korea differed from the closed one of North Korea. Dusk here seemed always ready to tip over into dawn and birdsong. Earlier, she'd heard the chirping of birds—nightingales, nightjars, whip-poor-wills—and the hooting of owls. But how did they live down here?

Moreover, West Sporangium's rocks seemed to have endured a pounding that had smashed them all to pieces. The pieces had broken down into soil. Now the free sporule farmers—*not* soldier sprols—worked dung into this dirt and grew mushrooms in it. They had also fed earthworms into it, or the worms had wriggled into it, and there had *always* been insects and spiders, creepy crawlers that gave Addi the heebie-jeebies, and nocturnal songbirds—and owls—that ate the creepy crawlers. Also, the sporule farmers, who traded with Big Box Bonanzas, set out birdseed, just as topside bird lovers did.

And don't forget the gorgástrogons.

Whoa, where had *that* name come from?

Most likely from hidden memories now unpredictably awakening. Anyway, she had actually meant slugs, whose slime trails provided lots of light down here. The arabesque patterns their trails made on the rocks also let the eaters of slugs hunt them down by sight, smell, taste, and feel. Not all slugs drew birds, for some tasted vile, and the body snot—*mucus*, Addi meant—

made by other slugs did not allow birds' beaks or talons to seize them easily. Still, they *were* a good food source for bats and other winged cavern critters, even as they stayed busy ruining the farmers' mushrooms.

Anyway, gorgástrogons played a crucial role in West Sporangium. For one, they discouraged most human beings from coming down and trying to take it over. Indeed, its current crop had created the dark, cool, moist, and mildewed dominion they liked. And gorgástrogons—gastropod mollusks without clear outer shells—*loved* West Sporangium. Addi furrowed her brow at the sight of all the shiny slug trails.

"What's the matter, Addi?" Mr. Valona asked.

"I sort of feel like I've been here before."

"Have you?"

"I'm not sure. I can't quite get past that 'sort of,' you know."

"But you'd planned to lead us to the Lollises, right?"

"It's straight on to those western foothills." Addi pointed past the flyke's parasail. "There, we'll climb to Condor's Cote, Mr. Borsmutch's cliff dwelling."

"How do you know *that*?"

"It occurred to me just now—really." And it had, bursting into her head as the goo in a cream puff bursts into your mouth when you first bite into one. But she'd never heard of, well, Condor's Cote before. Or had she?

Joel-Brock returned the yNaut to Mr. Valona and peered at the purple foothills that Addi had pointed out. "That looks like a really long way."

"Yes it does," Mr. Valona said, following his gaze.

"So please, sir, call Mr. Hudspeth."

"And ask him to send us some flyke fuel?"

"Yes sir, I believe you should."

Mr. Valona looked at Addi, who shrugged. The length of their remaining journey had softened her objections to calling Augustus, and so, sensing her mood, he opened the yNaut and rang him up.

"*Thank God,*" Mr. Hudspeth answered. "*You're safe.*"

"If you were so worried about us," Mr. Valona said, "why didn't *you* call?"

"*I feared what I might find out.*"

"Augustus, only a fool would deny himself a call for fear it would bring bad news when calling could banish that fear."

"*What do you want?*" Mr. Hudspeth said, and all the Smalls heard him because Mr. Valona had switched on the yNaut speaker-phone.

"Fuel for the flyke," Mr. Valona said. "Gasoline."

"*Tell me where you've landed. I assume you're in West Sporangium and can give me landmarks.*"

"If I do, will you send us gasoline?"

"*No—because it's lucky beyond luck you've gotten as far as you have.*"

"You *won't* send fuel?"

"*Didn't you hear me? It's too damned dangerous to fly in a roofed cavern.*"

"But you directed us to the craft as a means of escape."

"*With the sprols aroused, I thought it your best chance to get away, but—*"

"But what?"

"*I didn't really expect you to survive your takeoff from the roof.*"

"Now you tell us!"

"*I knew you'd piloted a flyke before and that the Canon kept it up there, so I did think you had a* chance. *Give me landmarks by which to help me find you all now.*"

"The flyke had just cleared the western portal, and I landed us a mile or so outside the tunnel. Our nose still points toward Condor's Cote."

"*Okay,*" Mr. Hudspeth said. "*We'll get the aircraft later. You and those kids need to move. Look for slime trails. Steer clear of gorgástrogons in groups. Don't talk to them, or not for long. They talk in riddles. Sometimes they sing. They'll trap you in word mazes or slug slime before you grok that hunger, not fellow feeling, spurs their interest.*"

Addi took the yNaut: "How far do we have to go to reach Condor's Cote."

"Whatever I say, it'll feel a whole *lot longer. So don't make me say."*

Peeved, Addi said, "Whatever," and returned the yNaut to Mr. Valona. Then she circled the flyke repeatedly until Mr. Valona ended the call.

*

They walked toward the "foothills"—a massive jumble of boulders at the far end of West Sporangium. They'd have to climb them to reach Condor's Cote, Pither M. Borsmutch's underground villa and the site of the third-floor dungeon where the Lollises (minus Joel-Brock) were jailed. Addi knew this stuff, as the boy knew about the mycohumanification of mushrooms, through a kind of learning that mystified her. Unlike Joel-Brock, she had not fallen into quagslip to absorb her knowledge. She knew what she knew as if finding pieces of memory that she had long ago lost—like someone with amnesia slowly pushing back forgetfulness.

The West's middle valley consisted of fields of raised mushroom beds. Strips of copper or fences draped with coppery foil protected them. Many paths divided the fields. Farmhouses sat randomly amid the mushroom beds, but were plentiful enough to imply that they ordered the farmers' lives. Still, unlike East Sporangium's rugged terrain, most Western lands allowed you to stroll rather than to hike them, and the Smalls could amble rather than trek through the beds.

Slime trails on the ceiling outlined constellations. Lichen fires—not real fires, but bursts of bioluminescence on the twigs of mutated fungi—suggested novas, or nebulae, far beyond the Milky Way. Of course, the Smalls realized that here there was no Milky Way, just a vivid mimicry of it that made them feel truly small. Joel-Brock pointed at a "constellation": "What's that one?"

"I'd call it the Grocery Cart," said Addi, "or the Downhill Racer."

"Yeah, like a soapbox-derby car." Joel-Brock selected a dot-to-dot pattern directly overhead. "What about that one?"

"Gumby or the Stick Man," Mr. Valona said. He pointed to another pattern on the southern ceiling. "Name that one for us, kidster."

"I can't. I'm not good at—"

"None of that can't crap." Addi grinned at him. "Come on—*name* it!"

"Okay. Marty the Mars Rover? See its wheels and antennas?"

"Not bad, but drop the hokey alliteration. Try another."

Joel-Brock looked up to do as she said, but a low buzzing turned him toward the dark eastern sky. "Look—our flyke!"

At a height of sixty or seventy feet, their paraglider, the one they had abandoned, was approaching the mushroom field encircling them. Beneath its parasail, it tilted this way and that. Its pilot saw them just as they spotted him. He dropped the craft's nose and homed on them with a deft course correction.

"Hit the ground!" Mr. Valona yelled. "Curl up against that bed frame!"

The Smalls did so, locking their fingers behind their heads and pulling their elbows in. They all feared that the new pilot knew just what they had done to cause the deaths of two sprols in the Spawnifice. Indeed, the pilot dropped a cantaloupe toward the footpath where they'd taken cover. It hit a body's length from Mr. Valona, burst into pale shards, and spattered reddish-yellow glop everywhere. "You kids okay?" he shouted. Still in their roly-poly body curls, both yelled, "Yes!"

The flyke made a wide turn to approach them from the southwest, probably with more heavy fruit to drop. Mr. Valona scrambled up and foraged in his backpack for a golf ball. The flyke's buzzing intensified, and Joel-Brock flashed back to his father's favorite film, *North by Northwest*. But when the paraglider passed overhead, Mr. Valona gave the boy a golf ball. At that moment, a watermelon hit with a wet *crump* in the mushroom bed near them. Pieces of rind and red fruit flew out, more than had burst from the cantaloupe. In the dimness, these blobs looked like bloody human organs. At the melon's ***SCHPLAT!*** Addi had screamed, and she did it again when a vivid scarlet spray stained Mr. Valona's knickers and shoes.

"I'm okay!" he cried. "Stay down!"

The flyke hummed northward, but banked to the west to return for another melon drop. Joel-Brock thought this strategy ridiculous—except that a strike by a melon would not have been funny. Disobeying Mr. Valona, *he* leapt up and hurled his golf ball at the aircraft. It bounced off the parasail and dropped harmlessly into a farther mushroom bed. "I told you to stay down!" Mr. Valona cried.

"But how many more melons has he got up there, sir?"

"At least one more or he wouldn't be making another pass."

"Use the detonator function on your yNaut, sir," Joel-Brock advised.

"Why? What in this bleak underworld would I be detonating?"

The flyke buzzed more loudly, yawing as it re-aimed at them.

"Sir, before we left our aircraft, I put three armed golf balls under the bench of its trundle seat."

"And then *forgot* what you'd done?" Mr. Valona asked.

"Yes sir, or I'd've never let that flying toadstool drop two fat melons on us."

Addi waved at the descending ultralight. "Sir, key the detonator!"

Using his yNaut, Mr. Valona typed in the detonator code.

Three balls in the paraglider's trundle seat, all with telltale blue mushroom-cap symbols on them, exploded. Fragments from these plastic explosives ripped through the aircraft's frame—as well as its pilot—and the flyke, disintegrating, plunged under its collapsing sail toward the mushroom field. If Mr. Valona had waited longer to type the code, Joel-Brock thought, it would have exploded right above them, and its falling parts would have sliced them into raw hamburger. The Smalls huddled on the footpath beholding what the yNaut had *un*wrought.

"Don't!" Mr. Valona told Addi when she stepped onto the raised bed.

"We've got to see if he's alive, don't we?"

"Not if *we* want to survive," Mr. Valona replied. "Look." He nodded at a nearby croft house. Its lights had blinked on. The end of the flyke's buzzing and the whoosh of its fragmenting fall had summoned a sporule family— four squat shadows under pancake hats—outside to examine the scene.

"They've got pitchforks," Joel-Brock observed. "Let's book!"

Stooped like arthritics, the Smalls hustled away from the flyke's wreckage. They fled westward through the mushroom beds until fences forced them to improvise routes through the fields themselves. Then, having outrun the pitchfork-toting family and afraid that their exposure in the fields would make them easy to locate, they rested beside a low copper fence, pulses racing.

Addi said, "We should travel by the ridges to our north or our south."

"That'll slow us up," Joel-Brock said.

"Not as much as capture or death," Addi countered.

"Who do we have to get past now?" Mr. Valona asked. "The only *real* enemies we've met so far were those zombie sprols in the Spawnifice."

"And Mr. Borsmutch controls them," Addi said, "just like he controls everything related to his stores and everything Sporangial down here. So maybe Mr. Hudspeth is a bigger enemy than the Canon's zombie sprols."

"I don't get Augustus at all," Mr. Valona mused. "He does seem to be tailing us."

"For Pither Borsmutch," Addi accused.

Joel-Brock dared to change the subject: "What's the deal with these little fences wrapped in reddish-yellow foil?"

"They're slug barriers," Mr. Valona said. "Slugs avoid copper and copper-based substances like copper sulfate. So sporule farmers put up those things to safeguard their mushroom beds."

"Some farmers," Addi said, "leave a few beds unfenced to keep the gorgástrogons down here happy." This knowledge had welled up in her magically.

"Why would they want to do that?" Joel-Brock asked.

"Because the gorgástrogons terrify the Sporangians," Addi said.

"Addi, are they slugs or gorgástrogons? I don't get it."

"Down here," Addi said, "they mean the same thing, sort of like *horse* and *steed*. But *gorgástrogon* puts *Gorgon* and *gastropod* into one scary term. Some sprols call them *snotfeet*—or *snotfoot* if it's just one."

"For the Greeks," Mr. Valona said, "a Gorgon was a snake-haired woman whose glance could turn to stone anyone she looked at."

"Is that what the Sporangians think a slug can do?" Joel-Brock asked.

"Maybe," Addi said. "Look around. You'll see slime trails everywhere and lots of standing rocks and stony walls for the creatures to crawl over."

"Augustus offered a friendly warning," Mr. Valona said, "when he told us to give a wide berth to slugs in groups."

"He also told us they tell riddles and sometimes sing," Joel-Brock said. "Maybe he ate too many of the wrong kind of mushroom."

"Maybe," Addi said. "Maybe not."

*

The Smalls detoured to the south to hike the rock tiers on the long cavern wall. The sprols here lived in hamlets consisting of a few conical houses, a plaza of mushroom beds, and a stone church with a wheat-straw roof. The

towns had names like Mycothorpe, Dorpwick, and Yokelton. Each had a pillar on its outskirts with its name on it in indigo letters, but so few sprols lived
in them that many resembled ghost towns, as if poisonous fog banks had
emptied them. To avoid their wary leftover populations, the Smalls hurried
through these hamlets and, as the terrain allowed, hiked westward below or
above them.

At length, they reached a slate tabletop and ate. A convex dome the size
of a carp pond hung over them. In fact, they chose this spot because the
dome offered them both a ceiling and a view. As if starved, they devoured
beef jerky, mandarin oranges from cans, and low-fat energy bars. Then, ex-
hausted, they slept.

*

Lying on a poncho from Big Box Bonanzas, Joel-Brock awoke. He didn't
have to pee. He hadn't had a bad dream. But *something* had awakened him.
He opened his eyes. When he beheld what he beheld and disbelieved it, he
shut them again. Maybe a fresh look would banish what he'd seen and restore
to the cavern a semblance of everydayness. But when he looked again, the
same dismaying sight hung there.

Three pale slugs—*gorgástrogons*—dangled in harnesses of slime from
the dome above them. As large as legless ponies, they slid down on bright
cords of mucus to the ledge on which the Smalls had slept. Each ugly
snotfoot *glowed*. The leprous sheen from their thick bodies—"a cylinder of
gut on a big sticky foot," as Mr. Valona had described them earlier—put
Joel-Brock in mind of a plug-in nightlight that Sophia had placed in his
bedroom when he was a littler kid. This sheen pulsed in their bellies like the
flame of an unending digestive process, giving their campsite the aura of a
crypt lit with pig tallow. Joel-Brock lifted himself on his elbows.

Each gorgástrogon turned all four of its feelers toward him, the seeing set *and* the smelling set, as if to catch him in a sensory cage. He should run. But if he did, would the other Smalls have the sense to rise and scamper too? *Do it*, Joel-Brock thought. *Come on, kidster, do it!* He tried to stand, but his legs would not obey, as if the critters had disabled the nerves allowing his will to drive his body—not *all* his nerves, but lots of them. In any case, they'd paralyzed him from the bellybutton down. How had they done that? He had no idea, and he hated that he had none.

Joel-Brock looked from one gorgástrogon to the other and the other. At first, the snotfeet seemed identical—triplets or clones. Closer scrutiny revealed subtle differences: a broken feeler in one, ivory spots on the saddle-like back of the second, and, in the third, fewer of the in-leaning teeth that work a slug's food deeper into its maw. But, together, they could paralyze, as did the Gorgons who, with a look, turned men to stones. These gorgástrogons paralyzed by stealing the feeling from one's legs rather than by petrifying all the cells in a person's body. What could Joel-Brock do to reverse the crippling effects of the slugs' energies? He had no clue, but maybe Mr. Valona or Addi did. He must enlist their help: *One for all, and all for one.*

"Mr. Valona, sir," he whispered. "Addi Coe. Please wake up."

Mr. Valona sat up and took in the Smalls' predicament. Three lion-sized slugs—each of which had set one long foot on the rock face—meant to eat them. He tried to rise, but had no more success than the boy.

Joel-Brock was grateful his voice box still worked. "Addi, you wake up too."

Addi neither sat up nor peered about in panic. In a throaty alto, she said, "I sort of hoped they'd eat me as I slept. No, I actually hoped this was a nightmare." She contrived to roll to her back but, like her companions, could not get to her feet.

The three gorgástrogons slid their tails around in order to trap the three

Smalls in a triangular corral. Joel-Brock noted the pale orange fibers in their foot mucus—"treads," which enabled them to climb or descend walls and to cling like flies to overhead surfaces. They all had the same see-through skim-milk skin, and the thin wedges of shell within the humps on their backs were faintly visible.

"This *is* a nightmare," Joel-Brock said belatedly.

"I am Eugenifer," said the snotfoot nearest him, "but call me Gean." It spoke in a high-pitched brogue.

"I am Sami," piped slug two, the nearest to Mr. Valona. "Short for Samuelantha, and friendlier. I love this li'l guy." Sami touched Mr. Valona with an optical feeler. "He's got spunk and soul."

And *you've* got snot and ooze, Joel-Brock thought.

"I am Charlamann," said the third gorgástrogon in Addi's ear. "Call me Charli. I like colleen cutlets."

Amazingly—at least to Joel-Brock—Addi did not scream. Maybe she felt that if they could not talk their way out of becoming unhappy meals, there was a cruder solution to their problem. "You guys speak awfully good English," she said.

"Thanks," Sami, said. "A year ago, in Dorpwick, we ate a sporule pastor and two preachers from Chicago and ever since we've spoken like Emily Dickens."

"Sami," Mr. Valona said, "you must mean Emily *Dickinson*."

"No," Sami said. "I usually say what I mean, and I mean Emily *Dickens*."

"Maybe you meant *Charles* Dickinson," Charli proposed.

"Nonsense," Sami said.

"Think about it a little," Gean urged Sami.

"Okay, maybe I did. But I never meant what *this* sweetheart"—kinking a feeler at Mr. Varona—"just suggested. I greatly dislike unhelpful help."

"We know," said Gean, showing big back-slanting teeth. "However, you might've meant Eliot George or Carol Lewis, mightn't you?"

"I'm tired of talking," Sami said, "and very hungry."

Addi said, "You guys aren't really meat-eaters, are you?"

"In truth, we're not *anything* that restricts our intake, speaking gastro-nomically." Gean seemed to smirk. "Why else pay you this visit?"

Joel-Brock felt his nape hair stiffen. "I've got some beef jerky."

"I never decline an appetizer," Charli said.

Gean and Sami wriggled feelers to second and third this sentiment.

Mr. Valona opened his own backpack and foraged. Joel-Brock hoped that maybe the jerky would buy enough time for a rescuer—Mr. Hudspeth, say, or a passing sprol Samaritan—to sweep in and slay these vermin. Given the Smalls' paralyzed legs, he had no idea how they could prevent their own deaths once the slugs stopped dithering and started to dine. Sami was moving in on Mr. Valona now.

"Wait!" Addi cried. "Save that for later, sir. I'll give them my jerky, Joel-Brock will kick in his, and we'll find plenty for *all* these guys to have their fill." She dug in her backpack as Mr. Valona and Joel-Brock searched theirs. The gorgástrogons swung their twelve feelers toward her in great expectation.

But instead of beef jerky, Addi held a heavy-duty cordless hairdryer, which she set on **High** and directed at Sami. The slug's horned helm flopped away from the blast and its body shrank into itself. Hot air flowed over its slick body, evaporated the slime, and dried out its otherwise naked flesh. Sami grew more and more compact and rigid. Soon, it had shriveled into a wind-scorched gray bag.

With Sami dead, Mr. Valona was able to scramble to his feet. Addi turned off the hairdryer and tossed it to him. He grasped it like a handgun and pointed it in turn at Gean and Charli. He did not press the button to trigger a blast of hot air, for at the dryer's first sound, these slugs had also begun shriveling. Joel-Brock believed Sami had broadcast so much mental distress that the slugs could not tolerate its weakening effects. They lay like drawn-up lumps beside Addi and Joel-Brock.

"Addi and I still can't move," Joel-Brock told Mr. Valona. "Help us, sir."

"How?" Mr. Valona asked. "Should I finish them off?"

"No," Addi said. "Maybe you could—"

"Wait!" With his foot, Mr. Valona rolled Charli away from Addi and Gean away from Joel-Brock. Although both children remained paralyzed from the waist down, the slugs' inward-leaning teeth no longer menaced them. So Joel-Brock and Addi relaxed, and Mr. Valona, kneeling before Charli, told the slug to release Addi from its spell or to suffer Sami's fate. Her release took a few minutes, but eventually Addi had full control of her legs. She stood to shake the kinks out, and Mr. Valona carried word to Eugenifer that it must free Joel-Brock from *his* paralysis.

Freed, Joel-Brock stood, stretched, and walked over to Addi. "That was really smart, riot grrrl."

"Right," Mr. Valona told her. "Of all the crap you brought, that thing struck me as by far the stupidest."

Addi stared at the dead gorgástrogon and its inert partners in slime. "I'm glad you never said that aloud, sir."

The slime cords on which the slugs had lowered themselves from the dome hung down like cheerless strands of fat yuletide tinsel. Addi nudged Charli with her foot, and Mr. Valona said, "How'd you know you'd need that contraption? How'd you know that it would even work?"

"I got the hairdryer for me. I *didn't* know it would work. It popped into my head as a possible help when I realized these snotfeet planned to eat us."

"Bless your Sporangial intuition," Mr. Valona said. "Now let's go. Few things smell worse than a decomposing slug."

"Sami won't get to decompose," Joel-Brock said, startling himself again.

"When Gean and Charli come to, they'll scarf down that defunct horn-head."

"These things cannibalize one another?" Mr. Valona asked.

"Yes sir. They're recyclers. They scavenge as well as hunt for food."

Mr. Valona grimaced. "Maybe we should blast-dry Sami's pals too." To soften this suggestion, he added: "To keep them from coming after us, I mean."

Addi said, "I'll bet they've had more than enough of us, sir." She grabbed her backpack, slipped it on, and circled away from the gorgástrogon-littered camping spot to another westward-leading footpath.

Joel-Brock and Mr. Valona followed. Addi had saved them from three huge and gluttonous slugs. She had also saved their mission. Joel-Brock was grateful that he had awakened before the slugs began to eat. Otherwise, Addi could not have performed her hairdryer magic. But give her credit for preventing a Smalls disaster. Also, none of them would have heard a slug talk, as Augustus had said gastropods could do—unless they met up with other snotfeet later. Joel-Brock hoped no such meeting would occur, but regretted one thing about this last near-fatal encounter:

"The slugs never sang for us," he said. "They never sang."

19

Untoward Events at Oathwick

Until they reached Condor's Cote, the Smalls kept to the long southern ridges of West Sporangium. Returning to the valley would expose them to more sprol assaults, but in the uplands they risked meeting gorgástrogons.

As so the Smalls did not walk but *hiked*, for the terrain placed heavy demands on any traveler. No Small begrudged another a break. Joel-Brock rarely called for one, but even he sometimes had to stop. Addi welcomed these respites as much as did Mr. Valona. Three hours into their hike, they reached a high ledge with many dark vistas of the valley plain and of the lower switchbacks of the rugged ridges on either side. Here, the Smalls perched in Sporangium's dusk, a twilight lit by slug-trail stars and the torches of many hovels and hamlets. Joel-Brock pointed into a western draw.

"We're being followed. And over there"—pointing at mushroom beds—"we've got more company." He then pointed east. "And there's *another* posse."

"That's a party of sprols from the Spawnifice," Mr. Valona said.

Joel-Brock nodded at some figures in the mushroom beds: "And those?"

"Farmers," Mr. Valona said. "Sprols called by the flyke crash. I don't think they want our blood."

"But the other two groups do?" Joel-Brock asked.

"I didn't say that." Mr. Valona yanked a thumb at the distant party from

Condor's Cote. "What would you all say about that posse?"

Addi squinted at it. "Human gobbymawlers and mycohumanified sprols together. I count five or six of each kind."

"You can *see* them to count them?" Mr. Valona asked.

"My eyes are better than twenty-twenty," Addi said. "More like twenty-fifteen."

"That sounds *worse*," Joel-Brock said.

Addi touched his wrist. "Sorry, but it's better. Ask an eye doctor."

Joel-Brock accepted her word, for this mixed bunch of gobbymawlers, human and sprol, kept coming. Then all twelve vanished, one by one, behind an ogre-shaped rock spire on the switchback. Meanwhile, perhaps fifty sprols from the Spawnifice trudged in pairs along the ridge—except where the path was too narrow—and the sprols on the plain marched west-by-southwest with modest urgency, stalking the Smalls and checking their beds for signs of slug damage or fungal blight.

It was the other two groups' pincer movements that implied catastrophe for the Smalls. Their options were to find a westward course hidden from the two parties, to go to ground until both left, or to meet one group head-on and persuade it that the Smalls' march on Condor's Cote had justice as its goal—the biggest pipe dream of all. Joel-Brock recalled a line from an old baseball poem, "*The outlook wasn't brilliant for the Mudville Nine that day,*" and recited it aloud.

"Are you saying our name is Mudd?" Addi asked. Joel-Brock shrugged. Addi turned to Mr. Valona. "So what do we do?"

Mr. Valona adjusted his pack. "Keep going—at a pace quicker than the sprols' on a route more cunning than the gobbymawlers'."

*

The path the Smalls chose avoided overlooks that would have given occasional glimpses of their stalkers. And, not seeing their pursuers, Mr. Valona thought less about them and more about how best to reach Condor's Cote.

Sometimes they slid rather than hiked. Sometimes they climbed hand over fist up small escarpments. By this time, they had all gulped down a Big Box Bonanzas canteen at least twice, but, on this southern ridge, they had little trouble finding trickles of sweet water with which to refill them.

"Shhh," Addi shushed her fellow Smalls. "Listen."

Sounds of sliding gravel came from the opposite slope. A birdlike chattering cut through these funneling sounds. Joel-Brock feared his own heartbeats would betray them. Mr. Valona patted his sternum and nodded at a hidden rock chute from their footpath to a cramped grotto below. *Hurry*, his patting said: *Hurry, but quietly*. They ran ahead of him and squeezed into the hole, a lopsided pit about three feet deep. When Mr. Valona ducked in, they flattened like octopi against its rear wall. Facing them, the detective squatted and wrapped his arms around both kids.

The posse from Condor's Cote trudged over the rise.

Joel-Brock could barely see them padding down slope toward them. Wow, those dudes have really booked it, he thought. Either their climb had not been too hard or they had been training with Navy SEALs. Anyway, here they came, twelve in total, six human gobbymawlers—the chatterers, he'd bet—and six sprols, who had lately done jobs in Big Box Bonanzas fit only for mutes: shelf stocking, floor mopping, forklift driving, and so on. All twelve wore khaki uniforms, or flesh so near-akin to BBB uniforms that only an expert could have told the difference. All wore pancake hats or mushroom berets. All had chains for belts, with handcuffs dangling from the chains.

Weirdly, the six sprols had budgerigars—budgies—on their shoulders or caps. Joel-Brock regarded these birds with yellow heads and green bodies as parakeets, and they did belong to a variety of the species. But these six budgies looked like soapstone statuettes, with pale lemon heads and pinkish bodies.

"*I taut I taw a puddytat,*" a bird said as the posse limped downhill.

The lead human halted and turned around. "You haven't seen a blasted thing!"

"*I taut I taw a puddytat,*" repeated the budgie, from the cap of a sprol behind the uptight human leader.

"Street 'Keet," the leader said, "I always tell my kids, *The first time it's funny, the second it's silly, and the third it's a spanking.*"

"*Spanking,*" the bird whistled. "*Spank me?*"

"I don't spank birdbrains. I wring their necks. But if you say '*I taut I taw*' again, I'll punch your two-legged host right in your mushy mouth. Got it?"

"*Soitainly,*" the budgie doing beak-work for Street 'Keet said, and the irritated human leader waved everyone forward to resume their search. In a matter of moments, they had bypassed the Smalls.

"Whew," Addi said. "I taut we'd been busted."

The Smalls crawled from their hole. Joel-Brock's feet tingled, as if he had soft cockleburs in his socks. As they readied to march again, Addi asked Mr. Valona about the gobbymawlers' handcuffs.

"Well," he said, "I think they're meant for us."

"Really?" Addi asked.

"Yes. And that's a good thing. Pither M. Borsmutch wants to take us alive. None of those guys had rifles or handguns."

"Maybe he wants to kill us himself," Addi said.

"Maybe. But I haven't a clue what the sprols coming up behind us plan to do—maybe kill us at first contact."

"You make them sound like evil aliens," Joel-Brock said, understanding that West Sporangium had proved frighteningly hostile.

*

They gnawed on jerky, with gummy bears for dessert. Then to reach a high junction with four paths to choose from, they climbed the hill the gobbymawlers had just gone down. Clearly, the Condor's Cote posse had hit on the best trail to permit them to overtake the Smalls rapidly. So, if they determined which trail the posse had taken, they could shorten their own trek time to Condor's Cote. Unhappily for the Smalls, the firmer paths beyond the posse's last loose-graveled slope gave no clue to how much foot traffic each path had recently hosted.

"Let's vote," Mr. Valona said. "The path with two out of three yeses wins."

"What if there's a tie?" Joel-Brock asked.

Addi gave him a just-kidding sort of head slap. "*Think*, Lollis! You *can't* have a tie if all three of us vote."

Joel-Brock glared at Addi. "I plan to abscond."

"Abstain," Mr. Valona said. "But why would you abstain?"

"I don't have enough facts to make my vote worth anything."

"Look," Addi said. "We're not so much *voting* as *casting lots*. None of us have enough facts to make our votes 'worth anything.'"

"But we each must cast a lot," Mr. Valona said. "Make it count, Joel-Brock."

"How can I do that, without all the facts?"

"Listen," said Addie, "if you're wrong about our best route, you'll have a partner to share some of the blame."

They each voted for a different path, a frustrating development. Mr. Valona then announced that the only route *without* a thumbs-up—the southernmost trail—had won by default. So they must follow *it* to Condor's Cote. If it led to disaster, well, the fault would lie with fate and not with any individual Small.

"Or with all of us," Joel-Brock said.

"No matter," Addi said. "If snipers on the ramparts don't pick us off, other sprols will catch us and lock us up when we get there."

"I love you upbeat kidsters," Mr. Valona said grimly, and the Smalls set off along a footpath that none of them had chosen.

*

They hiked a ridge near the southern wall, but at one point got high enough to look down on the army of sprols still dogging them. This group now included a robed figure on a pit pony. It had drawn much closer since the Smalls' last look at it, and its relative nearness suggested that the Smalls had chosen the *worst* possible path. If not, how had these sprols gained so much ground?

"We're switchbacking too much," Mr. Valona said, "and they're using an express route." He looked at Addi. "Can't you help?"

"*Me*, a teenage runaway with a pink slip from Mister Pither?"

Mr. Valona started to joke about how she was wearing denim shorts, not a pink slip, but, realizing that girls seldom wore slips today, he said, "Who else? You know a lot of stuff that made us decide to let you come."

"Okay. Let's go." Addi broke from their former trail and climbed through a chute with rocks for stairs and cracks in its walls for handholds. Wary of the advancing sprols, Mr. Valona and Joel-Brock blundered up this chute behind her. Did she know where she was headed? Did they dare follow a fourteen-year-old female? It scarcely mattered, and when the Smalls reached the chute's crest, they stood atop it to study not only the nearby terrain but also its far western reaches.

"Is that Canon Umphrees on the pony?" Mr. Valona asked.

"I think so," Joel-Brock said. "And the pony's probably Shaftoe."

Mr. Valona peered harder. "I didn't think the pudgy fungus had it in him."

"He's probably only obeying orders," Addi said.

"Whose?" Joel-Brock asked. "Mr. Borsmutch's?"

"So I'd best reckon," Addi said. "But he's a Sporangial cleric. Maybe Archbishop Meece sent him. Maybe Augustus didn't like us downing that flyke and sicced the Canon on us. Or maybe Umphrees set out on his own." When neither Joel-Brock nor Mr. Valona spoke, she added, "Come on," and led them off the tabletop through a tunnel of boulders to the outskirts of an up-cavern village. A pillar bearing a single indigo word shouted its name: **OATHWICK**, and its kirk—or church—had a bent steeple that scraped the cavern's ceiling and fungal ivy on its walls that would have pleased the Smalls if it had not been a scorched-looking, scrolled-up gray.

"Great," Joel-Brock said. "Addi's brought us to a town called Oatmeal."

"Oathwick," she said, patting his head, "not Oatmeal."

"Whatever we call it, if we hang around the place, either the gobbymawlers or the sprols will get us."

Addi shook her open hands beside her ears. *"Boogita-boogita."*

"Stop it," Mr. Valona said. Coming to Oathwick and lollygagging in front of its name placard must have seemed as unwise to him as they did to Joel-Brock. The fastest way through Oathwick took them past its quaint church, with its bell-tower-and-steeple fused to the rocks overhead, so Mr. Valona herded Joel-Brock and Addi toward it. The kids dragged their feet, rubbernecking like tourists. So Mr. Valona grabbed them in yoke-locks, just as he had done in the Spawnifice, and marched them along the street like two trussed turkeys.

"Hey," Addi said. *"Hey!"*

"Ow," Joel-Brock said. *"Ow, ow, owwwww!"*

Behind them, a voice cried, "Interlopers, *halt!*"

Mr. Valona tugged the Smalls even faster. Joel-Brock felt like a contestant in a six-legged sack race, *and* as if he was about to fall on his nose and drag the other Smalls down with him.

"Interlopers, *halt!*" the same voice cried. "Halt or face the consequences!"

Mr. Valona released the kids and turned to face the leader of the party that had nearly trapped them in a hidey-hole. At the leader's back, his posse stood like warriors, almost like samurai. But these twelve samurai did not look very imposing. Mr. Valona put his hands on his hips and glared.

"What consequences? A rattling of chains? A clacking of handcuffs?"

"Get them!" the gobbymawlers' leader shouted. "Take them alive!"

Mr. Valona turned and tripped on Addi's ankle, for she had assumed a fist-on-hips superhero pose just like that the boy had assumed. The gobbymawler posse swarmed forward. Addi and Joel-Brock struggled to get Mr. Valona up and to drag him toward Oathwick's church. With six budgies flying above them, the Borsmutch-deputized posse chased the Smalls, their chains chattering and their handcuffs held aloft as threats of capture and repression. We're doomed, Joel-Brock thought. But two unexpected events occurred to thwart that doom.

Addi triggered the first, but only by a hair. In tugging Mr. Valona forward, she had found herself studying Oathwick kirk. Her gaze fixed on its door, which featured a large bronze knocker shaped like a mushroom—a toadstool like the one represented on the inner side of the GillGate. Addi paid no heed to the *variety* of mushroom modeled by this knocker, but focused on its *meaning*, realizing almost at once that it could save them from their gobbymawler pursuers.

"We'll apply for sanctuary!" She dragged Mr. Valona toward the church-yard by his arm. *"Sanctuary!"*

Mr. Valona shook her hand free. "Nobody asks for sanctuary nowadays, and why do you suppose we'll get it here?"

"I don't *suppose* we'll get it. I *know* we will. Hurry." Addi broke for the church, trusting that Mr. Valona and Joel-Brock would follow. They did. But this route shortened the posse's angle on them, increasing their likelihood of capture. Still, Addi knew that just *touching* the toadstool knocker's brass would win them sanctuary: shelter and escape from punishment, inside. But a cleric must open to them and affirm their right to asylum, or the gobby-mawlers would seize and haul them off.

Now, less than thirty feet away, shaking their handcuffs and advancing en masse, the gobbymawlers seemed unstoppable.

Joel-Brock cried, *"You can't do this! You have no right!"* But the gobbymawlers swept on until—the second of two untoward events—a pair of dogs ran past the Smalls from the far end of Oathwick toward the posse, yapping as they darted at one enemy or another. The bamboozled gobbymawlers turned and fled, their budgies departing over the eastern rise with them, shedding pinkish feathers as they flew. Tails up, the dogs scurried back to the church.

Actually to Joel-Brock, who knelt to embrace them. *"Sparky! Leo!"* He could not believe that two of the family dogs had found him—in the knife's-edge of time. Sparky the terrier and Leo the King Charles spaniel mix had rescued them! The dogs wriggled and fawned. They leapt on Joel-Brock and cavorted all about him, licking his face when they could and nipping at each other when they couldn't.

"Sparky! Leo!" Joel-Brock kept saying.

"These are *yours?*" Addi said. "How in Holy Hades did they get here?"

"I have no idea," Mr. Valona said for Joel-Brock, "but thank God they did."

Addi ran to the church and tumped its knocker three times on its imported oaken door. Each knock echoed like a thunderclap. Then the door began to open. "Now to ask for sanctuary," she told her companions.

"But why?" Mr. Valona said. "We've escaped the gobbymawlers."

Archbishop Basil Sydney Meece stood in the door, with the mynah Mortimer on his shoulder. Members of the sporule army, presumably under the command of Canon Miles Lee Umphrees, crested the last incline into Oathwick. Indeed, a robed figure on a pit pony—Shaftoe?—led these foot soldiers, marching two by two, into the hamlet and straight toward the church.

"I'll be waxed and shellacked," said Mr. Valona.

"Sanctuary!" cried Addi. "Grant us sanctuary!"

Archbishop Meece opened the door wider and nodded the Smalls in, including the two wriggly dogs that had foiled the Condor's Cote posse. Inside, Joel-Brock winced to see Leo peeing spaniel juice over the flagstones and Sparky heading to the Archbishop to leap on his mushroom-colored priestly robes.

20

Asylum

Despite the dogs, Basil Sydney Meece closed the door and barred it with an oaken plank. A dankness of mood and spirit settled on everybody, and the Archbishop clasped his raw-looking hands and hung his head.

"What are *you* doing here, Archbishop Meece?" asked Mr. Valona. "I thought you worked in a *cathedral*."

Oathwick Kirk had a higher ceiling than Joel-Brock would have expected, going by its outer dimensions. But it held only six short pews, three to each side of its center aisle, and an altar with a large bronze *Amanita* mushroom atop a squat pedestal. Other rooms abutted the sanctuary, none much bigger than a small closet, and only twenty or so congregants could sit comfortably in its pews. From his shoulder, Mortimer spoke for the Archbishop: *"Call me Father, not Archbishop. Mr. Borsmutch has restored me to my favorite churchly rank."*

"Archbishop to Father?" Addi said. "That's a demotion, not a restoration."

"That depends on one's perspective," the mynah whistled. *"But Mr. Borsmutch did mean to demote me."*

Father Meece led the Smalls to the first split row of pews. Then he paced before them with Mortimer still speaking for him: *"Pither Borsmutch doesn't like suggestions about company policy. For him, what's good for Big Box Bonanzas benefits not only the USA but also all who work for his franchises, human or sporule.*

All his buddypards rise with the tides that lift the stores in which they labor."

Mr. Valona said, "But *you* asked Augustus to stop sending so many spor-ules into his Cobb Creek work force?"

"Exactly," Father Meece said through Mortimer. *"And he didn't like me talking so candidly with you three human gobbymawlers either."*

Sparky and Leo climbed all over Joel-Brock in his front pew. They clearly found Mortimer's speech annoying. Father Meece ignored them, gesturing as he spoke through the bird: *"When Mortimer and I left you all and soared toward Windcatcher Cathedral, near Condor's Cote, I got an impulse message from Mr. Borsmutch. He reduced me in rank in stages—archbishop, bishop, vicar, canon, deacon, and priest. I've always loved the priesthood. Years ago, I budded in Oathwick. So here he posted me as a priest, and here I was ordained. From here, I traveled all about Sporangium while BBB's engineers worked to convert it from a series of hollow caverns into a real country."*

At the church door, an alarming pounding began. All the Smalls had expected it, but Father Meece looked up as if astonished that this sprol stalking party had returned to harass them further.

"Please protect us from Mr. Borsmutch's evil minions, Father," Addie said.

"Evil minions?" Archbishop Meece said through his mouthpiece. *"Such a harsh assessment, child."*

"They want to kill or imprison us, Father."

"You used the sanctuary knocker, and I opened to you. I must protect you— unless you've profaned the sacred Spawnifice or killed someone."

Had the Smalls insulted the Spawnifice by entering it? And did the fatalities there qualify as murders or as acts of self-defense? Addi said, "Canon Umphrees waved us into the Spawnifice. We followed, but from the start he may have meant to back-stab us. If all that's so, we're innocent of any wrongdoing."

The pounding on the door began again. The Smalls held their breath.

"Then you do indeed warrant sanctuary, and I must protect you."

"*Can* you protect us, sir?" Joel-Brock asked.

"Better than you know." Father Meece strolled up the short middle aisle and laid his palm against the door. *"Stop that pounding!"* But when the pounding did not stop, he urged the Smalls and their dogs up to the door and asked them to cry out, "STOP THAT POUNDING!" The Smalls cried out, Joel-Brock's dogs yipped and yapped in chorus, and the pounding ceased.

"Go away," Father Meece shouted. *"These wayfarers have invoked their*

right to asylum in this franchise of the Holy Subterranean Assembly of Greater Sporangium. And so I say again: GO AWAY."

Joel-Brock did his best to hush the dogs, and the person demanding entry gave the door a last angry thump. Then a strangled-sounding voice said, "Open, so I may speak a message from Pither Borsmutch. You have my word that no one will seize or in any other way harm your asylum seekers."

"That sounds like Augustus!" Mr. Valona said.

Addi said, "Please, Father, don't let him in. Something weird's going on."

Sparky stood on his hind legs and clawed at the entry door.

"Open to me," Augustus's voice demanded. "What I've sworn, I've sworn."

"No," Joel-Brock said. "Don't listen to him, sir."

But Father Meece lifted the plank and shoved it aside. It clattered to the floor. He opened and revealed Augustus Hudspeth wearing the clerical clothes that, from afar, had made him resemble Canon Umphrees.

"Ah, Vaughnathan!" said Augustus, extending his hand.

The Smalls stepped back, Joel-Brock shushing Sparky and Leo as they did.

"I never figured you for a religious guy," Mr. Valona said. "And I can't say that a canon's robes truly suit your cockerocity."

"I can't arrest you here," Augustus said, "but, aboveground, you could face child endangerment or maybe even kidnapping charges." He pinched his nose. "Pardon me, but you three smell, uh, out-and-out gamy."

On the narrow street beyond Mr. Hudspeth stood a host of dumpy sprols, all with staves, slings, or stone hatchets, all appearing tired of their forced march and resentful of the Smalls for having occasioned it.

Augustus said, "You must know, sir, that these blood-thirsty midgets you shelter killed your old colleague, Miles Lee Umphrees."

"We didn't," Addi said. "No, we did not."

Augustus hurried on: "But they did. They caused the crash of the ultralight that Canon Umphrees was piloting. He didn't survive, and Mr. Borsmutch appointed me to bring them to justice—not that I relish the task."

Joel-Brock pointed a shaky finger at Augustus. "Canon Umphrees tricked us into the Spawnifice. Then, when we had to escape that goofy place, *you*"—stabbing with his finger—"sent us up to the roof for the flyke that, later, the Canon used to drop fat melon bombs on us."

"I never told you to hijack his ultralight," Augustus said.

"What else could you have meant?" Mr. Valona countered. "When we got to the roof, we had no other way to escape."

Father Meece looked confused. Addi growled at Augustus, the dogs barked, and Augustus tried to force his way in. The armed sprols behind him feinted toward the kirk. Father Meece slammed the door in Augustus's face, and he and the Smalls hurried to bar it with the plank. Mr. Hudspeth pounded as if with a hatchet, and Sparky and Leo set up a deafening doggy holler.

"Hush!" Joel-Brock scolded. "Shut your noisy yaps!"

shouted Addi in support. "Shut your noisy traps!"

And whether they had yaps or traps, the dogs kept barking.

Father Meece grabbed Mortimer and flung him at the dogs. The mynah snapped a tuft of hair from Sparky's ear and swung about to dive-bomb Leo. Both dogs scrambled under pews.

Outside, the pounding continued. Inside, the noise dwindled to foot scuffing and raspy breathing. Mortimer flapped back to Father Meece, and Mr. Valona approached the door. After the next three pairs of Augustus's thumps, he cried, "*Stop!*" and the pounding ceased and a final forehead bang put period to it all.

"*What now?*" Mortimer said, and the bird itself had spoken.

Mr. Valona called out to Augustus: "What 'message' did you bring us from Pither M. Borsmutch?"

"Surrender!

"Or?"

"Or, if you do not, one Lollis a day will be turned into human sausage!"

"Gross," said Addi.

Joel-Brock squeezed forward to the door. "*You can't!*" He could not imagine this man, a BBB supervisor, authorizing such a horrible act.

Mr. Valona spoke over the boy's head: "Augustus, even Mr. Borsmutch wouldn't stoop to such wickedness."

"I'll surrender!" Joel-Brock cried. "Just let my family go!"

Addi pulled him away from the door and hugged him. "They'll do whatever they want, Joel-Boy, whether you surrender or not."

"She's right," Mr. Valona said. "I don't know what's got into Augustus, but if he's lowering himself to blood blackmail—" He shook his head.

"I always figured him for a creep," Addi said, "but not for *this*."

"He likes the Braves," Joel-Brock whispered in helpless incredulity.

And outside the real Mr. Hudspeth yelled, "You have until three to open this door and come out: **ONE!**"

No one inside Oathwick Kirk spoke or moved.

"**TWO!**"

Addi held Joel-Brock more tightly. "Shhh," she said. "Shhh."

"**THREE!**"

Joel-Brock sobbed, but did not dispute Addi's words about the folly of doing as Augustus bid, but he did fear that Augustus would slay them or have them slain if ever they left the church.

Augustus said that his sprols would guard the church for as long as necessary to starve them all into surrendering, even the dogs.

Joel-Brock wriggled clear of Addi and went to the door. "You disgrace the human race," he said through its keyhole.

"Ah, the prodigal abandoned shrimpkin speaks," Augustus said.

"A jerk like you rooting for the Braves insults every real fan everywhere."

"Nanny-nanny-boo-boo," retorted Augustus mildly.

"You don't even qualify to root for the *Yankees.*" Joel-Brock made *Yankees* sound as vile as *puppy-eating savages.*

Outside, Augustus screamed, and a battering ram *thwack*ed loudly against the door. Father Meece and the Smalls, fearing additional oak-splintering blows, retreated farther into the sanctuary.

But nothing happened. And nothing went on happening.

Sparky and Leo sneaked out from under from their pews. Addi picked up Sparky, and Joel-Brock picked up Leo. A crisis had passed, but no Small supposed that Pither M. Borsmutch and Augustus Hudspeth as his top lieutenant would long ignore their defiance. For now, though, they begrudged a scanty lick of respect for the Sporangial Church and Addi's plea for asylum. Clearly, the Church had instituted sanctuary to offset some of the power of The Powerful, but it was a rare defense against the practices of their omnipotent Borsmutchian overlord.

So Father Meece told the Smalls they could stay in his church for a long time, or until they starved to death.

"We're doomed," said Addi.

"*No, no,*" said Mortimer Mynah for Father Meece. "*Just joshing.*"

"Are you sure?" Joel-Brock said.

"Listen: I love Oathwick Kirk. Its sporule builders had more mother wit than their tyrannical human taskmaster ever imagined."

The Smalls traded wary but hopeful looks.

·

21

Father Syd

Father Meece urged the Smalls to call him Father Syd and stepped through an inner door just off the sanctuary, but soon returned with a basket of mushroom wafers and four cups of elderberry wine, all on a tray with a thin bamboo rail around it edges.

"We won't starve all at once," Mortimer said for him, *"but we'll hardly thrive on this modest fare."*

Sparky and Leo perked up. They'd traveled far, from Condor's Cote itself, as the cuts on their footpads testified, but still they trotted over to the tray that Father Syd set on a pew bench. Joel-Brock shook his finger at them: *"No!"* Addi and Mr. Valona moved two other pews to form a triangular pen with the pew holding the tray. Near the altar, the dogs looked on hopefully. Everyone else sat inside the pen to eat a snack. Mortimer got a dried mushroom wafer.

"Isn't eating that sort of like cannibalism?" Joel-Brock asked.

"I'm a bird, not a mycohuman," said Mortimer, speaking for himself . . . although it was sometimes hard to tell.

"I was talking to Father Syd," Joel-Brock told the mynah.

Father Syd sipped his elderberry wine and said, through Mortimer, *"No more than taking Holy Communion would be for you."*

Mr. Valona rebuked him mildly: "Father Syd."

"What? Can't we be made holy as well as actually fed by that which we find truly sacred?"

"Couldn't these chips be made of something other than mushrooms?" Addi asked Father Syd. "Like tofu or eggplant paste?"

"Why eat a symbol of holy substance instead of the substance itself?"

"Duh," said Addi: "To avoid cannibalism."

"Such squeamishness!" Father Syd ate another wafer. *"And do you all hate your very selves so much?"*

"No sir," Joel-Brock said. "Just mushrooms."

Father Syd held out a wafer to him. *"Try this."*

Joel-Brock made an almost comic face of refusal.

"Just one, young man." Father Syd re-extended the wafer, and Joel-Brock at last accepted it. *"'Oh, taste and see that our mycelial presence is good.'"*

Joel-Brock didn't get "mycelial presence," but realized that it was holy, tongued the wafer, and quickly chewed it up. It was okay.

Addi chewed one too. "What do you mycohumanified guys believe, anyway?"

"Criminy," Mr. Valona said unhappily under his breath.

"I mean, who or what do you worship? Not Pither M. Borsmutch, I hope."

"Our Oneness," Father Syd said, eating and drinking as Mortimer "talked": *"The underground root system from which we all take our being and our food. We love others because we are both ourselves and others, you see."*

Mr. Valona cradled his aching head.

"Okay," Addi said. "That's cool. I sort of get how mycohumans would think up a fungus-fiber-based religion and teach it to every bud and spore."

Joel-Brock said, "Just as long as you don't worship Pither M. Borsmutch."

"Yeah, he's not just a lousy god," Addi said. "He's an utter sleazeball."

"Would you two stop chewing this issue, please?" Mr. Valona said.

"Why should they?" asked Father Syd.

"Because this is neither the time nor the place," Mr. Valona replied.

"*We have only the time we have.*" Father Syd's gaze came to rest on the *Amanita*-mushroom statue before the altar. But he said no more, and everybody ate and drank in silence . . . until, obnoxiously, the dogs began to whine.

"Have we got anything for Sparky and Leo?" Joel-Brock asked.

Father Syd said, "*There's plenty of water here.*"

"How'd they escape?" Addi asked. "How did they reach us just when we needed them to?" From her backpack, she dug out some jerky and salt-water tuna, and the dogs, wiggling, jostled nearer.

In *his* backpack, Joel-Brock found only some D'Lisssh Chocolates. They were not good for canines, so he let Addi offer them jerky, which they gnawed as they might old extension cords, and tuna, which wafted its fishy stink throughout the sanctuary.

"Either my mother or Arabella helped them," Joel-Brock said. "It's too bad the dogs can't talk, like Mortimer or those slugs you blasted."

"*I despise gorgástrogons,*" Father Syd said. "*No more destructive creature exists in Sporangium, but our salt-mining sprols would have no distinctive work without them.*"

Impatiently, Mr. Valona stood. "Father Syd, please help us escape."

"*All right,*" he said. "*Giving you Smalls asylum was just the first step of what I'd planned to do, anyway.*"

Mr. Valona said, "Truly?"

"*Yes, but I must discuss a matter with Miss Coe. Please, would you others retire to the sacristy?*" He nodded at a door to the altar's right.

Mr. Valona raised an eyebrow at Addi.

"Go on," she said, even if mystified by Father Syd's request. "I'll be fine."

*

Father Syd restored the pews to their original places, and Addi studied the kirk's interior. Its uneven stained-glass windows bore pictures of fungi, gastropods, or laboring sprols, while a yellow banner featuring a tangle of vegetable fibers hung behind the altar as a backdrop to the toadstool lectern behind which Father Syd preached.

Indeed, Mortimer flew from Father Syd's shoulder to the cap of the bronze altar mushroom. The bird sought purchase there. Doing so, it resembled a large black butterfly just out of its cocoon, drying in candlelight.

"Sit beside me," said Father Syd, through the mynah. He patted a spot in a front pew. When Addi joined him, the priest took her hand like a doting uncle. *"Thank you, child."*

"No problem." Addi freed her hand to scratch her nose.

Father Syd laughed, and Mortimer hissed, *"It'ss ssoitainly ssweet ssitting next to you, Miss Coe."* Father Syd glowered, to remind the bird to speak for him, not itself, and again took Addi's hand. She let him, for, wisely or not, she *trusted* him.

And then Father Syd, via Mortimer, began to speak: *"If Sporangium feels familiar to you, Adelaide, it's because you've been here before. No, wait. I'll explain."* Mortimer began to pronounce *esses* much less sibilantly: *"As a sprol sprout, I was a bud and then a boy here in Oathwick, but later I was taken to East Sporangium to work in the mushroom beds in the Spawnifice. I did so for an earlier canon, a sporule divine who liked me. He liked me so much that he asked his best gene-twisters to mycohumanify me because he thought that, over time, I'd make a good priest. After my gene-quirking, though, I heard of other sporule humans who passed through the GillGate and reached topside to become gobbymawlers for Pither M. Borsmutch. He gave them 'money' to work in his Big Box Bonanzas emporium. With 'money,' they traded for goods impossible, then, to imagine down here. And so I, too, rode upstairs to sign my gobbymawler papers and to become a drudge in BBB, a realm so much bigger than ours that I felt ant-sized. I worked as a box packer in the warehouse; later, as a late-night shelf stocker; finally, as a number crank in back-office accounting. I never spoke to anyone. I lacked, as I still do, vocal cords, but their absence never bothered me until a beautiful human female hired me as an assistant number crank in the back-room box-slot next to hers."*

"Is this a love story, Father Syd?"

Father Syd squeezed Addi's hand. *"You decide, child. We began to see each other outside work, this young woman and I—to date, as humans say—about once a week, and then more often, an upgrade that humans called 'going steady.' My chosen didn't mind that I could not talk. She told friends I was the 'strong, silent sort.' And then a manager, Ms. Smogor, told me that Mr. Borsmutch frowned on office romances. As I learned later, he actually frowned on romances between humans and sprols because the sprols always learned from their lovers that sprols made less money than humans for the same kinds of work. But I kept seeing your mother anyway. In fact, a justice—"*

"What?" Addi said, withdrawing her hand. "What did you say?"

Mortimer kept talking: *"A justice of the peace secretly married us. He didn't even check my phony blood test, and we lived in upstairs rooms close to Big Box Bonanzas in Cobb Creek. Then Tara Abbot Coe, your mother, started getting big. Or bigger, for she was a small person. In five and a half months, you popped out, not a preemie at all but a child the size of a human toddler! You had your mama's red hair but little from me other than the shapes of your mouth and ears."*

"I'm your *daughter?*" Addi's breathing had quickened.

"Yes, Adelaide. Now you may call me 'Father Syd' with total aptness. Tara, your mother, asked for raises for both of us—to help us raise a child of your surprising stature and liveliness. And, soon, Ms. Smogor handed me a dismissal notice. An evening later, as Tara worked overtime without *overtime pay, some sporule gobbymawlers kidnapped you and me from our rooms and whisked us back to Sporangium as a warning to other sprol-and-prol sweethearts tempted to marry and, worse, create a bud. Back in BBB, Tara was 'promoted' from a mid-level number crank to a triple-section manager. Her hours were extended from forty to seventy-five a week so that she could keep making what she had in accounting, and a pox on Mr. Borsmutch for his heartlessness."*

"I had a sense," Addi said softly, "but I don't fully remember."

"Adelaide, you were maybe a week old, even if you looked like a human toddler. Both human and sporule sprouts need time for their brains to mature."

"Wait. Stop. I need to know— "

"That's just the way we're gene-quirked in the mycohumanification process."

"—how long I lived in Sporangium, sir."

"Over a decade, possibly a dozen years."

"How could I live so long in Sporangium without a single solid memory of the place? Explain that to me, Fa—I mean, sir."

"They took you from me. They gave you brain-freeze drugs. They hypnotized you. They held you in deep sleep in isolation tanks. And yet you do have a few real memories of Sporangium. How could you have come so far without them?"

"Mr. Valona's smart and Joel-Brock learned a lot from the quagslip he fell into. But *what* real memories do you mean? *Who* hypnotized and iso-tanked me? And *where* did they do all this rotten stuff?"

"In a cell in Condor's Cote. Borsmutch's stooges did the dirty work. Hence, your real memories include a deep sense of the mystery of Sporangium and a full picture of the layout of Condor's Cote and its surrounding terrain."

"But I *don't* remember what you say I do."

"Adelaide, you will. You assuredly will."

Addi strode to a spot under the church's steeple and gazed up into its cone as if expecting to see God. "What happened to you and my mom? And how did I get back to Cobb Creek thinking I'd run away from a human family?"

Father Syd stepped to the altar and gave his arm to Mortimer. The bird hopped to his hand. *"Can't you believe I'm your father, Adelaide?"*

"I don't know!" More quietly, she said, "But why would you lie?"

"I wouldn't. I absolutely wouldn't."

"Then tell me about my mother, if Tara Abbot Coe was really my mom."

"I don't want to tell her story's ending, Adelaide, but I must. If you don't like it, remember that you asked and that this story is yours. Your names, Adelaide and Bridget, come from Tara's mother, Adelaide, and your mother's sister, Bridget. Coe was Tara's father's surname. Tara said he was a good man. And at Big Box Bonanzas, she was told that if she did her new work well, and held her tongue, she'd advance quickly. Also, BBB would update her not only about me and my assigned

work in Sporangium, but also about you, in your school not far from my classroom in the Spawnifice. Tara obeyed. She had little choice. Somewhat later, Mr. Borsmutch took out a Corporate-Owned Life Insurance policy—also known as a COLI or a 'dead peasant' policy—on your mother without her knowledge or consent."

"Why?" Addi asked. "And why a 'dead peasant' policy?"

"Because BBB received tax deductions on the money it paid for the policy, or it did until lawmakers made this practice illegal when you were two. Early the next year, your mama died from her efforts to move a heavy hand-truck from the docks out back to the dairy lockers inside. That was Borsmutch's second reason for taking out the policy on Tara. At her death, BBB got half a million dollars, but neither you nor I received a single penny. In fact, I knew nothing about this policy until the turn of this new century, shortly after the Church made me a bishop in Rockthorpe."

"What total slime buckets," Addi whispered, awed.

"Shhh, child. Shhh."

"You defend Mr. Borsmutch and his brownnosing greedies?"

"Big Box Bonanzas is far from alone in taking out policies—under the table, so to speak—on its own employees."

"Who else does it?" Addi demanded.

"Companies don't have to publicly disclose which policies they buy, which hires they insure, or how much of a benefit they purchase."

"That really stinks."

"Over two hundred US companies, many with offices or outlets in or near Cobb Creek, have their own company names as the payees on the insurance policies of many, many unsuspecting employees."

"So company bigwigs don't cry if some of their workers die?"

"Not even if their company has to send out thousands of flowers or arrange a hundred funerals."

"That stinks too."

"The higher a person on a ladder to the top, the colder the temperature of that person's blood."

Addi recalled the faces of Augustus Hudspeth, a rung climber; Melba Berryhill, a ground-floor worker; and the people in her department who'd taught her her job and who later threw her a surprise un-birthday party. There were *some* good bosses, but not always where she could see them and only rarely out among their store's customers. Addi shook her head.

"Tell me about my mother. Tell me why you loved her."

"Sure," Father Syd said. *"I loved her because she loved me. I loved her because she loved you. I loved her because she worked so hard and did it all for you and me . . . at least as much as, if not more than, for herself."* Father Syd halted to sift further through his memories.

Addi felt pity not only for herself but also for this being who was not fully human and who claimed to be her father. She sat down again and placed an arm around him. Her fellow Smalls must be wondering at the length of their talk, but she sought to console him and thus to also console herself.

"Why didn't you tell me all this in front of my friends?"

"I feared you'd tear me into spongy strips and feed them to Joel-Brock's dogs."

"They don't like mushrooms either."

Father Syd—he, *not* Mortimer—laughed silently. And Addi, at once laughing and crying, leaned her cheek against his chest.

22

Hope

The sacristy in Oathwick Kirk resembled a cabin aboard an old whaling ship, even if it stored censers, prayer books, salt medallions, mushroom wafers, candles, and two chairs in which a priest and an acolyte could pray before a service.

Joel-Brock and Mr. Valona sat in these hard chairs waiting for Addi's talk with Father Syd to end. Sparky lay in Joel-Brock's lap, his eyes wide open, as Leo fidgeted in Mr. Valona's. The boy calmed Sparky by stroking his wiry hair and fiddling with his ID collar. Now that the excitement of the run-in with Augustus had passed, Sparky was pooped, and when Joel-Brock caught his pinky under the collar and pulled it free, a strip of paper inside the collar also emerged.

Mr. Valona looked at him curiously. "What you got there, kidster?"

Joel-Brock unfolded the paper. Someone had written on it in small rust-

red letters, with a straight pin or a fingernail. He recognized the printing as Arabella's. Also, he had no doubt that his sister had used blood—from one of her frequent nosebleeds?—for ink. Excited, he read her message in silence:

Dear Joely,

The villain who ordered our kidnapping, Pither M. Borsmutch, has so far not harmed us, and we are not broken by our captivity. With help, as you see, we found a way to loose the Dogs of Lollis, for I believed that you or someone you'd sent would try to release us. I write these lines to assure you that all will be well.

Condor's Cote, a subterranean villa, gives the maniacal Mr. Borsmutch shelter, privacy, and self-indulgence. We do not hobnob with him in its loftier chambers, but live on Level 3—on a floor consisting of many padded cells, with built-in hand- and footholds (for climbing these walls), and lots of terrible piped-in music.

This music ranges from "It's a Small World, After All" to "It's a Small World, After All." It hasn't yet driven us mad, but it will. So, Brother, I send you these words by way of Sparky and Leo. A person you know took them from us 3 or 4 days after we came—until, at some danger to herself, she freed our dogs.

Anyway, I hope these words ease your trials as you and your friends try to find us. We cannot take much more of this—especially the stink of sweat-infused foam. Often, we huddle and hug, until we almost pop our hearts out and the hidden day at long last rises . . . if day actually does still rise.

I love you, Joely. Please come soon.

Arabella

Knuckling his eyes, Joel-Brock read this message to Mr. Valona. The paper on which it was written looked like a napkin spotted with dried catsup.

"Look," Mr. Valona said. "I've got one too." He held up a strip of paper that he'd just taken from the inside of Leo's collar. "Do you want to read it?"

"No. You go ahead."

Mr. Valona told Joel-Brock, "It's a poem. Here goes."

HOPE

An original poem by Arabella Lollis

When Tragedy shows itself,
And Disaster becomes all we know,
When Grief is our only companion,
And Despair is our single belonging,
Hope appears.
And suddenly,
The Tragedy is not so tragic,
The Disaster is not so disastrous,
The Grief is easier to cope with,
And the Despair is drowned,
By the Hope,
A single light at the end of the tunnel,
Leading the way for all who seek it.
So have Hope,
Embrace Hope,
Absorb Hope and radiate it wherever you go,
So that others may have it as well.

Mr. Valona looked up. "How old did you say your sister was?"

"I *didn't*. But she's twelve."

"*Twelve?* And she wrote the message you read me and this poem too?

"Yes sir."

"Pretty sophisticated for a twelve-year-old."

"It's okay, I guess. Arabella reads all the time."

"Caboodles of people read all the time, but still don't—" Mr. Valona stopped and finger-flipped the paper so that it *popped*. "Hold on. Here's something at the bottom." He lifted the paper so that he could read this something:

Joely, if you or a companion gets this message, you must have Hope to become our Hope. We love you, sweet Home Run Hitter of the Future.

Joel-Brock could not speak.

"There's a postscript to her postscript." Mr. Valona held out the sheet, and Leo leapt down from his lap when he did. Joel-Brock read the PS to himself:

When the piped-in music stops, I play my oboe—usually my part in <u>Estampie</u> or the duck in Prokofieff's <u>Guide to the Orchestra</u>. Hear my sad moans.

"My sister's blowing the blues on her heckelphone," Joel-Brock said.

"Heckelphone?"

"Only a hundred and sixty-five heckelphones have ever been made. They're a big sort of oboe. Daddy says that from what we paid for Arabella's, we must have bought the composer Haydn's *personal* heckelphone."

Mr. Valona web-searched *heckelphone* on his yNaut.

"You're still getting coverage here?" Joel-Brock asked.

"I am." Mr. Valona studied the yNaut's screen. "But it says nothing here about Franz Joseph Haydn ever playing a heckelphone."

"Sir, Wilhelm Heckel wasn't born until almost fifty years after Haydn died."

Mr. Valona gave Joel-Brock a peculiar look.

"Actually," Joel-Brock said, "we *rent* my sister's oboe. So that's just Dad being funny, or trying to be. But if it makes you feel any better, the inventor Heckel actually did give his name to a magpie in some old movie cartoons."

The sacristy door opened, and Addi, Father Syd, and Mortimer came in. Leo leapt on Addi, and Sparky leapt on the priest.

"This *person*," Addi said, touching Father Syd, "is my father."

"Of course he is," Mr. Valona said. "He's a priest."

"No, I mean that Father Syd is my *daddy*."

Joel-Brock's and Mr. Valona's eyes got very round. Why such an absurd claim? Addi put an arm around Father Syd's waist, and for the first time both Joel-Brock and Mr. Valona noted the family likeness in the shape of Father Syd's and Addi's mouths and ears.

"My mother is a dead peasant," the girl said.

Huh? Joel-Brock thought.

Mortimer hopped from Father Syd's shoulder to Addi's . . . to sip the tear skating morosely down her cheek.

*

Even in the sacristy, they heard fresh *hammering* at the door of Oathwick Kirk. The issue of Addi's parentage, so crucial a minute past, fell away as Father Syd gathered the Smalls so that Mortimer could address them:

"The entrance to Sporangium Salt, Incorporated, lies through the galley attached to our sanctuary. Enter the galley. Go through a door and down an access shaft into the mine. Then heed Mortimer's counsel and directions—speaking for me at a distance—to travel from Oathwick to the rocky foothills of Condor's Cote."

"But what will *you* do?" Addi cried. "Aren't you going with us?"

"I'm too big to get down those stairs. And as long as the sprols outside continue to pound, I must stay. I am the captain of this ship." Desperate to lead him away, Addi tugged at Father Syd. *"Child, I have my duty,"* he said, *"and you have yours."*

"But we can't lose each other now."

Wincing at each blow to the outer door, Father Syd smiled forlornly.

"Let him go, Addi, so that *we* may go," Mr. Valona said.

"I may never see him again!" But she released Father Syd's arm.

"Have Hope, Addi," Mr. Valona said. "Embrace, absorb, and radiate Hope."

Clearly torn, Addi stared at the flagstone floor.

Joel-Brock took Addi's arm. "You said you'd help rescue my family from the evil Pither M. Borsmutch."

Addi shook Joel-Brock's hand from her arm, but stepped away from

Father Syd, a single step to signal her intention to carry out her promise.

"What about the dogs?" Mr. Valona asked.

This question posed a challenge.

Did Sparky and Leo return to Condor's Cote with them or stay in Oathwick until their rescue attempt ran its course? And if it failed, what then? Joel-Brock argued that the dogs could lead them straight to the cell holding his family, but the other Smalls favored leaving the dogs. They could easily thwart their rescue attempt and end up as victims of Mr. Borsmutch's reprisals. As for Augustus and his sprols, they seemed ready to kick the outer door off its hinges and tramp over it like a gangplank to nab them.

"Go on," said Father Syd. "I'll reassert your right to asylum and keep these dogs as canine claimants of that same right."

So the Smalls, following Mortimer, went from the sacristy to the sanctuary to the galley and through the galley door to the stairs leading down into Sporangium Salt. Joel-Brock wondered how far these stairs spiraled down and how likely it was that they might all fall to their deaths.

*

Alone with the dogs, Father Syd reflected on the name Mr. Valona had given his crew, *The Valorous Smalls*. Despite never having traveled anywhere but Sporangium and parts of Cobb Creek, Father Syd *was* a learned man.

As such, he thought to tell Sparky and Leo that whatever the word *smalls* meant elsewhere, he respected Mr. Valona for giving the word all the dignity that the detective brought to his own small form. But he could not do so because Mortimer, his voice, had left to lead the Smalls through Sporangium Salt. Thus stymied, Father Syd turned again to the knocking at Oathwick Kirk's entry door.

23

Sporangium Salt, Inc.

At odd points down its maw, the entry shaft had newfangled blue-white bulbs to cast light into the pit. Not counting the mynah, which undulated down this shaft on a weak updraft, Mr. Valona went first, Addi next, and Joel-Brock last.

Joel-Brock thought it weird that in the catacombs of East and West Sporangium, the sprols had dug out other under-levels from which to dislodge big blocks of salt-rich rock. Did further lower floors exist? He wished he'd started counting stairs at the top of the shaft. Before he did start, the Smalls descended over a hundred iron steps. Moreover, each Small, at each step, considered returning to Oathwick Kirk to escape this mad drop to hell. Sometimes they saw Mortimer on a stair below, resting, but before Mr. Valona reached the step above that one, Mortimer flew down another thirty steps before resting again. But, still, there was a "single light at the end of the tunnel," and this light spiraled up to them like a halo of rising water.

Four hundred and thirty-six steps after Joel-Brock started his count, the Smalls reached a snow-white floor and stepped down onto it . . . like astronauts onto the Moon. Blasted salt walls thrust up around them, with drill-bearing iron rods pointed at the walls to bore holes for dynamite sticks. This mine, built on the room-and-pillar model, with pillars to support the walk-through rooms atop them, also featured faceted salt boulders around the bases of its walls.

"*Sporangium Salt,*" Mortimer said for the absent Father Syd, "*mines mostly rock salt. Big Box Bonanzas sells it to help Good Old Boys churn homemade ice cream and pour on icy winter roads.* We *use it as stumbling blocks to the gorgástrogons that raid our mushroom beds. But since production began here, Oathwick—right above us—hasn't had one slug infestation. You'll never find a gorgástrogon in a salt mine, unless a cruel human has introduced it to make it suffer.*"

"Without benefit of a hairdryer," Mr. Valona told Addi.

At shaft's bottom, Addi and Joel-Brock appeared shaky. Neither of them laughed at Mr. Valona's joke. Few sprols moved about the mine or along the salt road leading from this shaft to destinations westward. One path was an exit through the rocks sloping up to Condor's Cote. A huge truck ground forward on seven-foot-tall tires and turned a corner behind them, to halt beside the Smalls. Joel-Brock had never seen so enormous a truck, like a dinosaur on wheels. He feared that its exhausts and weird gut gurgles would make him faint dead away.

Mortimer flapped from the mine floor to the truck's side and perched there. He may have spoken to a sprol inside the cargo hold, but the engine growls kept Joel-Brock from hearing any word out of his beak. But soon a ladder with hooks on its two facing rails dropped over the truck's side and clanked down to the floor in stages. It landed in front of the Smalls, an invitation to climb it to the top.

"Down and then up," Addi said. "Wish our guides would make up their minds."

Now Addi led, Joel-Brock was next, and Mr. Valona third, ready to catch anyone plunging past the ladder's collapsible rungs. But no one did. When Addi crawled over the truck's gunwale, she imagined herself falling into an abyss, but instead came eye to eye with two sprols in hardhats standing on a ledge inside the cargo hold. Grotesque lumps of salt-laced ore filled the hold. The sight made Addi shudder, but the two sprols helped her in, and then Joel-Brock and Mr. Valona.

Seated in a box in its lofty cab, the truck's driver put the monster into gear. With a grunt and a chug, the salt walls lurched past in jerks. As the Smalls realized, the truck was creeping forward—not the walls sliding back—but Joel-Brock's feelings told him the opposite, mostly because of its great size and the lack of any reference points beyond the salt walls. At length, the delivery road widened. On either side, intricate salt statues, standing on boulders, jogged by.

Most represented famed heroes from the Holy Subterranean Assembly of Greater Sporangium, but seven depicted mushroom growers and sprol scientists responsible for spore multiplication and gene-quirking. Other statues were of planners or patrons of the salt industry, but all looked like plaster-of-Paris figures in a white-washed crypt. Then the mine's floor plan opened out, to accommodate dozens of white tables bearing candles and the salt chandeliers scintillating above those candles. Joel-Brock, who felt that the truck was carrying them into an unfinished museum, clung to its side to avoid slipping into the cargo bed or headlong to the distant floor.

"Would you like me to pray for your enter-prise?" Mortimer asked.

"Sure," said Mr. Valona, "yNaut?"

Joel-Brock had lost track of time since last trying to sleep, an effort that three big snotfeet had interrupted. And when Mortimer prayed, *"May the efforts of these human beings, including the son and brother of the Lollises and the daughter of a sinful sprol, go as well as they deserve to go,"* Joel-Brock nodded off.

"Hey!" said Mr. Valona to the bird.

"By which I mean," Mortimer added, gripping the truck's side, *"extremely well indeed."* The bird looked at Joel-Brock napping—*"Good for him"*—and at Mr. Valona and Addi: *"And, you two, close your eyes and dream of peace."*

Mr. Valona glanced at Joel-Brock, asleep on his feet, like a salt-mine pony, and replied, "Thanks."

"Don't mention it," said Father Syd, his hands on the church's oaken door but his voice several hundred feet deeper underground. When would Augustus and his sprols depart? Or force their way in?

The truck climbed a steepening grade. The mine's rooms and pillars contracted, the road narrowed, the walls pulled in as in a funhouse.

Addi felt a salt-fed dizziness that made her observe things *not* there. Even in the undergound chill, she sweated. She lacked the sleep-assisted balance that Joel-Brock had learned and that kept him safe from sudden

lurches. So Mr. Valona held her arm while the sprols in hardhats totally ignored the Smalls.

"*Now take a nap,*" Mortimer told Addi.

And the girl slid into a slumber as image-free as Joel-Brock's. Mr. Valona envied the kids, but fought not to join them. As the adult here, he had miles to go before *he* could sleep. . . .

*

Ka-boom! Ka-bang-bang-bang! Ka-rumble!

Mr. Valona had dozed. And now the enormous truck was backed up to a conveyor belt dumping boulders and crushed rock from its cargo bed into a hopper that fed the belt. What a sight. What a racket.

Meanwhile, the floor of the metal box in which the Smalls and two Sporangium Salt workers had ridden did something marvelous. A gyroscope in the box held its floor horizontal to the road even as the cargo bed tilted up to spill its contents into the hopper. Like Mr. Valona, Addi and Joel-Brock awoke to hear and watch the rock grind its way down, an obstreperous avalanche. Soon, bits of it swept from the sunken hopper to ride a conveyor belt up the inner flank of the salt mine to a hole—an exit, the boy supposed—into West Sporangium.

When the cargo bed had emptied and righted itself, the sprols in the passenger box tossed their ladder over the side and scrambled down to the hard-packed turnaround on which the truck had parked.

"This is the end of the line," Mr. Valona said. "Let's go."

"You first," Addi said.

"Suits my cockerocity. But follow quickly—no lollygagging, hear?"

"I'd never gag a Lolly or any other Lollis, either," Joel-Brock said.

"Touché," Mr. Valona said.

"I don't wear one," Joel-Brock said.

"He said *touché*, not *toupee*," Addi told him.

"I know that," Joel-Brock said. "Sheeesh."

Then the Smalls climbed out, over, and down, Mr. Valona leading, Addi last. The flank of the truck gave a feeling of shelter, but the looseness of the ladder and a dizzying view of the well-lit mine reversed that feeling with every downward step. Joel-Brock set his foot on the top of Mr. Valona's head and almost slipped.

Mr. Valona said nothing, but steadied Joel-Brock by raising his arm and holding a palm against Joel-Brock's thigh. From that point on, the Smalls proceeded with hardly a hitch, and, at the bottom, Mr. Valona caught Joel-Brock and Addi as they dropped, one at a time, from ladder to roadway.

All took their bearings. Mortimer was gone. They should have noted his absence earlier, but the grumbling of the off-loading rocks and the loftiness of the passenger box had distracted them. Addi asked if something terrible had happened.

"Like what?" Joel-Brock asked.

"Maybe a sprol wrung Mortimer's neck. Maybe Mortimer fell into the rock salt and got crushed when our driver dumped it."

"Probably," Mr. Valona said, "he's winged his way back to Father Syd."

"But *now* what do we do?" Joel-Brock asked.

Mr. Valona said, "Adapt. Improvise. Go on." He pointed to a crooked set of stairs climbing the mine's western flank beside the conveyor belt. It did not rise quite so high, however, stopping midway up the rock face at a rusty red door.

"An elevator to the caverns above," Mr. Valona said.

"You don't know that," Addi said.

"One way to find out." Mr. Valona circled the truck and trudged to the stairway's base. When Addi groaned, Joel-Brock yanked his backpack straps and followed Mr. Valona. With few other options, Addi fell in behind Joel-Brock so that the Smalls all got to the lowest stairway platform almost at once. Then they climbed to the rust-red door of the elevator . . . if it wasn't a dumb waiter to hell. Frustratingly, this door had no button to push or any speaker to give them instructions.

"Don't you want to ask us something?" Addi asked the door.

The door kept its own counsel. Mr. Valona knocked on it, rapping out a seven-beat cadence: *Shave-and-a-haircut,* **two bits***!*

Nobody behind the door—if any such soul existed—bothered to reply.

"Now what?" asked Addi.

"If it doesn't open," Mr. Valona said, "we may have to go back to the conveyor-belt feed and ride the belt to the top."

"Oh, no," said Addi. "I'd rather have it ask us a question."

"*Very well,*" said the door through a narrow bolt-hole. "*Just one: What did the open-pit mine say to the strip mine?*"

Addi rolled her eyes but hazarded the guess, "'Would you be mine?'?"

"I sort of like that, miss," said the audibly nonplused door, "but you couldn't be more irritatingly wrong! Try again!"

Joel-Brock held his palms to the door and said, "*Open, Sesame!*"

The door slid open, revealing a big cubicle with a metal floor. The Smalls stepped into this crate and faced the closing door. Then, with a downward lurch of their stomachs, the Smalls rose with the creaking crate.

"That shouldn't have worked," Addi said. "'*Open, Sesame,*' I mean."

"Why not? My baba once read me 'Ali Baba and the Forty Thieves,' just like my memaw read me Hans Christian Andersen."

"Your *baba*? Meaning Ali Baba, the guy who said '*Open, Sesame*' to get into the forty thieves' treasure cave?"

"No, I mean our grandfather, Arabella's and mine."

"You call your granddad 'Baba'?"

Joel-Brock hesitated. "I don't—anymore. Arabella still does."

"Baba," Addi said thoughtfully. "That's sort of sweet."

"Yes it is," Mr. Valona agreed.

Addi rocked on her heels. *"Baba,"* she repeated. Trek fatigue had blurred her talent for tenderness, but now she was getting it back.

As it rose, the elevator whistled. Eventually, it screeched, slowed, and slammed to a halt that left the Smalls atremble. They waited for something encouraging to occur—a welcome from a ceiling speaker, for example.

But nothing happened. And nothing went on happening.

Open, Sesame!" barked Mr. Valona, without effect. And the Smalls felt a surge of panic. They were trapped in a cage with no alternate exit. "Try the yNaut," Addi told Mr. Valona. He did. Although it had worked nearly everywhere else in Sporangium, it did not work now. yNaut? Maybe because they were inside an elevator cage within a shaft inside a mountain under a cavern beneath a country. Addi felt the door like a blind girl and then squatted and tried to pry it open with her fingernails.

"You say it," she ordered Joel-Brock. "Say, *'Open, Sesame!'"*

Joel-Brock obeyed, but nothing happened. Addi pounded on the door, and they all recalled Mr. Hudspeth beating on the door in Oathwick. Her pounding had the same lack of result. So Mr. Valona felt for a button or switch that would let them escape to . . . well, what? Total darkness?

And then Joel-Brock said, *"Emases, Nepo!"*

His friends looked at him as if he had spoken Phrygian pig-Latin. And a hydraulic *whooosh* sounded at their backs and a door behind them slid open, only to clang shut like a prison door slotting into a paneled sheath. The Smalls turned to confront an ugly prison yard, where the prisoners had erected chain-link fences and hammered salt blocks into a beach of white pea gravel.

Joel-Brock chuckled. Elevators don't always open on one side only—but this part of Sporangium Salt did not much resemble Cobb Creek Medical Center.

"Let's go," Mr. Valona said. "*Now!*"

No one guarded the fenced causeway.

Outside, they sensed rock, uphill trails, and trickling water. They crunched across the pea gravel and through the chain-link maze beyond the elevator. They were on their way again and so near Condor's Cote that they could smell its acrid ozone and the grilled hotdogs and burgers that Mr. Borsmutch ate or fed to mysterious guests in the Cote's luxury suites. But what did the imprisoned Lollises get to eat?

Joel-Brock hurried to the nearest west-leading trail and clambered up it in quest of his lost kinfolks.

24

Condor's Cote

The Smalls pressed upward to a vantage on the far western edge of Greater Sporangium. They gazed in awe at the seven-story face of Condor's Cote, a fortress fitted to the cavern wall. On this strange façade, huge images flickered, telling odd tales or advertising items for sale in Big Box Bonanzas.

Joel-Brock found it hard to distinguish the stories from the ads because the ads featured slogans in big letters—**BUY AT BBB**—or cartoons of shoppers loading their carts with TVs, swimsuits, soccer balls, can openers, *et cetera*. And then there flashed images of rushing waterfalls, whales splashing in deep-blue bays, and the greenish ribbon whips of the Northern Lights as seen from outer space. These shots alternated with close-ups of clownfish swimming in schools, a lemur in Madagascar, and an immense praying mantis stilt-walking through a jungle of Bermuda grass. Sometimes, fireworks drifted across the face of Condor's Cote. Sometimes, a California condor soared across it and hovered there until an image of the Eifel Tower, or Pikes Peak, or a desert of sand dunes, or the marbled Earth itself replaced it.

"I hate to say it, but that's pretty impressive," Addi said.

"Yeah," said Mr. Valona, "but who's the Big Boss trying to impress?"

"Us," Joel-Brock said. "He knows we're coming."

The Smalls stared longer at the light show, which used programmed projectors set in the rocks yet ahead of them. And Joel-Brock was grateful to Mr. Borsmutch for trying to impress them. Otherwise, given the few shiny slime trails here, they would have had only fungal glow and their feeble flashlights to see by. The light display had no sound track except for their breathing and the gurgling of nearby streams, but they all felt both expectant and very small before it. Then a faint brown alto melody sounded in the cavern, issuing from Condor's Cote. It started at the sudden appearance of a gigantic newborn lamb struggling to stand in a summery green meadow.

Joel-Brock's heart kicked into a higher gear.

"What's that?" Addi asked.

"It's 'Mary Had a Little Lamb,'" Mr. Valona said.

It was indeed, but "Mary Had a Little Lamb" stripped down to its most elemental self and played like a funeral dirge.

"I meant, what *instrument* is that?"

"It's an oboe," said Joel-Brock, aching inside. "It's Arabella's oboe."

For such a thin brown tune, it had freaky power. And then the lamb on the face of Condor's Cote tottered out of sight, followed by hundreds of galloping wildebeest. These creatures ran—to this side, then to that—as if "Mary Had a Little Lamb" terrified them even more than would have a pride of hungry lions.

"The notes don't sound amplified," Mr. Valona said. "How can we hear her while we're still so far away?"

"Oboe notes carry," Joel-Brock said. "Besides, Arabella has a wicked lip."

Addi turned her ear toward the sound. "And, apparently, a mighty heart."

They listened until Arabella—it *had* to be Arabella—stopped playing and a vast quasi-silence hung over all.

"If they already know we're coming, how do we get there without being seen?" Joel-Brock wondered.

"We don't," Mr. Valona said. "We just go. Or we turn back."

Joel-Brock gripped his backpack straps and set off down a path toward the rocky valley and the foothills between it and Condor's Cote.

*

Mr. Valona sensed that Mr. Borsmutch and his henchmen were watching as the Smalls crossed this no-man's-land. Soldiers during World War I must have felt this way moving from trench to trench across fields booby-trapped with mines and barbed wire. When the light show on the wall ceased, crisscrossing searchlights roamed, as if trying to pinpoint the whereabouts of escaping inmates. The Smalls hunched over like convicts and, when the searchlights rippled over them, dropped to their bellies and crawled.

Crawling, Mr. Valona said, "Keep going, Smalls. Keep going." The villa seemed to retreat rather than draw nearer. Moreover, the absences of natural light and their daily routines had scrambled their inner clocks, but finally they stood again and trudged ahead under the dueling searchlights. To each Small, the beams hit like disorienting waves, but, helping one another, they hobbled on toward their long-sought goal.

Then the searchlights shut off, and they stood in blank perplexity until a phony sun—a glitter ball as big as a water-tower tank—snapped on, **BLAAAM!** It rained light in buttery gouts. The Smalls ducked, but, once adjusted to this light, saw before them . . . *Augustus Hudspeth*, dressed in crimson robes, astride the pit pony Shaftoe. An army of sprols—or a platoon—carrying half-pikes and slings followed him, glaring ahead with piggy eyes.

"OMG," said Addi.

In an instant, the sprols encircled them with a stunningly effective maneuver, and the Smalls were caught.

"By order of Pither M. Borsmutch," Augustus said, "you're all under arrest."

Addi Coe said, "Which of the Four Horsemen are you? Death?"

"Ha-ha," Augustus said. "You thought you'd escaped me, but—just look!—you haven't. I am the Horseman of your Communal Comeuppance."

"If we're under arrest," Mr. Valona said, "what's our crime?"

"In Pither M. Borsmutch's view, it's the unforgivable worst: treason."

"Treason?" Joel-Brock said. "We're trying to right his wrongs."

Augustus winked, creepily. "So you say, and so you may believe, but you're none of you in any position to judge, Master Lollis."

"Who better?" Mr. Valona said. "Who better to—?"

Obedient sprols came up behind the Smalls and poked them on toward Condor's Cote, which, in the false sun's raw light, now resembled an unused factory on a shabby winter beach.

*

At the base of Condor's Cote, Augustus Hudspeth and three pike-bearing sprols forced the Smalls through a gate in the villa's outer wall. The other sprols stayed outside while Augustus led the Smalls to a glass portal that opened automatically. The sprols behind the Smalls prodded them into the villa, jabbing them with their pikes if they hesitated. Joel-Brock's guard kept sticking him in the lower neck—until Joel-Brock spun about with his hands fisted.

"Knock it off!" he cried, trembling.

The sprol lifted his pike threateningly, but Augustus grabbed it and turned it aside. "Get back to the courtyard—all of you!" The sporules hesitated. "Go on! I know these people. They won't try to harm me."

"Actually," Mr. Valona said, "I was thinking of clever ways to do just that."

Augustus curled a lip at him but spoke again to the guards: "Why would they try to escape now that they're Mr. Borsmutch's guests?"

"As a frog in a boiling pot is a guest?" asked Mr. Valona.

But the sporule guards retreated, and Augustus nodded the Smalls toward an elevator bearing on its door a mushroom sign like the one on the GillGate's warehouse side. Stirring music by Tchaikovsky, familiar from Christmas concerts, assailed them as they approached the elevator. There they saw that a car was dropping to them from the third of Condor's Cote's seven levels, and Joel-Brock asked if Augustus planned to turn them over to Mr. Borsmutch.

"Do you want me to?"

"I'd like to see my family," Joel-Brock said. "And we've come so far together, I think Addi and Mr. Valona would like that too."

The elevator car from the third floor arrived, and Joel-Brock took Addi's arm to help her inside when its door slid open.

The door did just that. There stood a girl in a pinstriped baseball uniform, with **GOBBYMAWLERS** on her shirt and the letters *G* and *M* on the front of her cap. When she tilted her head the better to see the Smalls, her silver-blonde ponytail plumed through the hole at the back of the cap. Joel-

Brock, who knew her as a classmate at his school, noted that she was tall and slender, like a model, and that as usual she had arranged her hair to show off its slivery-blonde sheen. Also, she held the elevator door open and posed as if Addi and he might like to ask for her autograph.

"Is that your sister?" Addi whispered.

"N-No way," Joel-Brock whispered back.

"She's like a Willowy Wendi doll. Do you know her?"

"He certainly does," the girl, who had heard Addi quite well, told her. "I'm Fractoria Scampi, a member of the Big Box Bonanzas Gobbymawlers in our Cobb Creek Cubby League."

"She means she's a ball girl for them," Joel-Brock said.

"Not just a ball girl, Joely," Fractoria Scampi said. "Since you've been away, I've become a fully invested Gobbymawler constituent."

"Constituent?" Joel-Brock echoed her quizzically.

"That's *player* to you, Joely. I actually pitch. I've won two games and saved a third in relief."

"Good for you, Fractoria," Addi said. "Did you have to sue the Cubby League to make them let you play?"

"No," the girl said. "Papa Pither threatened to cut off their funding."

"Ah," Mr. Valona said. "You're Mr. Borsmutch's great-granddaughter."

"Yes," Fractoria said. "Mama's his oldest daughter's middle darling, and I'm the apple of Papa Pither's crossed right eye."

"So he bribed the boys' league to take you?" Mr. Hudspeth said. "How proud you must be, young lady."

Fractoria turned to Augustus. "I can flat-out *play*, sir. And Papa Pither's threat to cut off funding was *not* a bribe. It was an *anti*-bribe."

Joel-Brock reckoned that if, in two weeks, the girl had won two games and saved a third, she had justified Papa Pither's faith in her. His father, Bryden, liked to quote an old player named Dizzy Dean's favorite comment

on this subject: *"It ain't bragging if you can back it up."* And the supposedly evil
Mr. Borsmutch had supported Fractoria's right to play.

"Why are you dressed like that?" Fractoria asked Augustus. She meant,
like a high-ranking Sporangial cleric.

"I'm taking these traitors to your great-granddad, Fractoria. May I
proceed with them up to his command center?"

"Traitors?" Fractoria said. "Joely is searching for his family. Would you
call it treason if *you* had to rescue kidnapped family members from an underground prison far from home?"

"My parents are dead, I have no siblings, and I'm *not* married."

"Maybe you would be, Augustus, if you were nicer."

Augustus curled his lip again. "So I may *not* deliver my captives, eh?"

"A good person would first take them to see the Lollises."

"I don't know where the Lollises are," Augustus lied.

"Go up to Papa Pither alone. Maybe he'll be glad to see you. In any case,
Joely-Pistoley must see his family."

Addi stage-whispered to Mr. Valona, "I like this girl."

Mr. Hudspeth, who clearly loathed having to bicker with an over-
privileged kid, spat out a single word: "*Criminy!*"

"Augustus," Mr. Valona said, "let Miss Scampi take Master Lollis and
Miss Coe to see his family. I'll go up with you to testify that you did your
duty."

"A wonderful idea," Fractoria Scampi told Mr. Valona.

And so, Mr. Valona and Augustus caught the express elevator to Bijou-
Lo, the Big Boss's private command center, and the three youths rode a
freight elevator to Level 3, where Mr. Borsmutch kept his prisoners, to let
Joel-Brock see for himself that the lost Lollises were still alive and kicking.

25

Reunited

Joel-Brock put a hand to his heart to muffle its pounding. He eyed Fractoria with equal measures of suspicion and interest, for he still viewed her as an abettor of his family's abduction. She had free run of all of Condor's Cote as well as Mr. Borsmutch's blessing to greet newcomers. But, despite her gawky height, she remained just a kid, a kid with an obvious sympathy for Joel-Brock's family. She'd even admitted that the old guy had had them kidnapped!

On the jailhouse level of his villa, Fractoria pushed a button to keep the freight-elevator door from opening. "We've taken *very* good care of the Lollises," she told Joel-Brock and Addi. "I've become a very close friend to Arabella and a second daughter to your parents, Joely-Pistoley—sort of, anyway."

"I'm not sure I'd brag about those things," Addi said.

Puzzlement colored Fractoria's face. "Brag? Who's bragging?"

"I just mean it's not unusual for hostages to develop ridiculous feelings of trust toward their captors."

"*Ridiculous?*" said Fractoria.

"Kidnappers have no right to a hostage's gratitude or friendship. The relationship of a kidnapper to a hostage has its basis in a crime, a *violent* crime."

"There *was* no violence," Fractoria said. "Some sprols brought the Lollises down here to learn more about Big Box Bonanzas."

"Against their will," Joel-Brock said. "They were pulled from our house by—"

"—brainwashed sporules," Addi concluded for him.

"That's just not so," Fractoria said, red-faced.

But Addi persisted: "How would you like it, Fractoria, if a crew of thugs dragged you out of your split-level home and carried you to, say, the county landfill . . . to 'learn more' about, say, waste disposal?"

"That's all wrong." Swaying like a young bamboo stalk, Fractoria wept.

Joel-Brock said, "Let us out. *Show* us the people you've made *friends* with." He saw Fractoria as a dupe of her great-grandfather's greed and ego, for she was clearly off-base about the old man's plans and motives.

"I sort of get," Fractoria said, "that Joel's family wasn't, like, *glad* to be here. That's why I let the dogs go. I knew you all were coming—Papa Pither said so—and I figured they'd find you."

"They *did* find us," Addi said. "If they hadn't, well, we . . ." She ran down.

Joel-Brock deliberately did not say that they would have reached Condor's Cote earlier if they had not had to dodge the sprol and gobbymawler posses trying to stop them dead in their tracks.

Fractoria said she'd fallen in love with the Lollis dogs, Sparky and Leo, canines taken from the Lollises' cells shortly after their arrival. Although they were fun to play with (and she had played with them a lot), feeding and cleaning up after them had grown tiresome. Sprols later assumed these duties, but Sparky and Leo found the sprols, even carrying food, so provoking that they could not stop barking or snapping at them. Finally, through the air ducts of some nearby cells, Arabella heard the dogs and asked Fractoria to somehow free them. Fractoria knew that Papa Pither would see that act as a betrayal and punish her severely.

"Still," said Fractoria, "I did it. I put Sparky and Leo on leashes and rode with them down to the sentry court. I told the guards that because Papa

Pither didn't want these yappy pooches in Condor's Cote anymore, he'd told me to let them go. The silly guards believed me and released them."

Addi asked, "Didn't you care what might happen to them in the caverns?"

"No. We've all heard stories about dogs, dumped far from home, finding their way back despite the dangers."

"Dangers like gorgástrogons?" Joel-Brock asked.

"Of course not. Anyway, Sparky and Leo sniffed you out, right?" Fractoria wiped her face and smiled toothily. Neither Joel-Brock nor Addi melted.

Joel-Brock said, "Release *us*, please."

Fractoria hit the button. The elevator door slid back, and a familiar tune flowed in upon them. Joel-Brock knew it as Arabella's oboe solo on "Mary Had a Little Lamb," with some very pretty grace notes.

*

The express elevator to the top floor of Condor's Cote and the sanctum called Bijou-Lo rose so fast that Mr. Valona hardly had time to blink before he and Augustus stepped into the domed rotunda there. On this dome, images from a stormy Himalayan sky moved in graceful hypnotizing sweeps. Mr. Valona covered his eyes.

"What's the matter, Vaughnathan—sick to your tummy?"

"You've been up here before." But *up here before* sounded funny to Mr. Valona, given that they had first traveled down to travel up.

"No," Augustus said. "This is my first time."

"I don't think so," Mr. Valona said, uncovering his eyes. "I think you and Pither M. Borsmutch are just like this." He crossed the index and middle fingers of his left hand and showed them to Augustus.

"Look, Vaughn, I've *never* set foot in this fortress before—Sporangium, yes, but Condor's Cote, no."

"Pardon me, but you're lying."

"You mistake me for someone who *cares* what you think. Come on. Let's go see Mr. Borsmutch now."

Augustus led Mr. Valona around the rotunda, a ring of alcoves in which various kinds of BBB merchandise were displayed. His slow progress around the circle soon led Mr. Valona to suspect that Augustus really had *not* set foot in this place before. Then they came to an alcove fronted by a ticket machine with a metal door. The door had a poster on it depicting purple mountains topped by a floating king's crown. A gold scroll beneath these mountains said:

Bijou-Lo, My Personal Promised Land

"Here—I think." Augustus rapped on the door. A light on the machine flashed on. Mr. Valona hit a button, and a slot spat out a ticket that read **Admit No One.** On its other side appeared these words:

Please sit in the rotunda until summoned.

Mr. Valona gave the ticket to Augustus, and each man sat on a stool, a tall one for Mr. Hudspeth and a short one for Mr. Valona. Both stools boasted round leather seats that sagged when sat upon, and the two men perched uncomfortably on these stools for what seemed a full hour.

Augustus finally said, "This sucks."

"Does it always happen this way?" Mr. Valona asked.

"I've already told you, twice—I've *never* met Mr. Borsmutch here."

"Yeah, right: You usually meet in a tobacconist's shop in Toronto."

"Hey, you're the security specialist. I've worked in Electronics two years, and this is my first top-secret assignment and just my third descent into Sporangium."

"Then you've done very well in a very short time."

"Thanks." Augustus's tone implied that he deserved even better treatment from Mr. Borsmutch. More minutes passed. Overhead, the stormy time-lapse sky yielded to one shot through with fluffy white clouds. Trying to rise, Augustus caught his foot on a rod at the stool's base, tripped, and fell over. He rolled to his knees, kipped to his feet, kicked clear of the stool, and peered down on Mr. Valona with a mysterious plea in his eyes. "You're my friend, aren't you, Vaughn?"

Mr. Valona had no idea how to reply. A short while ago, Augustus had said, "*You mistake me for someone who cares what you think.*"

"You don't wish me harm, do you?"

"No, but I'll lay more than harm on you if you threaten any of us Smalls again."

"Would you go easier on me if I told you my recent 'hostile' activities all stem from my following orders for an important secret purpose?"

"No," Mr. Valona said.

"You're not curious about what that purpose might be?"

Mr. Valona disliked this question. He could have replied, "No, you mistake me for someone who cares," but that seemed—well, *small*, in the absolute worst sense. And so he said nothing.

"Vaughn, I'm a double agent for Wardell Monger of Mongermart, Inc. BBB is eating Mongermart's lunch, but BBB's success derives from unfair practices and tricky workarounds of established business regulations."

"Have you considered that this rotunda might be bugged, Augustus?"

"Sure, but who puts bugs in his 'Personal Promised Land'?"

"We're not *in* Bijou-Lo. We're cooling our heels in its antechamber."

A speaker above them blared: **"Gentlemen, you may enter Mr. Borsmutch's command center, Bijou-Lo."**

And Mr. Valona thought, If the rotunda is bugged, poor Augustus may have more to worry about than I do. . . .

*

Addi, Joel-Brock, and Fractoria followed the strains of "Mary Had a Little Lamb" down the corridor to Arabella's cell. The corridor's walls were covered with ash-gray wallpaper printed to resemble bricks. At intervals between the real cells' doors were large cartoons of half-naked prisoners hanging from iron rings. These figures included classic comic-strip characters, the last three American presidents, three international beauty queens in tattered ball gowns, and Wardell Monger of Mongermart Inc.

Often, mechanical rats scurried along grubby baseboards in well-hidden grooves, and automated bats swooped on whoever was walking through, but veered off before hitting these pedestrians. Beneath Arabella's "Mary Had a Little Lamb" oboe melody, there played disquieting recordings of snapping whips, moaning prisoners, and torturers demanding confessions.

"Isn't this great?" Fractoria said. "It's almost like a real medieval prison."

"Except for Popeye, George, Miss Brazil, and that guy there," said Addi, nodding at the cartoon of skinny Wardell Monger in gray cartoon chains.

"They're just for grins," Fractoria said. "Papa Pither has a great sense of humor."

"It isn't great," Joel-Brock said. "It's sick."

"No, it's funny," Fractoria insisted.

Joel-Brock banged his fist on the wall. "It's sick. What if *you* were locked up here and you hadn't done anything wrong?"

"Who says the Lollises haven't done anything wrong? Your mama has slammed and labeled Papa Pither's wonderful store again and again."

"I think she means slandered and libeled," Addi said.

"My mama's told only the truth about BBB," Joel-Brock said. "And even if she'd lied—which she never has—what about my daddy and Arabella?"

Hands on hips, Fractoria said, "What about them?"

"What did *they* do wrong?"

Fractoria looked at Addi and turned ripe-tomato red.

"Nothing," Joel-Brock said. "They did nothing wrong, and neither did my mother. She just told some truths that pitiful Papa Pither *didn't like.*"

Fractoria glared at the boy. "Do you want to see your family or not?"

Addi stepped in front of Joel-Brock. "Of course he does. Why do you think we faced so much danger to get here?"

"Here!" Fractoria stopped at the door of the fifth room on their right, as Joel-Brock knew she might because of the oboe music issuing from behind it. The cartoon on this door—a skinny kid kneeling on a platform with a guillotine blade about to behead him—was horrifying. "She's in here. It's a room a lot more like a room in the Oglethorpe Suites than it's like a pig sty."

Joel-Brock wanted to believe her.

Fractoria slid a card shaped like a dollar sign into a slot on the door. A green light flashed there. Joel-Brock opened the door. Arabella stood inside with the reed of her oboe between her lips and her feet planted on reddish gym mats. The walls and ceiling were hung with this same reddish material, which would have muted the sound of her playing but for the microphone above the door and the speakers in the hall.

Arabella wore a garment combining the worst features of a hospital gown and a straitjacket, even if it left her arms free and did not expose her backside when she rushed to Joel-Brock to hug him. She was barefoot and covered with gooseflesh from a chill in the air like that in Sporangium Salt, Inc. *"Joely, Joely!"* she cried, scraping his neck with her oboe. Joel-Brock hugged her, but also gaped in disbelief at the cell Fractoria had just described as swank.

For a toilet and toilet tissue, the cell had a zinc bucket and scraps of torn-up cereal boxes. For bedding, it had cardboard boxes folded out for "mattresses" and "blankets." For wall decor, it had rips in the gym mats and

sayings scratched in them by fingernails or inked with smuggled-in Sharpies. Its walls also had hard-rubber hand- and footholds here and there so that prisoners could climb them for exercise.

Joel-Brock looked at Fractoria. "You call this *dump* an Oglethorpe Suite?"

"In comparison to a sewer in lower Cobb Creek, yes—yes I do."

As he had done in the corridor, Joel-Brock fumed. That Arabella, who at home endured from him such insults as *"Idiota"* and "Prisspot," should have received such treatment—well, it seriously steamed him. He was about to scold Fractoria from foot to forehead when Addi covered his mouth, and his sister, still crying, cradled her oboe and lowered her chin.

"You came," Arabella said. She looked at Addi, whom she thought she knew. "Thank you." She glanced at Fractoria, her recent confidante and playmate. "You won't put my friends in jail too, will you?"

"Me?"

"Your great-grandfather, I mean."

Very slowly, Fractoria said, "That's completely up to Papa Pither."

*

Mr. Valona entered Bijou-Lo seven steps behind Augustus Hudspeth. He half expected the old codger to slay them with a poison dart for their trouble. After all, Mr. Valona had taken the side of "traitors" and, even scarier, in the rotunda Augustus had admitted spying for Wardell Monger of Mongermart, Inc. But when Augustus and Mr. Valona entered, nothing happened—at least at first. So they looked around. The walls here consisted of aquarium tanks in which barracuda, gar, and several sharks swam like ancient fish in a dream world made of water only. Blessedly, the room enclosed by these tanks was itself *free* of water.

Its only furnishing was a wheeled scaffold within which Pither Borsmutch now rolled toward them. Two male gobbymawlers pushed this gantry and the booth inside it, which served its occupant as bedroom and office. The booth had curved plastic doors that his servants had opened outward, wholly revealing Papa Pither, like a prize inside a big holiday egg.

Papa Pither wore blue sunglasses and a thin blue robe that made him look like a big butterfly in a split cocoon. Straps held him in, though, so he would not tumble out. His aides had combed his thin white hair straight forward. His pale baby-slick skin was the hue of new mushrooms soaked in weak orange juice.

Oddly, Papa Pither of Big Box Bonanzas looked tiny, feeble, old, and no threat to anyone, much less to a hulk like Augustus Hudspeth.

Still, Mr. Valona kept up his guard.

Once they had pushed the living ghost of Pither Borsmutch into the center of his personal paradise, his aides stepped aside. They wore black suits, red ties, and polished slip-on shoes. The helper to their right picked up and held a bright-eyed dog that had waddled into the room after its owner. It had foxy ears and a bib of snow-white fur on its chest. With its white whiskers and grizzled amber coat, the dog looked ancient. Mr. Valona said, "A Welsh corgi. That breed came from dogs taken to Wales by Flemish weavers a thousand years ago."

The man holding the corgi ignored this remark and said, "Welcome, Augustus—and Vaughnathan."

"Who *are* you guys?" Mr. Valona asked.

"Agent Madison." The man glanced to his left. "And Agent Monroe." The second man smiled. "We're Mr. Borsmutch's sense organs. We assist and protect." The men had ordinary faces that would melt into forgettability as raindrops do into lake water.

"Can't Mr. Borsmutch speak for himself?" Mr. Valona asked.

"Sure," said Agent Madison, lifting the corgi, "with some help from his pal here."

Grinning, the corgi licked its lips. *"I am Pembroke,"* it said, *"and I am more or less pleased to meet you gentlemen. However, I am here under a sort of compulsion akin to your own."*

"You're the old man's mouthpiece," Augustus said.

"I don't dispute that I'm old, but I'm not your old man," said Mr. Borsmutch via Pembroke. *"If you can forgive my pickiness on that point, Augustus."*

"Oh, yes sir, of course I can."

"Tell me why you failed to capture Mr. Valona and his little friends before they got to Condor's Cote? You've hardly wrapped yourself in glory."

Mr. Valona said, "He *did* capture us. And we Smalls fought very hard to keep him from doing so."

"A midget and two kids? I wouldn't call you a formidable foe, detective, and yet you flummoxed our blundering Mr. Hudspeth repeatedly, didn't you?"

Agent Madison set Pembroke down, and he and Agent Monroe helped their Big Boss undo his straps and step from his gantry onto Bijou-Lo's floor, where he tottered like a wind-blown reed. His agents, both with pistols under their coats, backed up to give him and Pembroke more room. Meanwhile, a hammerhead shark in one tank caught sight of the corgi . . . or perhaps not. (Sharks have atrocious eyesight.)

"Sir," Augustus said, "I succeeded where a party from Condor's Cote failed."

Pembroke sniffed Augustus's shoes and then Mr. Valona's. He then sat up and asked, *"Where are the other two interlopers?"*

"On the detention level with your great-granddaughter," Augustus said.

"You should have brought them here too, Augustus."

"Why?" Mr. Valona asked. "What do you plan for them?"

Pembroke dogged his master's heels to the tank holding the hammerhead. *"Feed my fish, Madison,"* he told the agent who had held him. Then, to the other agent: *"Feed my fish, Monroe."* Mr. Borsmutch's words, Mr. Valona thought, strongly implied that he wanted to turn the Lollises and the Smalls into shark chow.

"No sir," Mr. Valona said: "You must let us *all* go."

"Feed my fish," the old man said through Pembroke. *"Feed my fish!"* Dapples of light from the shark tank rippled through Bijou-Lo. ***"Feed my fish!"***

*

Fractoria led Addi and Joel-Brock through Arabella's cell to a door hidden in the wall's matting. She slid her card into a slot, and the door cracked to reveal an adjoining cell. In it, two adult persons lay in each other's arms under a big piece of cardboard they'd torn in two to share with Arabella.

Joel-Brock thought of these cells as *rubber rooms* because the mats on their floors and walls were meant to keep the inmates from hurting themselves. He did not recognize the people as his parents—except by the cell's nearness to Arabella's—and he was afraid to check now. Maybe Papa Pither had engineered a cruel trick.

"That's why I compared these rooms to Oglethorpe Suites," Fractoria said.

Addi said, "Because they have a *connecting door*?"

"How many prison cells have connecting doors?" Fractoria asked.

"Just the ones whose wardens hope their inmates will go through them to knock each other's brains out," Addi said.

"Well, we don't do that here."

Joel-Brock walked into this second cell and knelt by the sleeping—*not* dead, thank God—couple. Eureka! There lay his dad, Bryden, and his mother, Sophia. Arabella knelt across from him, set her oboe aside, and smoothed back Bryden's hair. When Joel-Brock kissed Sophia, her face knotted as if she had seen something ugly in her sleep. When he kissed her again, Sophia's eyes opened in a way suggesting that they were tracking cruel dream images. Then her eyes, one with an ugly purple bruise beside it, focused, and she sat up, grabbed Joel-Brock, and rocked him.

"Joely, Joely, Joely," she said.

But to Joel-Brock's great pain, his hunger for this display of Sophia's love fled an instant after it had seized him. He could not rest in it, and Sophia, sensing his struggle, let go of him and lay back down.

Bryden awoke. Arabella nodded at the reunion occurring beside him. Bryden's eyes widened. He reached for Joel-Brock, lifted him over Sophia, and rubbed his bristly beard all over Joel-Brock's face.

"Stop," Joel-Brock said. "Stop, stop, stop, stop, *STOP!*"

"Who's going to gobble you up? Who's going to gobble you down?"

"Make up your m-mind," Joel-Brock cried, wriggling. "Is it up or d-d-down?"

Arabella tickled her brother lustily. He squealed and twisted even harder. Across the room, Fractoria covered her ears, and Joel-Brock, seeing her, hushed and struggled to his feet. Bryden, Sophia, and Arabella rose, too, and all four Lollises hugged.

Fractoria uncovered her ears. "I wish my daddy was as strong as yours."

"My daddy needs deodorant," Joel-Brock said. "And a razor, and a toothbrush, and some toothpaste."

"Well, *excuuuuuuse* me," said Bryden.

"Fractoria," Addi said, "why couldn't you all give your prisoners those things?"

"We could," the girl said. "Papa Pither's stores have caboodles of that stuff. But why would anybody in jail need them?"

Addi and the Lollises looked at her with undisguised scorn.

"Personal hygiene," said Bryden.

"Cleaner teeth," said Arabella.

"Better breath," said Joel-Brock.

"Fresher underarms," said Addi.

"A little self-esteem in a setting of stupid institutional cruelty," said Sophia.

And all five speakers nodded to one another in mutual satisfaction.

"How rude," Fractoria said. "We've been really good to you all."

Joel-Brock turned to her. "Then trade places with my family?"

"Pardon me?"

"Free them all and take their place in this . . . *suite*."

"Which isn't all that sweet," Arabella said.

"And see how *you* like it," Joel-Brock concluded.

Fractoria actually mulled this proposal, it seemed, but finally said, "Papa Pither would kill me."

"Would he *really* kill you?" Sophia Lollis asked. "Or *really* have you killed?"

"You know what I mean, ma'am."

"I do. So remember that he *really* had Bryden, Arabella, and me kidnapped. And because I questioned his business practices, he clapped us in these stinking rooms."

"I don't know what that means."

"*Clapped?* It means 'locked up' or 'jailed.'"

Joel-Brock grabbed Fractoria's wrists. "If you won't trade places, then loan us your key."

"My *key?*"

Addi said, "A device used to lock, or unlock, a door, window, or diary."

Fractoria said, "Ha-ha."

"Come on," Arabella pleaded. "Help us get our lives back."

"Loan us your master key," Joel-Brock said.

Fractoria lifted her head higher—it was already higher than Joel-Brock liked it—and sniffed his parents' funky prison chamber.

"All right." And she handed her dollar-sign card to Joel-Brock, who studied it as if it were the 1951 rookie baseball card of the great Willie Mays.

"Let's go," he said.

*

"Are you threatening to have us fed to these fishies?" Mr. Valona approached Mr. Borsmutch and Pembroke and knelt before the dog as if it were the smarter. The dog waddled backward, and Mr. Valona said, "Maybe you should feed the *fish* to your human prisoners, sir."

"*Nonsense,*" the corgi said. Because the movements of the dog's lips looked like cheap TV animation from Mr. Valona's boyhood, he seized

Pembroke's snout. The two agents started to close on Mr. Valona, but Mr. Borsmutch raised a frail hand.

"Speak!" Mr. Valona ordered Pembroke.

But because Pembroke could not now say the words that Mr. Borsmutch sent him, he moaned and whined instead.

And the old man, irked and out of patience, apparently stopped sending.

"If you won't speak," Mr. Valona told the corgi, "then *listen.*" He glanced at Papa Pither and got a slight nod. Mr. Valona let go of Pembroke, who again retreated. Then Mr. Valona stood to his full height, as unimpressive as most would have found it, so that he and the Big Boss faced each other eyeball to eyeball.

"Think of your legacy, sir," Mr. Valona began. "Think of your—"

Mr. Borsmutch turned to Agents Madison and Monroe, and Pembroke, his voice, told them to get out of Bijou-Lo *now* and to leave him in peace with his visitors from his foundational Cobb Creek store.

"We can't do that, sir," Agent Madison said. "We're under orders to—"

"*I said, Get out,*" Mr. Borsmutch said. "*I cancel those orders and direct you to the fourth-floor employee lounge for funnel cake and peach schnapps.*"

"But, sir, we can't just—"

"*Of course you can.*" Mr. Borsmutch pointed at the door. "*Go!*"

And the two agents slunk out. Mr. Valona and Augustus traded a look. Even with Bijou-Lo under surveillance, it seemed that by dismissing his agents Papa Pither had left himself at their disposal, maybe even their mercy.

26

Free at Last, Almost

G rab your heckelphone and come on," Bryden told Arabella, who picked up her oboe and trailed her dad out of their shabby cell.

Joel-Brock, Addi, Fractoria, and Sophia had already gone on ahead.

"He'll kill me, he'll kill me," Fractoria muttered.

Bryden surged past those now in the hall and seized Joel-Brock by his shirt. "Give me the key card, Joely."

The boy obeyed, and Bryden moonwalked past Addi, Fractoria, and his family down the hall, *away from* the elevators. At each door, he slotted the card, opened the cell, and bid its prisoners forth. As they emerged, he asked them to join their march on Bijou-Lo. Some did, but others, broken in body or soul, stayed in their cells. Those who came out, though, joined Bryden,

Addi, the other Lollises, and a sub- dued Fractoria at the bank of eleva- tors.

Bryden asked Fractoria how many people could ride the express elevator up. Ten, she said, but may- be seven *comfortably*. What about the freight elevator? he asked aloud.

Fractoria said twenty-seven could board it, but that it ran only between the first and fifth floors, down to the courtyard or up to the Level 5 offices. Up

there, anybody wishing to meet Papa Pither had to get clearance and take the express elevator.

"What about the sixth floor?" Bryden asked Fractoria.

Fractoria said that no one got off there but family. She *lived* there, along with her grandmother, Bambi Borsmutch Scampi, and her folks, Jake and Natalie Scampi. Natalie ran an online mail-order business from Level 6, a business in direct competition with Big Box Bonanzas—but everyone pretended that she sold only specialty items like lifeboats for yachts and gold hubcaps for luxury cars. As for Jake, he traveled to Sierra Leone, Bangladesh, Singapore, and Saint-Tropez for Papa Pither and maybe even for Natalie. Mostly, it was *boring* on the sixth floor. That was why Fractoria often roamed Level 3 making friends with Papa Pither's happy captives.

Gathered in the hall in ripe clothes and riper bewilderment, these happy captives waved at Fractoria. Or a few did. Most, Joel-Brock noted, looked weary and unsure of what Bryden had planned. Besides his own family and Addi, he counted sixteen captives. Fractoria, of course, did not qualify as a prisoner.

"We'll take the freight elevator to Level 5," Bryden said.

Fractoria's face clouded. "You want all these people to see Papa Pither?"

"You've got some say-so with those Level 5 employees, I'll bet. Persuade them to let us *all* go up to Bijou-Lo."

"I don't think Papa Pither would like that."

"He doesn't have to like it," Sophia said. "But justice demands he hear us out."

Fractoria looked around for Justice, a blindfolded woman with scales and a sword. The absence of Justice gave her pause, and then an inspiration.

"You're probably right," she said. "Let's go."

"Wait," Bryden said. "You can really get us permission?"

"Piece o' pancake." Fractoria keyed open the freight-elevator door and bade them enter. Twenty-one persons did, and, before the door shut, she joined them, with a last-second assist from Bryden.

Despite his natural shyness, Joel-Brock moved about introducing himself to the other passengers. He squeezed among them as agilely as a mouse exploring a block of Swiss cheese, popping up now and again to ask each prisoner why he or she was being held in Condor's Cote. He met a former greeter from Grand Junction, Colorado, who had recruited other BBB workers to join an anti-BBB organization called Stall-the-Sprawl. He met a truck driver from Trabzon, Turkey, who had tried to start a union among the BBB drivers at work across Eurasia. He met a checker from Hardy, Arkansas, who had written letters to the *Memphis Commercial Appeal* and the *Little Rock Democrat-Gazette* complaining of unpaid overtime work, and a shelf-stocker from Sheboygan, Wisconsin, who had blown the whistle on managers who'd locked him and his fellow workers overnight in their store on eight separate occasions. None of these people struck Joel-Brock as malcontents, loafers, or troublemakers. But what did he know?

Fractoria knew all these people too. But the inmates had never met *one
another* before. Now, they traded stories about their ill treatment at the hands
of buddypards, sales clerks, managers, and public-relations chiefs. Shaking
from scalp to toe, Fractoria gaped at these animated people in surprise and
resentment.

"What's the matter?" Addi asked. "Didn't you ever ask Papa Pither's prisoners to tell you their stories?"

"I told them," Fractoria replied, "about how I'd be the first woman to
pitch for the Yankees. I took them sausage biscuits and cinnamon rolls from
our personal chefs. I told them how one day I'd open a restaurant on Broad-
way and—" She broke off and eyed the chattering captives. "They never told
me *any* of the stuff they're saying now."

"They didn't trust you," Addi said.

"I was *good* to them!"

"They thought the Big Boss had sent you down to spy on them."

"I was their friend."

"Not if you didn't ask them their stories, Fractoria."

Creaking in its cables, the freight elevator hit Level 5 and released
its passengers into a suite of glass-partitioned offices. Fractoria, Addi, the
Lollises, and sixteen refugees from the cells on Level 3 bumbled about here
like smoke-drugged bees until a woman in a black jacket-and-skirt outfit
came over from the glass-walled office nearest the elevator. Fractoria seized
her hands.

"Ms. Herbroth," she said, "these people want to see Papa Pither."

"Are they detainees undergoing second-step retraining procedures?"

"Is that Greek for 'brainwashing'?" Joel-Brock asked.

"Don't call Security," Fractoria said. "They just want to thank Papa Pither
for his efforts to return them to work as buddypards in good standing."

"They must first return to work as buddypards in good odor."

Sophia Lollis snapped, "I was *never* a buddypard of any standing or odor, just a shopper offended by your store's many unchecked abuses."

Fractoria took Sophia's hand. "Here at Condor's Cote," she told Ms. Herbroth, "Mrs. Lollis has come a long way managing her anger. She plans to *become* a shopper in good standing, and they *all* want to thank Papa Pither."

In a much more respectful tone, Sophia said, "Yes, it's true."

"Papa Pither likes to meet persons being retrained," Fractoria said.

"I don't know," Ms. Herbroth said. "I should *ping* Mr. Borsmutch."

"Go ahead. Tell him his great-granddaughter has a special request."

Ms. Herbroth smiled a mouth-only smile. "Give me a minute." She withdrew to a glass cubicle to confer with a male coworker.

"Way to go," Addi told Fractoria.

Sophia apologized for nearly ruining Fractoria's efforts to get them all up to Level 7.

"It's just that everything about this upsets me," she finished.

"Like what?" Fractoria asked.

"Our kidnapping," Sophia said. "Our imprisonment, my worries about Joel-Brock and our animals, Papa Pither's horrid brainwashing sessions, But do you know what really steams my clams? Nearly everyone here assumes that lies or bribes will buy me off and make me join the bad guys."

"Lies?" Fractoria said. "Bribes? Bad guys?"

"Okay, call the lies half- or quarter-truths. As for the bribes, they're disguised as gifts or as payments for services to come later, so they're also partial truths. But, usually, only bad guys lie and bribe, right?"

Joel-Brock's nerves began to twist. Ms. Herbroth and her fellow worker in the glass cubicle appeared to be arguing.

Meanwhile, Sophia reported that on Condor's Cote's second floor, Papa Pither's questioners showed his hostages videos hailing the riches that Big Box Bonanzas brought to any city it took root in. They touted "wonderful products at unbeatable prices." They celebrated the company's plans to offer better service, fairer hiring practices, better pay, more locally made goods, *et cetera, et cetera.*

"All that's true," Fractoria said.

"Maybe," Sophia said. "But your great-grandpa does a lot of that just to offset bad press and public anger with his stores' regular practices."

"That's sort of vague, ma'am."

"Talk to the greeter from Colorado, the fellow from Turkey, Miss Childress from Arkansas, or the guy from Wisconsin." Sophia waved at those milling about between the elevator and the glass cubicles. "They'll give you details."

Addi said, "Ask me about dead-peasant insurance or my mama, Tara Abbot Coe."

Ms. Herbroth returned, smoothing her skirt. "Only the *boy* can go up with you. Everyone else stays here until we've received word that Mr. Borsmutch really wants to see this, well, this unkempt rabble."

"Didn't you ask him that?" Fractoria demanded.

"Mr. Borsmutch said he was 'momentarily indisposed.' We don't know exactly what he meant by that, but—"

"It means he doesn't feel too well, Ms. Herbroth."

"Yes, Fractoria, we got the 'indisposed' part. It's the 'momentarily' part that confuses us. How *long* does he need to give us a solid answer?"

Fractoria asked her own question: "Didn't he tell you?"

"No. He asked us to send you and Master Lollis up to see how your session with him goes. Then he'll decide what action to take next. He can't tolerate a crowd right now. Take it or leave it."

Addi blurted, "Well, I'm going too."

Ms. Herbroth gave Addi a sharp look. "Everybody knows three's a crowd. You can't just invite yourself."

"They've already got a small crowd up there," Sophia said.

"Oh?"

"A pair of buddypard bodyguards and two hires from the Cobb Creek store. How will this sweet poppet of a girl make that group any more of a crowd?" Sophia's speaking up for Addi gave Joel-Brock a toasty glow.

"If Sophia and I can't go," Bryden said, "I second my wife's endorsement."

Ms. Herbroth looked over her glasses at Addi and Joel-Brock. "You two are *not* joined-at-the-hip Siamese twins. The girl stays here."

"Then *I* won't go," Joel-Brock declared. "We'll spread out and hang around here until you all get used to a *real crowd*, okay?"

Ms. Herbroth said, "Wait," and left to talk to her coworker. She quickly returned to report that Fractoria could escort the two remaining Smalls up to Bijou-Lo. However, she wanted an authorized end to the "refugee situation" on Level 5 and timely word that Mr. Borsmutch was all right.

Joel-Brock Lollis and Addi Coe traded a soft high-five and boarded the private lift to Level 7 with Fractoria Scampi.

27

Crisis in Bijou-Lo

As soon as Mr. Borsmutch's two aides had left, a device in his wheeled gantry emitted a *ping*. The old man tottered over to it, reached inside it, and tapped out "I'm here" to his caller. Via Pembroke, he muttered, *"What a bother,"* but typed equally curt replies to two other brief messages.

"Is everything all right?" Mr. Valona asked.

"Is anything ever *all right?"* The old man returned to his visitors in front of the aquarium wall, and the hammerhead shark swam by.

To his shame, Mr. Valona had just considered dropping this old man into the tank as shark chow. He felt sure that Augustus, even dressed as a cleric, would have helped him. But all the tanks rose to this paradise's ceiling—or higher—and he couldn't find any place through which to insert Papa Pither into the water.

'Now, Vaughnathan," Mr. Borsmutch said. *"What did you mean by advising me to 'think of my legacy'?"*

"Adding kidnapping to your sins will soil the Borsmutch name for decades."

"You've more faith in public memory than I. The day after I die, the name Pither Borsmutch will have less resonance than does the great Alvah Roebuck's."

Mr. Hudspeth stepped forward. He towered over Mr. Valona and Mr. Borsmutch, whose profits he hoped to sabotage by spying for a rival just as corrupt, the avaricious Wardell Q. Monger. His vivid red robes lent him a bulk verging on the terrifying.

"Why are you dressed like that, Augustus?" Mr. Borsmutch said.

"I'm recruiting sprols to overthrow your regime, and I thought this a potentially effective way to do it."

"You're in my domain now, and we're recording everything you say. In less than five minutes, you'll be surrounded, hog-tied, and totally neutralized, Augustus. What do you think about that?"

"You haven't got five minutes, sir." Mr. Hudspeth bent as if to seize the old man, but Pembroke darted forward, bit him on the nose, and waddled aside as blood gushed from the gash that the corgi had inflicted. Mr. Hudspeth dropped to his knees and cupped both hands over his nose.

As the shark in the aquarium whipped into view, Mr. Valona wondered at this violent outburst as well as at Mr. Borsmutch's lurch toward the fish tank and his collapse in front of the hammerhead. Mr. Hudspeth hadn't even touched him, but the founder and CEO of the most profitable business in the world lay on his side before the walleyed gaze of a hovering shark. Pembroke began to bark.

"Help me," Mr. Hudspeth kept saying: "Help me."

"In a second." Mr. Valona knelt to check the old man's pulse. He didn't have one, or not much of one. "I believe he may be in cardiac arrest."

On his knees, Augustus said, "Let the scumbag die." His fingers, wrists, and robes shone with a spreading redness.

"My CPR certification lapsed long ago," Mr. Valona said and ducked into the rotunda for help. "Hasn't anybody here got a defibrillator?" he demanded of its ceiling. Then he shouted, "Agent Madison! Agent Monroe!"

An elevator door in the rotunda opened, and Joel-Brock, Addi Coe, and Fractoria Scampi burst from it. Even in the elevator, they'd overheard the commotion in Bijou-Lo. Fractoria saw Mr. Valona and screamed at him to help Papa Pither. She tugged him back to the command center, where Mr. Hudspeth continued to strain his nosebleed through crimson fingers. Addi

and Joel-Brock entered and gaped at the fish-filled walls and the gantry housing Papa Pither's booth. They marveled at the shelves of old books, which ran like spokes from the middle of the command center to the curved glass aquaria. They also stared at the two men on the floor: one almost a giant, the other a pathetic ventriloquist's figure.

Fractoria shoved Mr. Valona. "Do CPR! You know how, don't you?"

"Chest compressions? I might be able to, but I could break the old guy's ribs."

"So what? He'll die if you don't."

As if not able to help, Mr. Valona lifted his arms.

Fractoria turned to Mr. Hudspeth. "What about you? Can you do it?"

"I don't want to and I won't," he said defiantly. "What about you? You're a big girl, and blood kin to the bastard."

Fractoria shook her head and began to blubber.

"I'll do it," Joel-Brock said. "Our ball coach, Mr. Mirsky, taught us." Fractoria hugged him so hard that he wriggled free in self-defense. "And I won't even crack his lizardy ribs."

"Joely!" Fractoria said, still blubbering. "But have you done it before?"

"Only on a practice dummy. The dummy lived, Coach Mirsky told me."

"Then do it. I'll go for help—*real* help." She broke for the door, but stopped to scold Joel-Brock for dithering: "Go ahead. Start now."

"Get out your yNaut," Joel-Brock told Mr. Valona.

"You're wasting time!" Fractoria screamed through her tears.

Joel-Brock straddled Papa Pither to give him a series of chest pumps at the one-hundred-beats-per-minute rhythm of an old rock anthem called "Another One Bites the Dust." Before he began, though, he asked Mr. Valona to put through a call to his elder self, J.-B. Lollis. Then he used the heels of his hands to straight-arm the old man's small, flabby pecs.

"Good," Fractoria cried. "Keep going." She hurried into the rotunda and hopped the elevator back down to Level 5 or lower. Pembroke followed, barking and wagging his tail, but Fractoria let the door close on him.

*

Mr. Hudspeth lay back and spread his arms like the wings of a mutant giant condor. Mr. Valona struggled with the yNaut. But, once, he *had* broken through to J.-B. Lollis, future Atlanta Braves star, and, now, he worked to do so again, and succeeded. "I've got him—I've actually got him!"

"Ask if I'm doing the right thing, giving Papa Pither CPR."

Mr. Valona obeyed and held the yNaut toward Joel-Brock so he could hear the reply of his future avatar:

"Joby," said Joel-Brock's older self, *"at this point in* my *trip underground, I just couldn't do what you're doing, and Mr. Borsmutch died. As a result, I never saw Mama, Dad, or Arabella again."*

"Gee," Joel-Brock said, still pushing and letting go. "Gee!"

"Did my refusal to help him trigger their deaths, or would their deaths have happened anyway? I think maybe it was me not helping, Joby."

Mr. Valona spoke into the yNaut: "Then he's doing the right thing?"

"I think so. If I were him—and I am him*—I'd keep the chest-only CPR going. Some people say 'no good deed goes unpunished,' but I don't believe that. I believe the reverse: No* foul *deed goes unpunished. Or I try to."*

Joel-Brock sort of got the gist of this philosophy and kept giving CPR: *"And another one bites . . . And another one bites . . . And another one bites the dust!"* But even his rhythmic chest compressions did not guarantee success. Coach Mirsky liked to note that after the shock and shutdown of a heart attack, *fewer than ten percent* of those receiving CPR survive. . . .

*

Then why even do it? Luc Winter had asked Coach.

Because without it a person in cardiac arrest has almost no chance at all, Coach Mirsky told Luc, Joel-Brock, and the other boys. Zilch. Nada.

But one out of ten is a crappy *survival rate! Luc Winter yelped. I'd feel rotten doing all that for nothing.*

Would you feel terrific sitting on your hands and watching the victim die?

Well, no. So they all had a whack at the practice mannequin and joked about how they hoped whoever had an "episode" at a ballgame turned out to be a "babe" like Luc's mama. Luc blushed, and the dummy, after their strenuous efforts, wound up looking more depressed than a Florida sinkhole.

Listen, guys, you're just trying to keep the victim's brain alive until a pro with a defibrillator shows up to restart the heart. You're trying to . . .

*

Addi knelt behind Joel-Brock. "If you get tired," she said, "maybe I can do it."

Papa Pither looked dead to Addi. His milky eyes were neither focused nor closed, and his body bucked every time Joel-Brock pressed his chest. If he had need of advanced care—and it seemed he did—he'd best come around before his ribs all shattered or Joel-Brock's arms dropped off.

"I'm okay!" Joel-Brock resumed humming, *un*tunefully, "Another One Bites the Dust." Meanwhile, the shark in the tank swam as near as it could to the boy's unceasing labors.

Mr. Hudspeth stood and used the sleeve of his robe for a towel. The sleeve was now a shocking red. Mr. Valona, agitated by this sight, looked back out into the rotunda again to see if any additional help had arrived.

It had. Fractoria exited the elevator pulling a sprol dressed like a 1950s high-school hoodlum: white T-shirt, crisp blue jeans, and black alligator loafers polished like mirrors. She and this lanky mushroom lad entered Bijou-Lo. The lad set a defibrillator box down beside Mr. Borsmutch and showed with a hand chop that Joel-Brock should stop doing CPR and move aside.

Addi sprang up. She knew the sprol and, to keep from saying his name, retreated several steps. She did not want to distract him from restarting the old man's heart. Even so, the sprol's name—the one he'd used as a gobby-mawler—tolled like a knell within her: *Manny Obello, Manny Obello, Manny Obello.*

For a time, they had dated, sort of. Worse, he'd driven the truck that had carried the Lollises from Crabapple Circle to the delivery dock of Big Box Bonanzas. Now, apparently, Manny lived in Condor's Cote, not as a prisoner on Level 3 but as a guest on Level 6. He had earned this reward for contributing to the capture of Sophia Lollis and her family—except Josie the Chihuahua, Will S Gato, and Joel-Brock the Brave. That he had not been demoted for failing to nab Joel-Brock along with the others amazed Addi, for everybody knew that the Big Boss hated slip-ups and punished each and every worker prone to them.

Here, Manny jolted Papa Pither's sick ticker into ticking again. He then gave two thumbs up and leaned back to give Mr. Borsmutch room to breathe.

"*Thanks, Manny,*" Pembroke said for the old man. "*You saved my life.*"

Addi moved forward and told Mr. Borsmutch, "Manny restarted your heart, but Joel-Brock kept your blood flowing and your brain alive till Manny could do that. Or you'd be a veggie now—a baby carrot, maybe—and not a live megalomaniac, with all of Sporangium, and a lot of the world above it, as your personal mushroom bed."

Mr. Borsmutch's pale eyes stared up into the light. _"Who . . . called me . . . a megalomaniac?"_

"I did." Addi knelt over the old man and alternately gave him and Manny Obello the stink-eye. Manny sidled away. "I'm Adelaide-Bridget Coe. You made the Lollises hostages to your greed. You also murdered my mama."

"That's enough," Pembroke said, and neither Joel-Brock nor anyone else in the room could tell if the dog or Mr. Borsmutch had spoken. _"It's more than enough."_ Ah, it was definitely Mr. Borsmutch talking. _"Where is this Joel-Brock kid . . . who rescued . . . my brain and me . . . from oblivion?"_

Joel-Brock moved so that Mr. Borsmutch could see him. He felt pride and horror at having saved the old man's failing heart, treacherous mind, and very life.

Mr. Borsmutch squinted up _"Thank you, Joel-Brock. I owe . . . I owe you."_

"Yes sir, big time."

And now Agents Madison and Monroe, along with security guards, medicos, and other Borsmutch family members arrived in the rotunda and edged into Bijou-Lo. Their arrival set the hungry hammerhead stirring, as if it hoped to slide by a watery magic into another tank.

"About time . . . you got here," Mr. Borsmutch said. _"I almost . . . passed."_ He opened and closed his eyes slowly two or three times. _"Right now . . . I feel so bad . . . I'd have to . . . uh . . . get better to . . . die."_

"Then don't get better," Joel-Brock said.

A flicker of surprise lit the old man's eyes.

"Here's what you owe me: Let all your hostages go. You're a business man, not a prison warden or a judge."

"Or the dictator of the world," Mr. Valona interjected.

"*Okay,*" Mr. Borsmutch managed, "*I hereby . . . free . . . my hostages.*"

"Next, let all the hostages from Level 3 come up here and tell you in person how you've like totally demolished their lives."

"*Uh-uh,*" Mr. Borsmutch gasped, "*I won't . . . do that.*"

A sprol medic put a line in his arm and electrode pads on his chest, flanks, and belly, and Agent Madison blurted, "Did none of you geniuses look for a defibrillator in Bijou-Lo?" He strode to the gantry, reached in, and pulled out a device just like the one Manny Obello had carried in.

"See this? See this? See this?" he chanted in scorn.

He's covering his rear, Joel-Brock thought. To Mr. Borsmutch he said, "Yes, you will. —Finally, pay a fine to everyone you ever locked up and give them their jobs back, if they want them. Then swear you'll never do anything like this again and write out the promise in your blood."

"*My blood?*" The old guy grinned in a ghastly way. "*I'll do it . . . in Augustus's blood. . . . He's got plenty . . . to spare.*"

Wow. Mr. Borsmutch had just said something funny. Of course, he'd said it at the expense of a two-timing double agent, Augustus Hudspeth.

28

Gobbymawler Park

Doctors and nurses filed into Bijou-Lo to treat Mr. Borsmutch with shots, IV drips, and other curious nostrums. Two interns lifted him into his gantry. Within it, he reminded Joel-Brock of the oyster-like Martian pilots in the walking war machines in *The War of the Worlds*. But the old man was easier to see in his booth than were those oyster brains in their huge tripods, and he *glowed* with health as Pembroke hopped up into the gantry and perched beside his master on a red satin cushion.

When the old man could see visitors, the freed captives from Level 3—Bryden, Sophia, and Arabella among them—came via elevator to Bijou-Lo. Owing to the shark and the other tropical fish in its walls, the room felt overstuffed, and Pembroke spoke up to deliver this message: *"We must all venture aboveground for a parley."* A doctor told Mr. Borsmutch not to overexert by talking, but he replied, *"Modern medicine has saved my life. I feel great."*

"Then you're a lucky man," Sophia said softly. "A very lucky man."

"So lucky that I will not further trouble my physicians. Medical personnel, take your leave. Everyone else, into the rotunda with me!"

When the medicos departed, Mr. Borsmutch drove his gantry into the rotunda and halted, with the Lollises, the Smalls, his former captives, and a few other annoying patrons—besides Joel-Brock's mother—gathered all about him.

"Draw up closer, you all. Pull in. Pull in."

Fractoria had also come, and she directed everyone to do as he asked. Promptly, a wide tubular lift in the center of the floor began to ascend: a pillar of flexible metal that had been coiled in the space between Levels 7 and 6. Everyone in the rotunda seized a neighbor for support, but the trucker from Turkey rolled off the rising disc and fell to the floor below with a thud. Panicked, he reached after his ascending friends, but they soon attained the dome, which split open to admit them into the cavern under the rocky ceiling of Greater Sporangium.

"Goodbye!" the trucker yelled to those departing. "Goodbye!"

Sophia and Bryden held Joel-Brock tight. Arabella, bracing herself, played part of a number called *Ascend* on her oboe. (How appropriate.) Also nearby, Mr. Valona and Addi clutched each other, but Mr. Hudspeth was nowhere to be seen. Well, Joel-Brock hardly missed him, and despite the dizzying rush of their rise, he had not felt this safe in weeks.

*

The wide top of the pillar stopped flush with a circular area at the center of four Cubby League fields in Gobbymawler Park, seven miles west of Cobb Creek. This was a recreational complex built by Big Box Bonanzas, Inc., meaning that Mr. Borsmutch had paid for it. He had also named the park—to spite those people who used *gobbymawler* to insult any person in his tyrannical employ. The townsfolk did not like the name, but they could not overrule the man who had funded the park.

In any case, once Mr. Borsmutch had lifted his ex-captives out of Sporangium, and the Smalls and Agents Madison and Monroe along with them, he drove his gantry to a field at one corner of the complex and parked in front of a set of three-tiered bleachers. Everyone who had ridden the pillar-lift from Condor's Cote hiked to them and clambered into the bleachers to find a seat.

It was night, but only Mr. Borsmutch's bodyguards knew the hour. Stadium lights came on, half-blinding everyone. Arabella, who had made a quiver of torn wall matting for her oboe, snuggled up to Bryden and breathed the air of freedom for the first time in a long while.

To Joel-Brock's amazement, Sophia stood near the gantry to act as Mr. Borsmutch's prosecutor. "You've starved thousands," she accused. "Your henchmen have browbeaten, brainwashed, starved, and stuck in solitary so many innocents that Justice herself cries out for justice!" Immediately, Agents Madison and Monroe leapt from the bleachers to silence Sophia, but when they tried to take over Pembroke's job and speak for him, his former hostages booed them and stamped their feet.

"It's our turn! It's our turn! It's our turn!" they chanted.

One at a time, they told of hardships that Mr. Borsmutch and Big Box Bonanzas had inflicted on them. Their stories painted their tormentor as a scofflaw and his various stores as torture pits. Joel-Brock began to feel queasy. Others shouted, wept, tugged their hair, or stared at the ground. Joel-Brock regretted not starting rescue efforts sooner and failing to imagine what his family had suffered. The stench of the victims' unwashed bodies heightened his queasiness and his pity. Many of them, along with Arabella and the other Smalls, sobbed quietly or in wrenching gulps.

Mr. Borsmutch peered from his gantry with annoyance, but did not drive away. Agent Madison tried to deny all the horrific stories, but Sophia squelched him every time with a stinging rebuke: "Hush. It's not your turn to talk."

The stars moved across the sky, and, eventually, every hostage who wanted to speak had spoken. Then, and only then, did Sophia grab a strut of the old man's gantry and tell him: "Okay, sir. You may respond."

Agent Madison spread wide his arms, as if offering the captives of Condor's Cote something valuable. "I don't think—" he began.

Mr. Borsmutch broke in raspingly, using his own voice box, not the phony one in Pembroke's throat: "I can *speak* for myself." He held the corgi's snout to keep the dog from talking, and when Agent Madison said, "Good for you, sir," he told his aide to shut up and sit down. Agent Madison tucked tail and sat.

Everyone else in the bleachers looked on expectantly.

"I've heard your stories," Mr. Borsmutch said. "I deeply sympathize. I will repay you for all the slights that my feckless middle-management gobbymawler underlings have inflicted on you, as either patrons or employees. I've noted all Big Box Bonanzas' lapses, and I will repay you for all your inconveniences."

"Reimbursing us for our 'inconveniences' isn't enough, sir," Sophia said.

Agent Madison stood again. "What would you consider 'enough'?"

"Shut up," Mr. Borsmutch told Agent Madison. "Sit down."

Glumly, Agent Madison again obeyed his boss.

Mr. Borsmutch said, "Why not, Mrs. Lollis? What would *you* consider enough?"

"Yes, you must make reparations, but you and your BBB accomplices must also go to prison."

"I'm sure they'll do that," Mr. Borsmutch replied pleasantly.

"And so will you," Sophia told him. "And so will you."

Silence fell on Gobbymawler Park. The stars jangled a little, and Joel-Brock felt a surge of adrenalin that somewhat offset the queasiness prompted by the stories of those wounded by the old man's machinations. Still, telling their stories had begun to ease their heartbreak and blunt their bitterness.

*

And then Fractoria appeared, walking from a restroom near the center of Gobbymawler Park. Joel-Brock surmised that after hearing one terrible story too many and heading to a toilet to throw up, she was now ready to speak for Papa Pither.

And so, wearing her clean Gobbymawler baseball uniform, fingering her silver-blonde ponytail, and towering over Sophia Lollis, she confidently addressed the crowd: "My great-grandfather is old and sick and doesn't belong in prison."

"Yes he does!" cried Henry Milburn, a buddypard manager who had traveled to a factory in Central America to settle with the families of workers burned to death in two separate fires there. But because Henry had been unable to talk the grieving Salvadorans into taking BBB's "remunerations," he came home to tell Mr. Borsmutch that the factory there skimped on fire-safety measures so that Big Box Bonanzas could undersell Monger Mart and other in-country competitors. Papa Pither fired Henry.

"My wife and I could no longer afford the medicines to keep our daughter Trudy alive," Henry said. "She died seven months ago. I got a lawyer. Shortly after, I wound up in a rubber room in Condor's Cote. So, young woman, your great-grandfather does in fact belong in prison."

Fractoria, crying now, said, "That was all the doings of crooked underlings, sir." She smeared away her tears, but, to Joel-Brock's astonishment, they flowed and flowed and flowed.

"And *they*'ll definitely go to prison," Mr. Borsmutch said.

Cascades of objections poured down on him.

"Wait!" Fractoria said. "Listen: We should play a Cubby League game to settle this. Our Big Box Bonanzas Gobbymawlers challenge an all-star team from our other league teams. If the All-Stars win, Papa Pither goes to prison. If the Gobbymawlers win, he doesn't. Whaddaya say?" Still crying, Fractoria faced the outraged crowd with as big a smile as she could manage.

Silence greeted her proposal. Earthworms plunged deeper, sprigs of grass on the infield uncoiled, and Joel-Brock heard them all. Then Sophia turned to the girl and said, "You're *kidding*, right? Nobody sane allows the outcome of a ballgame to decide a black-and-white moral issue, Fractoria."

Everyone laughed, but Arabella hurried down to the field to wrap her arms around Fractoria, and the laughter ceased. Then the sprinklers buried in the ball field came on, sparkling like tiny geysers, and many former captives ran from the stands onto the field. Almost everyone but Sophia, Mr. Borsmutch, his aides, and Fractoria joined in. And as the hostages ran, they tossed aside their clothes to dance in their underwear among the geysers like children. It had been too long since they'd last showered or romped, but now they did both, laughing as they spun, but in joy rather than in mockery.

This was a bad moment for Fractoria, reader, but she told Arabella to cavort with the others, and it may please you to learn that she grew into a humane adult who lived the remainder of her ninety-plus years with purpose and grace. . . .

A Cobb Creek police car pulled into Gobbymawler Park. It cruised toward them. As Sophia watched, Mr. Borsmutch leaned toward her from his seat and rasped, "Those imbeciles are dancing in sewage slurry. It's just not that cost-effective to irrigate with treated water."

Sophia cringed at these words, but said, "Well, they're having fun, and it's quite likely even sewage water is purer than your polluted soul."

Mr. Borsmutch blinked.

The squad car parked, and an officer strolled over to the bleachers. "Evening," he said, touching his cap brim. "What's going on here, ma'am?"

"We've escaped from an illegal underground prison," Sophia said. "Please arrest this man." She nodded at Pither M. Borsmutch, whom the lawman viewed with curiosity and amaze.

"On what charge or charges, ma'am?"

"Let me see," Sophia replied. "Start with kidnapping and go on to illegal human resource practices, illegal *non*-human resource practices, and, well, you name it."

"Yes ma'am," the officer said. "Stay here," he told Mr. Borsmutch. And walking like a bow-legged cowboy, he strolled to his car.

"I'll get you for this," Mr. Borsmutch told Sophia.

"No you won't," Sophia said.

Pembroke, now out of a job, dozed on and on.

29

Arabella's Coda: 2010

Just like everyone else tripping through the sprinklers on that lit-up field, I got *soaked*, but I didn't take off most of my clothes to do it. I just ran for the joy of running and the hope of washing from my skin the stink of captivity in Condor's Cote. You'd have done the same in my situation, I imagine.

As soon as we all got home, Mama made me take a hot bath. She sent me ahead of Joel-Brock because although he had carried out a valorous mission with the other two Smalls (Mr. Valona and Addi Coe), he had not spent as much time in Sporangium as we three abductees, the Malodorous Lollises. But did I mind? Oh, no! Soaking in steamy-hot water at my leisure felt scrumptious.

The officer who'd come to Gobbymawler Park at two in the morning called for backup. He listened to what my parents told him about what had happened to us and the released prisoners, but he also heard Papa Pither tell a lie about how we'd "crashed" his park while he, his bodyguards, and his sad dog were running a test on some new stadium lights. Anyway, when backups arrived and questioned the lame old coot, they decided he was either sick or spacey. His bodyguards clammed up, and Pembroke the corgi kept on cushion-snoozing.

Lawyers were summoned—not by us, but by Pither M. Borsmutch, whose middle initial, Daddy swore, stood for Menteur. *Menteur* is French for "liar," but I had not even known that Daddy spoke it. Mr. Borsmutch's lawyers couldn't prevent his arrest, but they did buy him a get-out-of-jail card with his own bail money.

Although Mama tried hard to stop that injustice, she could not. "Life isn't always fair," she told Joel-Brock and me. Then, using a line I have always loved, she said, "But that doesn't mean *you all* can't be."

*

I don't have a head for lawyering. And a lot happened after the arrest of Fractoria's great-grandfather. I'll tell some of that "a lot" as clearly as I can.

First, police and state and federal agents—*not* including Madison and Monroe—descended on the BBB store in Cobb Creek. They questioned employees. They confiscated many of its documents and turned them all over

to the court. They froze its assets, making it impossible for Mr. Borsmutch to reach some of his store's money. Federal agents went down into Sporangium to decide if the United States should take him to court for using the citizens of a foreign land—the sporules of Sporangium—as slave labor in his stores worldwide.

Upon our arrival back in Cobb Creek, Will S Gato had come up from his smelly pillow in the basement to greet us. (He had a cat door down there and kept himself fed by killing birds and rodents. Please forgive him.) Eventually, we got Sparky and Leo back from Father Syd's kirk in Oathwick. A man in a black suit brought them home in airline cages. When Mama and Daddy let the yappy mutts out, we laughed and bawled all at the same time. Later, Melba Berryhill came over from her Jarboe Street cottage to hand over Josie, our Chihuahua, who pranced around on toenails that crackled on our kitchen floor like roaches in a corncrib.

Next, Bryden, Sophia, Joel-Brock, and I tried to get back to normal as soon as we could. Mama asked Mr. Valona, Miss Melba, and Addi Coe to the house for supper as a reward for getting us home from Sporangium or for taking care of family members (Joel-Brock and Josie), and they were glad to come. None had jobs any more. Our local Big Box Bonanzas had gone into receivership. A court appointed someone—the receiver—to handle the money issues of the Cobb Creek store, the only BBB affected, but Mama still felt sorry for the so-called "little people" who had worked there.

Daddy cooked that night. He had had a lot of catching-up to do at his Lollywild Grills, but he was relaxed the night the Smalls and Miss Melba came over. Sparky tried to get Daddy to throw him his mushy yellow tennis ball, but Daddy would not. He likes to feed caboodles of people, people he wants to please with his meals and the resulting good talk when his guests eat those meals. Daddy made plate-sized pizzas for everyone, with fruit-salad sides.

The grownups had wine. Joel-Brock and I had root beer or crème soda.

Oh yes: We had one other guest, a lawyer named Lita-Gay Torres. She had come not merely to eat, but also to gather evidence about our ordeal. Bright and sassy-looking, she made her own necklaces, earrings, and bracelets.

After dinner, still at the table, Ms. Torres said, "Is Mr. Borsmutch a sprule? He had a Welsh corgi for a ventriloquist's figure in Condor's Cote, but once he came topside again, he did his own talking, didn't he?"

"The old guy's as human as you or I," Mr. Valona said. "But a few years ago, after decades of chain-smoking, he contracted throat cancer. He didn't lose his larynx, but almost. So he had surgery that let him talk mind-to-mind with animals modified to speak. However, BBB surgeons don't modify sprols to talk because earlier trials in Sporangium proved that, within days, they revert to muteness."

"And how do you know that?" Lita-Gay Torres asked.

"After we returned from our mission, *I* told him," Joel-Brock said.

"Okay. And how did *you* know it, young man?"

"Quagslip," Joel-Brock told her, and he did his best to explain what we all finally decided remains mostly unexplainable.

Then Lita-Gay Torres asked us to clarify the difference between gobbymawlers and sprols and between gobbymawlers and buddypards. Joel-Brock groaned. But Miss Melba and Addi explained the matter in a way that even a five-year-old could understand. So Ms. Torres, who was forty-three, got it. Then she glanced at us all in turn and asked, "But isn't 'gobbymawler' an ugly putdown?"

"I guess it shouldn't be," Mama said. "It's supposedly a neutral term, not an epithet coined by critics outside the store."

"A critic like yourself, Sophia?"

"I'm a critic, but I didn't coin the term gobbymawler, which even Mr.

Borsmutch uses approvingly. Give him his due. He's an evil old vulture, but a clever one."

"Fractoria says he's ill and just getting sicker," I told everyone.

"Even so, he should die in prison," Mama said.

"Is that a kindly way to think?" I asked Mama.

"Arabella," Daddy said, "he's committed more crimes than a Mexican drug lord, all with a fountain pen."

"*All?*" Ms. Torres asked.

"No way," I said. "He had Manny Obello and several other gobbymawler sprols kidnap us from our house and stick us in a grubby cell in Sporangium."

"Well," Mr. Valona said, "he deserves prison time for creating a whole race of innocent beings for his use as slaves, worldwide."

Daddy turned to Miss Melba, Mr. Valona, and my new friend Addi Coe. "So what will you good folks do now?"

"Search for other employment," Mr. Valona said, "in a deeply down job market."

"I'm sorry," Mama said, as if herself responsible. "I'm really sorry."

"Retire," Miss Melba answered Daddy. "It's past time, anyway."

"Play shortstop for the WorkOutWarrior Braves," Joel-Brock said.

"Visit Father Syd in Oathwick," Addi said. "I'm his daughter, and we've put in my papers for dual citizenship."

"Neat," I said. "You'll be like Persephone, living half the year topside with us and half underground with the Lord of the Dead."

And I wanted to slice my tongue out, for Father Syd was *not* another Hades. But Addi only smiled. I loved her even more and resolved to visit her one day in Oathwick. At least we probably wouldn't meet the vile Mr. Hudspeth down there. He had vanished, Addi said, vanished utterly.

At that point, Daddy cried, *"Is everybody happy?"* He did not yet realize that he had made a mistake by adding mushrooms to Joel-Brock's pizza.

"Not I." Joel-Brock lifted a slimy mushroom for us to behold. "Look— just look—at this coolinary abomination."

I patted his wrist in sisterly pride . . . for sounding just like me, almost.

30

Joel-Brock's Coda: 2023

I often recall what happened in the summer of 2010 because it changed our lives forever and several other lives too. And I'm grateful to an older version of myself who told me what to do in Condor's Cote when Mr. Borsmutch was dying. I not only saved that horrid scumbag's life (for a time), I also saved the lives of my folks and my sister without fully understanding how I had done so.

I still don't understand. Saving a life changes a life—everyone knows that—but what bizarre collisions of molecules, brainwaves, and time particles bring about those complicated changes?

First, I never grew into the Home Run Hitter of the Future that I aimed to be as a baseball-crazy ten-year-old in Cobb Creek. I am twenty-three now, and no one going by J.-B. Lollis has a roster spot on the Atlanta Braves, or on any other major-league baseball team. Also, despite what the FōFumm in Big Box Bonanzas showed Melba Berryhill, Augustus Hudspeth, and me thirteen years ago, no major-league club called the Nashville Cats exists today and there's still no travel agency up there or anywhere in the world offering vacation trips to the Moon.

Miss Melba remembers those pictures, however, and Mr. Valona vouches for the reality of my yNaut talks with J.-B. Lollis, major-league All-Star. But I retain my life, a fine one that I hope to live out with Faith, Hope, and Charity . . . if I can find three strong women with those names who will all marry the same man. That's a joke. Please forgive me. I often joke when I've hiked too far into the pits of subterranean quagslip for my own good. So I joke a lot. It more or less balances everything out.

Let me summarize a few matters: Pither M. Borsmutch had a trial for ordering my family's abduction and those of many of his own employees, and for confining all these persons in a prison in the caverns beneath Cobb Creek. His trial did not start until a year after our return from Condor's Cote, and it ended in a conviction. After the trial, he continued to live under house arrest in his Cobb Creek mansion for a time and got well enough to stop living inside his life-support booth. He did not go to prison at once because the state brought other charges against him: fraud, aggravated chicanery, villainy in the first degree. These trials lasted far too long, and on several charges he was found *not guilty* by reason of "undue influence and wealth." (Another joke, this one two-edged.)

But in the end he went to prison . . . in a Level 3 rubber room in Condor's Cote! Judge Hamilton could have posted him to a rich-guys' prison in Hawaii, but decided that making him serve time in his own junky jail better fit his crime(s). All who'd suffered at the old goat's hands cheered this decision.

Later, I learned that Mom *may* have nudged the judge to make up his mind by telling his wife (one of her WorkOutWarriors) that sending Mr. Borsmutch to a holiday lockup would alert voters that Judge Hamilton "mollycoddled crooks, especially rich ones." That sounded like Mom, but I have yet to verify the story.

*

A few months after Mr. Borsmutch wound up in his Level 3 rubber room, Miss Fractoria Scampi asked me if I would go with her to visit him.

"But why?" I asked.

"He wants to thank you for doing CPR on him."

"He's already thanked me," I answered with Mom, Dad, and Arabella all in the front dining room listening. "He thanked me by taking us on that crazy pillar lift up to Gobbymawler Park."

"He wants to thank you again."

"Fractoria, I don't want to go back down there. I don't like Papa Pither."

Fractoria began to cry. Arabella put an arm around her shoulders, but my folks, although not upset with Fractoria, could not work up any sympathy for her great-grandpapa. They stepped aside to let the girl and my twelve-year-old self work out the issue between us.

"The real problem," Fractoria said, crying harder despite Arabella's hug, "is that *no one* visits, not even my mother or his ugly stuck-up sons."

"Yes, but—"

"Okay, he can go," Dad said. "He'll be glad to. Won't you, Joel-Brock?"

And so I again went underground to visit a man I despised. However, Fractoria and I did not have to make the long trek that I had made with the Smalls. Instead, after riding to Gobbymawler Park with Dad, all Fractoria and I had to do to reenter Condor's Cote was ride the pillar-drop at the center of the four fields. And, *voilà*, we were in—not in a smelly rubber room, but in a chamber on Level 3 with plate glass between the bad guys and their visitors.

Inside, Condor's Cote now resembled a stern gray building like the ones built by the Soviet Union in Eastern Europe in the 1950s. It was in receivership, like the store in Cobb Creek, and all that was pretty or valuable inside it had been pulled out and hauled away. But, for irony's sake, the phony bricks and the cartoons of chained prisoners on the wallpaper in Level 3 still adorned its halls.

I don't recall much of what happened when we sat down opposite Mr. Borsmutch, except that Fractoria put her hand up to the glass to force him to hold his own palm up to hers, but he ignored her. Fractoria lowered her hand

and began to cry, while he smiled in a sinisterly chilly way.

Then I spoke the only words of my own that I can recall saying, and I still do not regret them: *"Sir, are you sorry?"*

"You acted bravely," he said. "You acted in a way belying the world's opinion of most persons of small stature, myself included."

I stayed mute.

"Persons like us," Mr. Borsmutch went on, "may have small bodies, but within our breasts we have—" He broke off.

Fractoria looked up. "What? What do you have?"

"—the hearts of giants." He patted the left side of his chest, even though he had just spoken utter, unmitigated gibberish.

Then his face twisted, like a latex mask of a Halloween demon near a hot torch, and he spat a big, moist, yellow gob at the glass divider.

We both recoiled.

Then Fractoria told him, "Papa Pither, that isn't nice." It was *so* not nice that this obscene, scornful, and petty act seemed to break her heart.

*

As the years rolled on, my dad found satisfaction in opening a new all-fresh-foods franchise that he called Bryden's Groovy Sliders. Mom gave up her job as a physical trainer to enter seminary and to apply her sense of justice in other front-line capacities. Arabella set aside the oboe, but, with Dad's help, took up the guitar and the ukulele and wrote poems that she turned into lyrics for original songs.

I continued playing baseball and video games, and I took great pleasure from the reopening of the old Big Box Bonanzas store under new management and a brand-new name, Beneficial Bargains Today, which nearly everyone now calls BBT. For a while, I even stocked shelves there.

Mr. Valona signed on as BBT's store detective and occasional special sale-item demonstrator. On breaks, he and I played kings-in-the-corner in an employee lounge in the rear of the store, for BBT's basement was still in the hands of government receivers and off limits to persons without clearances. But on at least two weekends every year, we used *our* clearances—given us for helping to convict Mr. Borsmutch—to visit our fellow Small, Addi Coe, at Oathwick in West Sporangium.

Addi serves as an acolyte for Father Syd, but also does social-service work among the sporules of Greater Sporangium. When she began, she was too young for her post, but passion carried her far, and now she impresses all who know her as an upright and caring person. Last summer, she spoke to Congress, arguing for amnesty for sporule workers forced topside to work for low or nonexistent pay. She also champions full citizenship for those passing qualifying tests. Moreover, although she still meets forceful opposition, she never loses heart.

Mr. Valona and I go underground every September 22, the autumn equinox, for Father Syd told Addi that that is her birthday. When we go, we take a well-wrapped gift. We carry it into Oathwick Kirk and place it on a pew directly before the altar. Father Syd sets out cake and ice cream, and we serenade Addi with off-key enthusiasm. Our upbeat caroling pulls in many well-wishers from Oathwick's stony streets: *"Happy birthday to you,"* etc., everybody sings.

"Well, what is it this year?" Addi hefts and shakes her package from us. It never rattles much, but she observes this annual rite, uh, ritualistically. And Mr. Valona, Father Syd, and I admire her for doing so.

"You'll never guess," Mr. Valona tells her.

"Three or four brand-new boxes of Lost-in-the-Woods golf balls?"

"Sorry, no."

"A bust of Father Syd, carven from Sporangium Salt?"

"No."

"A pullover sweater made from platypus tails?"

"Now you're being ridiculous," Mr. Valona scolds.

"Then I guess I must open your package to find out."

"Go ahead," everyone urges.

Addi removes its paper as carefully as a movie star takes off and lays aside a mink coat. Then she lifts the box, which features a photograph of her gift right on its front, and everyone applauds and gasps, "Wow—a heavy-duty cordless hairdryer!"

"Again," I say, not really apologetically.

"Again," Addi acknowledges.

And we glance around to see if a gorgástrogon has glided into Oathwick Kirk. Blessedly, one never has, and so, like starved flies, we all set upon the waiting cake and ice cream.

*

I went to the University of Georgia. Where else would I have gone? Yellow Jacket Tech? Maybe, but for a time I had my doubts about going to *any* college or university. It seemed an ordinary rite, and an expensive one, and a less exciting option than everyone makes it out. But I went, and even though I didn't *always* start on the baseball team, I played every game, and I throve. I actually throve.

Once, early in my sophomore year in Athens, several years after Mr. Borsmutch's imprisonment, Vaughnathan Valona drove up to meet me at the Snack Shack, not far from my dorm. By this time, he had won a golf tournament for persons of small stature, flown a flyke of his own in several cross-country rallies, and moved from his shoplifter-spotter position at Beneficial Bargains Today through management to a significant vice presidency with the franchise, which was working to do all the things that my mom had wanted BBB to do. Anyway, we occupied a booth in the mostly empty Snack Shack in Athens, with Braves and Bulldogs baseball photos on its walls and peanut hulls in small heaps all over its floor, and we talked.

"Vaughnathan," I said, because my dear old friend now insisted that I call him by his first name, "what's this all about?"

Wearing a striped charcoal suit and a brown fedora that he slapped down between us, he looked like a tiny gangster from a movie from the 1930s. He pushed his yNaut X9 at me. Its panel glowed like the well-lit windows of a big-box discount store. We stared at the device. "Pick it up, kidster."

We both said, "yNaut?" at the same time, and neither of us smiled, the joke was so old. Anyway, I picked up the sleek device.

"What time does it give you?" Vaughnathan asked.

The device's screen said **10:56 AM**, and I told him so.

"In four minutes, the X9 will sound and your caller will expect you to answer."

"Okay," I said. "And who will it be?"

"I'm leaving. Eat some peanuts"—he tapped the bucket next to his fedora—"and sip some lemonade"—a waitress set a glass before me—"until he calls. Then have a chat. Afterward, I'll return to retrieve my brain."

Before I could stop him, Mr. Valona leapt down and ambled into a connecting room as agilely as he had led Addi and me through the dim wastes of Sporangium when I was a kid. I sipped my lemonade, but a strong fear that I'd choke kept me from filching an unshelled peanut from the bucket. Four minutes passed like half an hour, and the ring tone—a snippet of a favorite song of mine, "Bells and Roses"—sounded.

I snatched up the X9 and said, "I'm here—talk to me."

"Hello, Joby," said a voice I knew, from a caller I knew, and my heart stiffened within me like a small leather bag baking in the sun.

"J.-B.," I managed. "Where are you? *When* are you?"

"I'm calling from Cobb Creek, or a version of it, in a year that Mr. Valona tells me falls thirteen sun cycles after your current year."

"I don't understand."

Ignoring this, he said, *"What happened in Condor's Cote in your own time when you and the other Smalls went down there to rescue Mom and Dad and Arabella?"*

"Surely, Mr. Valona has long since told you."

"Mr. Valona got back in touch with me only two days ago, right after he bought his spectacular yNaut X9. Anyway, Joby, you tell me."

So I told him everything, just as it had happened—to me, that is—all the while wondering what had prompted this tardy call from a troubled variant of my future self. He expressed his relief that my having performed CPR on Mr. Borsmutch had saved not only that horrible man but also our admirable parents, our older sister, and our animals.

"I didn't do what you did," J.-B. said. *"I let the nasty coot die, and our group's rescue efforts failed, probably as a direct result, and—"* He broke off.

"Your family died. You told me years ago." (By saying "your family," I actually meant "our family," even though *mine* had survived.)

"I'd forgotten I told you," he said in surprise. *"I'd forgotten."*

"You can't blame yourself for the bad result in your ... dimension, J.-B. You mustn't." He said nothing for so long that I feared he'd pocketed *his* yNaut (or whatever it was). Faint trilling birdsong came through the device, but no hint of his breathing or his movements. "What are you doing in a *version* of Cobb Creek?" I asked. "It's September. You ought to be playing baseball."

"I'm making cabinets. I design, build, finish, and market them. No one builds a prettier or tighter cabinet than J.-B. Lollis, kid."

"And baseball?"

Again he did not answer, and I began to think that he had severed our connection. Then he did talk, recounting how, in the fifth year of his career as a Brave, a high-thrown curveball had smashed his cheek bone. Complications during surgery made his recovery harder than anyone had expected, and when he tried to play again, he disappointed both himself and his manager. And so he retired at age twenty-nine.

"I'm sorry," I said.

And recalling his fluid play on that magical TV in Electronics, I spoke only the truth. But as I spoke it, my voice broke, as if, itself, made of bone.

"Best thing that ever happened to me," J.-B. said. *"I've got to go."*

"We'll talk again," I told him. "Soon."

"Thanks for playing me better than I did. But we don't walk the same earth, and I can't handle or pay for talks like this one again, ever. Goodbye, Joby."

Then he was gone, for good, and Mr. Valona came back to the table, with his own glass of lemonade, to reclaim his yNaut X9. He didn't try to console me with phrases like *"It's all for the best"* or *"Into every kitchen an occasional slug must crawl."*

So I tapped my glass against his, softly.

"Here's looking at you, kidster," Mr. Valona said, and we both blinked and sipped our bittersweet drinks.

*

Nowadays, I work as a recreational director and baseball and tennis coach at Borsmutch Commons, the new name for Gobbymawler Park, now increased in size. Four years ago, the old megalomaniac died in Condor's Cote, once the site of his "personal paradise," but later his place of imprisonment. His Last Will & Testament bequeathed the land making up additions to the old park and the former park itself, to the city of Cobb Creek. He did so with an unpopular decree, that the city rename the place Borsmutch Commons.

But, if the city met this demand, his estate would provide money not simply for repairs and fresh construction, but also for the salaries of its new officials and maintenance workers. And so Cobb Creek voted to take the deal.

My salary does not come from the BBB Foundation, but from user fees, charitable donations, and contributions from parents, or I could not work here. Right now, I coach fourth and fifth graders in baseball, acting as trainer, instructor, cheerleader, and dugout strategist. I select the smallest kids who appear here—runts that our more macho coaches love fobbing off on easy marks like me.

I always oblige them. I not only oblige them, I spotlight my players' lack of size by calling my team of pipsqueaks, male and female, the *Valorous Smalls*. Then I coach them with such fire and foxiness that sometimes—okay, rarely, but more often than most folks expect—my Smalls triumph. And, yes, I often get as much pleasure from our larger foes' chagrin as from the crowd's enthusiastic cheers.

Why do I choose these kids? Because although I am bigger than they are, I am still just their size, and vice versa. I often squat, stoop, or bend over, and, as a result, we always see things eye to eye. And at every practice—we practice twice a week—I break from teaching baseball fundamentals and get my team to go out and roll in the unwired world. I show them rocks, sand grains, mouse skins, garden slugs. I urge them to sniff—on the wind, I mean—rain, chicken trucks, cow manure, auto exhausts, hickory smoke, their own skinned knees, potting soil, pine cones, dog poop, deer hair, dandelion puffs, human sweat, and lightning strikes. Nothing is too big or too small for us to delve into, and although I am not sure where the ghostly J.-B. Lollis has gone, I have an idea, and I am content—at least for the time being, that time being now.

About the Author

Michael Bishop is the author of the Nebula Award-winning *No Enemy But Time*, the Mythopoeic Fantasy Award-winning *Unicorn Mountain*, and six previous Fairwood Press/Kudzu Planet Production titles, including *Brittle Innings*, *Who Made Stevie Crye?*, and *Philip K. Dick Is Dead, Alas*. *Joel-Brock the Brave and the Valorous Smalls* is his first novel expressly for young persons, "whatever their age." He and his wife Jeri live in Pine Mountain, Georgia, with far too many books.

Author Photo © 2015 Jeri Bishop

May 2013. Bellaria, Italy.
The author on a pig on a beach. Quoth writer John Kessel, "Silly man."

OTHER TITLES FROM FAIRWOOD PRESS

Amaryllis
by Carrie Vaughn
trade paper: $17.99
ISBN: 978-1-933846-62-0

Traveler of Worlds: with Robert Silverberg
by Alvaro Zinos-Amaro
trade paper: $16.99
ISBN: 978-1-933846-63-7

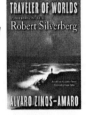

On the E yeball Floor
by Tina Connolly
trade paper: $16.99
ISBN: 978-1-933846-56-9

Seven Wonders of a Once and Future World
by Caroline M. Yoachim
trade paper: $16.99
ISBN: 978-1-933846-55-2

The Ultra Big Sleep
by Patrick Swenson
hard cover / trade: $26.99 / 17.99
ISBN: 978-1-933846-60-6
ISBN: 978-1-933846-61-3

The Specific Gravity of Grief
by Jay Lake
trade paper: $8.99
ISBN: 978-1-933846-57-6

Cracking the Sky
by Brenda Cooper
trade paper: $17.99
ISBN: 978-1-933846-50-7

The Child Goddess
by Louise Marley
trade paper: $16.99
ISBN: 978-1-933846-52-1

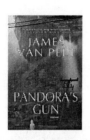

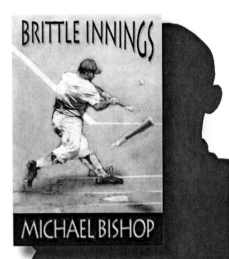
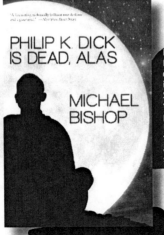

Michael Bishop

Mary Stevenson Crye, a recently widowed young mother known as Stevie depends on a balky PDE Exceleriter for her free-lance writing. Then the PDE Exceleriter goes noisily on the fritz, and so many other things begin to go wrong as a result, including her machine's insistence on typing segments of her everyday life as she either lives or hallucinates it. A novel of the American south, an alternately tender and scathing parody of twentieth-century horror novels, and an involving account of one woman's battle to maintain her sanity.

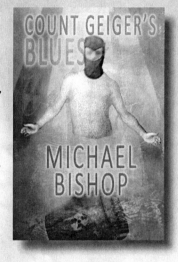

While skinny-dipping in a pool polluted with radioactive waste, Xavier Thaxton, arts editor at a major Southern daily, is afflicted with superpowers all his own and becomes that which he most scorns. A radiation-induced ailment, the Philistine Syndrome, forces him to assume the persona of comic-book hero Count Geiger to allay its career- and indeed life-threatening symptoms. This novel of intellectual heft and self-spoofing kitsch is a take on superheroes like no other: a rollicking foray into high and low culture that mines the vicissitudes and tragedies of everyday life for serious belly laughs and bona fide heartbreak.

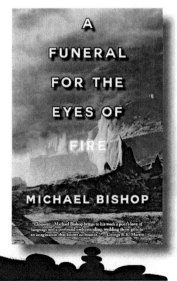

Seth Latimer, a human member of a family of clones, finds himself marooned on Gla Taus with no way home unless he joins a mission to a neighboring world to negotiate the transfer of a minority population from one planet to the other. Diplomacy devolves into brutal expediency against a background of complex gender and religious polarization. Alien settings and cultures are lovingly woven into this story of passionate individuals caught up in the sweep of history toward tragedy, change, and eventual renewal.